DATE DUE

		JUL 31 2001
AUG 07 2000		SEP 10 2001
OCT 16 2000		MAR 26 2002
		APR 03 2002
NOV 08 2000		
DEC 12 2000		
DEC 28 2000		
FEB 07 2001		
APR 26 2001		
MAY 10 2001		
JUN 16 2001		
JUL 09 2001		
JUL 16 2001		
JUL 23 2001		
AUG 23 2001		
MAR 26 2002		

GAYLORD   PRINTED IN U.S.A.

The Secret Keepers

The Secret Keepers

Julie Mars

GREYCORE
New York

For Farris

COVER ART: Valerie van Inwegen (V Scott V)
COVER AND TEXT DESIGN: Kathleen Massaro

Mars, Julie
    Secret Keepers/Julie Mars
    p. cm
    LCCN: 99-90345
    ISBN: 0-9671851-4-9

    1. Man-woman relationships—New York (State)—New York—Fiction.
2. Stalking—New York (State)—New York—Fiction. 3. Custody of
children—New York (State)—New York—Fiction. 4. Autistic children—
New York (State)—New York—Fiction. 5. Private investigators—New York
(State)—New York—Fiction 6. New York (State)—New York—Fiction
I. Title

PS3563.A7132S43 2000   813'.54
                        QB199-1383

Acknowledgements

My sincere thanks to the writers and friends who helped me with this book: Madalyn Aslan, Jennifer Egan, Robert Farris, Mary Beth Hughes, Michele Meyers, Theresa Park, Julie Reichert, Joan Schweighardt, Hilary Sio, Mary Anne Staniszewski, and Rebecca Stowe. I would also like to express my gratitude to the New Jersey State Council on the Arts for its generous financial support.

1

The day she left her keys on the counter at the Stuyvesant Post Office was not the first time he'd seen her. He had, in fact, watched her carefully for three months. It wasn't perverted, obsessional curiosity that compelled him to note each detail of her movements as she collected her mail. It was simply in his nature to observe.

Three times a week—Monday, Wednesday, and Friday—Steve Dant waited on the long post office line that snaked between frayed, dirty ropes in a complicated figure S. The line inched forward toward the three service windows. The clerks had long ago mastered the art of looking busy while doing almost nothing. They shuffled and stamped papers behind their grates and tossed priority mail packages into different bins in slow motion as the people on line shifted from one foot to the other and the tendons in their necks rose out of the skin and pulsated very slightly.

Steve did not share their impatience. The post office line marked the end of his work day and he used it as a cool down period. It was his equivalent of happy hour, a time to slowly unwind in a crowd of strangers. He pushed his box of "outgoing" mail along with his foot and enjoyed the spectacle. Hispanic women yanked their children along by their frail little arms and talked in loud voices in a language he didn't understand, despite three years of high school Spanish and two trips to Mexico. Aged Eastern European women with swollen legs and sunken mouths clutched letters in lightweight airmail envelopes, complicated addresses scrawled across the front. Tired looking interns in white jackets fiddled with the stethoscopes hanging around their necks. It was like a movie, Steve often thought, some art movie that didn't have an obvious, recognizable plot.

Steve worked in a four-person office one half block from the Stuyvesant P.O. It was on the third floor, where the sounds of the traffic on 14th Street amplified and the rumble of the L train passing by deep underground subtly shook the building at five to eight minute intervals. The vibration slowly dislodged more than a century's accumulated dust and filth which collected on the tops of the desks and filing cabinets. The computer screens became fuzzy and a small coffee spill soon became a small mud pie. The two-room office had to be swept at least three times a week or dust bunnies grew to unruly proportions behind the doors and under the creaky steam radiators.

Amid the dirt and the noise, they produced a literary quarterly called *Expression* which sold for $5.00 a copy. It was a labor of love for the editor and publisher, Janet Lawrence, who had started the magazine on a shoestring eleven years before. Janet handled her enterprise with an intensity that secretly amused Steve. She favored wall charts, push pins, and Post-its. Her profit margin, if any, was minuscule, but she often stated that relating profit to product value was an error primarily made by money grubbers with no taste, no sophistication, and no sense of aesthetics. A big brunette going grey, Janet spent all her time reading unsolicited manuscripts, fussing with the page layout of the next edition, and moving her color-coded push pins from one mysterious square to another. She had hired Steve three months before, after he answered a classified ad she'd placed in a free downtown newspaper.

"Look," she'd said, sliding her faux-leopard skin glasses up her nose, "I'm not gonna ask you why you want this job or how you're gonna live on the money. That's your business. But I want to make it clear that just because you work here, it doesn't mean you're automatically gonna get published in *Expression*." She'd looked at him and paused, and something about the density of that pause and the position of her head indicated a question. Steve wasn't sure what it was, but he felt expected to answer. Finally he mumbled, "I'm not a writer."

"O.K.," she said, her shoulders dropping a fraction of an inch. "For five bucks an hour, I don't expect you to stay forever. Just give me two weeks notice, that's all I ask." She'd stood up and extended her hand. "See you Monday at nine. That's in the morning."

He'd smiled at her little joke and let himself out into the dimly-lit landing. He went down two long flights and pushed through the metal door to the street, stepping over a full-time stoop sitter with a buzz cut and silver rings in both his nose and his upper lip.

"Spare change for beer?" the stoop sitter asked, thrusting his hand toward Steve.

"Why should I pay for your beer?" Steve answered, ignoring the fingers that nearly poked his leg.

"Fuck you," said the stoop sitter. "I want money, not conversation."

Steve disengaged. He walked around the corner to a bagel shop and got himself a cup of black coffee. He had a job, his first in eighteen months. As he stirred three packets of sugar into his coffee, he found his mind drifting back to the stoop sitter. The facial rings and studs were distracting, but Steve had noticed the derailed intelligence that leads to total cynicism behind his muted grey eyes. Steve gazed up into the cracked, gilded mirror tiles glued to the wall behind his table and considered his own eyes. Shit brown. Dull. He shifted in his seat and tapped his fingers on the Formica table top. A job, he thought. A crummy job, but a job.

That Monday he'd met the rest of the staff: John, the word processor, was a part timer, and Mary Anne, Janet's right hand, proofread and did all the accounting. Steve's modest duties included Xeroxing, sweeping, running errands, picking up the mail, and sending the magazine out to subscribers. Hence, his visits to the post office. He usually hit it around 4:15 and he wasn't really expected back in the office, though occasionally he returned for the last fifteen minutes of the work day.

He'd noticed the woman who left her keys on the counter at the end of his first week on the job. She seemed to ride in from 14th Street on a dark cloud, and then move like a streak toward the postal boxes that lined the eastern wall of the lobby. She was tall, perhaps 5'10", and her stride was long and smooth, despite her calf-length motorcycle boots and tight black stretch-skirt. There was a kind of precision to her, a single-pointedness that cleared a natural path. No one stepped in front of her.

The woman squatted down to fit her key into a box on the second to bottom row. She pulled out a single letter and stuffed her key ring, which appeared to Steve, twenty feet away on the line, to be a bright pink golf ball, into the pocket of her denim jacket and dropped her huge leather bag off her shoulder onto the floor between her feet. She slid her finger under the flap of the envelope and pulled out a hand-written letter.

The line shifted forward one person, and Steve moved with it, but his attention remained fixed on the woman, on the way she leaned against the mail boxes, effectively blocking one entire vertical row, while her eyes, brown like the hair that was piled on top of her head and tied with a black scarf, darted across line after line, down the page. She turned the letter over and read the last paragraph on the back. Then she tore it to bits and dumped it in the garbage can as she sailed out, shifting her sunglasses down off her head over her eyes.

"Move it up, bud," a voice behind him said. The person in front of him had made the final turn and was a full three feet closer to the windows. Steve quickly pushed his box of mail along the floor and fought off the urge to apologize to the group. Why should it make them so nervous, he wondered, if he didn't step forward the exact second it became possible? What unrelenting chaos could his slow response time unleash?

It was a small incident, the arrival of the woman into the periphery of his life, and he forgot about her until he saw her again later that week. She was, apparently, a creature of routine because she always arrived at 4:35 and always did the exact same thing: she'd open, read, rip, toss, replace the sunglasses, and disappear through the various dogs tied to the railing on the steps in the foyer. Based on his observations, she got one letter a week, and they mustn't have been too important because she discarded them immediately. Her face never registered anything as she read. No smile cracked along her lips, painted a dark, rich shade of red-brown, nor did she ever straighten up and begin to read with sudden intensity.

When she broke that pattern, Steve was, in a detached way, stunned. He'd just concluded his *Expression* business and turned from the window when he saw her there in her usual stance, leaning against the wall of mail boxes. She looked relaxed but distant, as usual. Then her face changed and she took a few steps to the counter and seemed to use it to steady herself.

Steve moved toward the stamp machine. A man in an orange shirt fed quarters into the slot, and Steve stepped behind him. The woman flattened her letter out on the counter and read it again. Her head fell forward and the sunglasses clattered to the floor. She fumbled twice, so unlike her usual abbreviated gestures, when she reached down to pick them up. Then she folded the letter back into its envelope and carefully tucked it into the inside pocket of her jacket. She almost ran out of the post office, her movements uncoordinated and clumsy.

And then Steve noticed her pink key ring sitting on the counter among the used carbon paper and bits of trash. He crossed quickly, picked it up, and started toward the exit. He waited impatiently as a woman with a stroller maneuvered through the one working street door. Then he stepped onto 14th Street, moving across the crowded sidewalk to the curb to get a clearer view. The woman was walking east, just making the right turn onto Avenue A. He picked up speed as he followed her.

A crowd of noisy kids, their pants drooping into puddles of cloth at their ankles, stood on the corner. Steve skirted around them in time to see her step into a liquor store a few doors down. He had her keys in his hand as he pushed through the heavy glass door. He even felt the "m" in the word "Miss" form in his lips, but he said nothing.

"A bottle of Tanqueray," she said, bending slightly to speak through the slots in the bullet-proof glass. An Asian man went to a corner shelf and using a step ladder, reached for the gin. It was, Steve later thought, the sound of her voice that had arrested him. It was musical, soft and somewhat timid. It sounded as if it had never been raised in anger, never lashed back in an argument. It surprised him. Until that moment, he had not realized he had acquired an unconscious set of expectations about her.

Steve tucked her keys into his pocket.

It was a reflex action, something unexplainable. There was no plot, no intention. It was the frailness of her voice and the way she counted, and then recounted, the money she finally passed through the slot. Steve left before the Asian man returned her change and handed over her bottle of gin.

When the woman emerged from the liquor store, Steve had the receiver of a broken pay phone pressed against his ear. He placed his arm against the top rim of the metal phone cabinet and leaned inward so his face would be hidden. An empty Gatorade bottle and a crumpled brown bag, left on the shelf, came into focus as he reran what had just happened. It seemed strange to him: on the one hand, he'd wanted to give her some privacy as she asked for the gin in her quiet voice; on the other, he wanted to keep the small part of her that he already possessed. The irrationality of that thought scared him.

The woman crossed Avenue A, dodging between a taxi heading south and a dented Chevy van heading north. She stopped in front of a Korean market and stared at the buckets of fresh flowers. She selected a bunch of lilacs, shook off the water, and went inside. Steve watched her take a bottle of tonic water from a cooler and place it on the counter. She left quickly, heading downtown toward Tompkins Square Park. At 10th Street, she took a left, and five doors down she climbed the cracked front steps of a brownstone. As she reached into her pocket and fished around, a look of irritation crossed her face. She set her shopping bags and her oversize purse on the landing and began to search in earnest.

It entered Steve's mind that she would soon retrace her steps. He could easily beat her back to the post office and think about this later. He started to jog north at an easy pace.

He was inside the locksmith shop before he was even complete-ly aware of noticing it.

"One of each?" asked a middle-eastern man with a huge head of wiry hair and a cigarette hanging from the corner of his mouth.

"Yeah. Please."

There were four keys on the ring. As the machine ground out a duplicate set of keys, Steve moved to the window and glanced down Avenue A. No sign of her.

"I can't copy the post office key," the man said over the whine of the machine. "It says right on it, 'Do Not Duplicate'."

"No problem. Forget it." Steve dug into his pocket for money. "How much?"

"Three bucks plus."

"Plus what?"

"Tax, man. Where you from? The moon?"

Steve laid four dollars on the counter and stuffed the keys into his pocket. As he bolted for the door, he heard the locksmith call, "Hey buddy, your change!" but he didn't stop. Through the front window, he saw the man shrug and drop back down onto his stool.

Steve ran around the corner and into the post office. He cut in front of the "Broken mailbox/pick up" line and shoved the keys through the gridwork.

"Found these on the floor," he said. The clerk glanced up without interest and tossed them into a box with "lost & found" printed on the side in blue magic marker. Steve stepped back outside and stood in front of a street vendor's table full of wallets. Nervously, he picked one up and pretended to examine it.

"Genuine eel skin," the vendor said. "Best price in the city."

She was coming around the corner.

"Just looking," Steve said, replacing the wallet.

Her eyes were covered with her big dark glasses, but her mouth was set in a tense line that created a squared off angle in her jaw.

She pulled the door open and disappeared into the post office. Steve slowly walked the half block to the entrance to the L train and descended.

2

Steve took the L train west two stops and then switched to the uptown #6. The five o'clock crowd was thick and pushy, like every day. Steve avoided the subways at this time. He usually walked down to the Jack LaLanne gym in the Woolworth Building where he had a lifetime membership. Or else he walked home, up First Avenue to 64th Street where he lived in a two room, tub-in-kitchen tenement apartment. It was a sublet, filled with things that were not his. It needed a paint job and a kitchen renovation.

A woman in a business suit and sneakers got off the train at 23rd Street, and Steve sat down. He pulled the keys from his pocket and ran his finger along their shaved edges and angles. He didn't look at the keys. He ignored the questions that tried to push into his consciousness. He felt enormous pressure from inside, as if he were under ninety feet of water and surfacing too fast. Exiting the train at 68th Street, he slowly walked home, stopping at 65th and First Avenue for a slice of designer pizza with black olives and roasted red Italian peppers. The counter man slipped it onto a white paper plate and into a white bag and stapled it shut. It was spotted with grease stains by the time Steve climbed to the 4th floor, rear, and let himself into apartment 4D.

He flipped on the overhead light and stepped out of his black slip-on Keds. In the bright glare of the bare bulb, the apartment looked depressing and worn. The wooden floor was buckled and uneven, and the stove and fridge were dented and stained. The bathtub, barely big enough to fit in, occupied most of the floor space. Steve left the pizza on the sink shelf, pulled off his long-sleeved grey tee-shirt, flipped it into a wicker clothes basket, and carried his dinner into the other room, a living room/bedroom combination that faced south. No buildings obscured his view of the Roosevelt Island tram, which crossed back and forth over the river every fifteen minutes.

Steve sank into an oversized, overstuffed couch and ate the slice of pizza slowly. It was warm, just the way he liked it. Between bites he stared at the color configuration on the slice: black, red, that pale yellow. It looked like a painting to him, something he'd seen magnified a thousand times on the wall of the Whitney. Bit by bit, he ate off the sides, studying the changing shape as he went.

When he finished, he wiped his mouth with a paper towel from the roll he kept on the end table and dropped his plate into a small plastic trash can. He took the woman's keys out of his pocket, lining them up on the coffee table according to size. Perched on the edge of the couch, he leaned forward and stared at them for a long time. Then he formed the keys into a triangle. He wanted to think about what he'd done, the strangeness and unacceptability of it, but his mind felt empty. He did not picture the woman's face. After a quarter of an hour, he simply added the keys to his own key ring and went into the kitchen for a bottle of wine.

Steve opened a bottle of California burgundy and rinsed out a lime green wine glass that was sitting in the stained porcelain sink. He carried his bottle and his glass back to the couch, where he turned on a small lamp and poured the wine. Then he re-read the Mr. Coffee operating manual which he had mistakenly brought home from work the week before. He fell asleep after finishing three quarters of the bottle of wine, the 75-watt bulb shining right into his face and his arm flung over his head to reveal a long purple scar along his inner arm. Needle marks.

Steve jolted awake when the usual nightmare started. Wake up, it insisted. It was better if he woke up, he knew. Anything was better than being trapped in the sleep state and subjected to the twists and tortures of that dream.

He reached up and pushed the off-switch on the light. The room became foggy and grey, lit by the weak, pale rays of the beginning daylight. Steve turned his head to gaze out the window. From this angle, there was nothing visible but a patch of blank sky that was the color of fresh concrete. His heart rate, accelerated by the start of the dream, slowly calmed. Steve made an assessment of the messages in his body and decided he would not be able to drift back into sleep.

He sat up and looked at the luminous dial on his dirty plastic alarm clock: 5:20. Not bad. He rose, undid the zipper of his jeans, stepped out of them, and carried them through the kitchen to his laundry basket. Then he stood in front of the toilet, one hand on his hip, and waited for the noisy stream of morning piss. He leaned forward to compensate for the initial trajectory, vaguely self conscious about the racket, though no one was there. The sound seemed to echo off the grimy walls of the closet that held nothing but an old toilet with the company name, Success, printed in black letters over the drainage hole.

Steve yanked on his jogging clothes, thrown over the top of the door, and sat on the rim of the tub to put on his sneakers. He looked around for his keys. Not on top of the fridge, his usual spot. He went to the living room. Not on the coffee table either. Retracing his steps, he took the black jeans out of the dirty clothes and felt the pockets.

Yes. There. He pulled his key ring out and then it all came back. The woman. Her keys. He felt a small thud in the pit of his stomach and moved quickly to the door and out into the hallway of the building. The fluorescent tube light blinked above as he locked up and zipped his keys into the front pocket of his windbreaker.

It was mid May. Red and yellow tulips bloomed in window boxes and the city's trees, despite the mist of car exhaust and toxic fumes, produced spectacular pink and white blossoms that rustled gently in the breeze. The streets were damp and quiet as Steve jogged north to 71st Street and took the stairs, three at a time, to the park along the river. He ran four miles every morning, counting his steps in sets of eight until the monotony set in and freed his mind. He called it the "Blank Zone," and he liked it. But eventually, inevitably, a thought, a feeling, a memory, something unwelcome would arrive and recognizing it would cause his breath to shorten, which threw his rhythm off, and he would begin to count again: one two three *four*, five six seven *eight*, one two three *four*, five six seven *eight*.

Today he wanted to analyze his impulses about the keys which pressed very slightly into his breastbone as he ran. Why had he copied them? Because the opportunity had presented itself, he admitted, and suddenly he remembered being a child, perhaps four or five. Sometime before kindergarten. His mother was sliding the size 34 blouses on their hangers along a metal rack in Kopald's Dress Shop, and Steve, bored with this shopping trip, had wandered to the counter, trailing his finger along the edge of the glass display case. At the corner, treasure: a bin of assorted gift boxes, just cardboard but covered with shiny, bright paper. Steve had reached for the one he liked—a long, slim one meant for one of the bracelets that glittered in the display case. He slid the box up the sleeve of his winter coat. The box had no value, but when it slipped out of his coat sleeve as he climbed into the car, his mother's eyes had widened and she had snarled at him in disgust. She forced him back down the street through the snow to Kopald's and stood outside the door.

"Now you march in there, Mister, and tell Mrs. Kopald what you did," she said. "March!" She shoved him inside.

He had not wanted to confess. He glanced over his shoulder at his mother's face glaring through the front window. The angle made the pupils of her eyes look red, which terrified him, and with down-cast eyes he quickly gave back the box. His heart pounded as he rejoined his mother on the street. She dragged him back toward the car in silence.

Even now, Steve felt the deep shame and hopelessness of the long drive up the mountain toward home. Why had that memory surfaced, he wondered, when there was no one to make him return the keys, no one to make him march in and confess? He suddenly realized that he felt guilt about the keys, but no shame. As a child, he'd felt shame but no guilt. What did that mean? But then his lungs tightened and his pacing faltered. One two three *four*, five six seven *eight*, he counted, and he turned his attention to the tugboats pushing barges of garbage down the slate colored East River and the lights coming on, one by one, in the hideous apartment cubes on Roosevelt Island.

Steve returned home and was scrunched up in his tub by 6:30. The water pressure in his building negated the possibility of a shower, but he'd become accustomed to his little tub. If he wanted to slide his shoulders under the warm water, he had to stretch his legs up straight and rest them against the edge of the sink. It was ridiculous, he thought, but no more ridiculous than all the other ways he just didn't seem to fit into life.

Steve took the bus down Second Avenue and got off at 9th Street instead of 14th. It was barely 7:30. No one would arrive at *Expression* for an hour or more. He walked north one block, then turned east on 10th toward the park. Between First and A, an old man whose skin sagged stood on the sidewalk in a polyester bikini in front of the Russian Bathhouse. He spoke in a foreign language to a man in an expensive dark suit. It made Steve feel good to stumble onto such an incongruous scene. It made him feel like part of New York, part of its color.

He bought a coffee-to-go in a smoky corner market and strolled along the northern edge of the park until he was across from her building. He stood facing it for a second, blowing into the steam rising from the hole he'd poked in the cover of his paper cup. Behind him was a fenced combination basketball court/baseball diamond with wooden benches placed on the periphery. Steve entered the gate and chose a place where he could watch her building. A lone roller-blader made high speed spins and circles and figure eights as Steve slowly sipped his coffee and stole occasional glances at the various windows of the brownstone.

She was probably asleep in there, he thought. She looked like a person who avoided the morning. Someone who took cabs home late at night and asked the driver to wait until she was safely inside her building before he moved along. With her black-on-black clothes and her sculpted sunglasses, which Steve had seen on display at the Glasses Emporium for $275, she seemed confident, like a woman for whom people saved a seat, hoping she'd come and anxious that she wouldn't. She probably had her morning coffee in the early afternoon and never accepted phone calls before two.

Steve himself had not received a phone call, aside from those from long-distance company representatives who tried to snatch his imaginary business back and forth, since he'd moved to New York five months before. The aspiring actress he'd sublet his apartment from had seemed so shocked when he expressed no interest in transferring the phone to his name or even, in fact, in keeping it at all, that he'd quickly reconsidered on the spot. It made him uncomfortable when a stranger got an unexpected glimpse into his private non-life. How could he explain that he didn't seem to stick to people, that he made no imprint on them despite what he could objectively evaluate as somewhat better than average looks and a lean, hard body that stood 5'11" tall and weighed 168 pounds, stripped. He was a thoughtful person, and he felt drawn to the places where people went for inspiration—museums, movies, exhibits—but neither his appearance nor his activities seemed to color him in and make him visible.

As a child, he had startled his rural school teachers. "Can you see me?" he would ask. Their fingers would flutter into wisps of dull brown hair and they would answer, "Of course I see you" in a distracted way that made Steve doubt them. "Do you like me?" he would persist, treating it like a survey question, devoid of emotion. "Of course I do. I like all the children. Now finish your arithmetic problems like a good little boy." The mechanics of arithmetic presented no problem to Steve. He just couldn't understand the point of doing it.

From his bench in the park, Steve saw three people leave the building on East 10th Street: two men (one in a baggy linen suit; one in a tee-shirt and dungarees) and one woman (elderly, with a sad-sack Basset hound). The old lady headed around the block, reappeared ten minutes later, at 8:20, and went back inside. Steve tossed his coffee cup into a wire trash can at 8:40 and sauntered across the street and up the steps. He wanted to look at the intercom, see if he could deduce which apartment was hers.

There were seven units in the building. He eliminated #1 because its entrance was at street level and he had seen the woman climb the stairs. That left #2 (B. Wertz, it said); #3 (Tio and Hart); #4A (Asher); #4B (Stanley & Steigman); #5A (C. Timberlake); and #5B (Benito and Sheffield). No clues there. He left the building before anyone appeared and walked north to 14th Street, feeling oddly at home in the neighborhood. He even stopped at the Korean market with the lilacs fading in white buckets and bought a Dr. Pepper for later.

The stoop sitter was in his usual place. He shifted aside a bit so Steve could use his key to open the door. They had maintained their disinterested truce since Day #1 but it didn't fool either of them. They were, in fact, very aware of each other. Their eye and body movements were choreographed to eliminate the possibility of conversation, yet Steve knew every detail of the stoop sitter's torn leather jacket and his steel-toed Doc Martin combat-style boots. Steve felt he could judge the stoop sitter's hangover by the level of green in his skin tones.

Steve squeezed into the door and climbed to the third floor. The *Expression* door was ajar, meaning that Janet was collecting the blue recycling bags and about to put them in the hall for collection. Later, the stoop sitter would jam his steel reinforced toe into the door after someone came in or out and sneak into the hallway to collect the deposit cans and bottles before the super did. He was furtive and sneaky, though everyone knew he did it. Steve had once opened the door and seen him rifling through a bag outside an office across the hall. Unnoticed, Steve closed the door and gave him time to finish.

"Oh Steve, I'm glad you're here," Janet said as he reached for the bag she had in her hand and put it down for her. "That coffee machine's throwing up all over the counter again. I had to unplug it."

"Janet," he said, patiently following her back inside, "it only does that when you forget to put the top on the pot."

"Yeah, well, I never had any trouble with the old one."

They crossed to the narrow table with a sign reading "Caffeine Fix" above it. The pot was empty, but water, thick with grounds, oozed out the cracks around the filter basket.

"It's because of the 'Pause 'n Serve' valve," he said as he carefully freed the plastic basket and dumped it.

"The what?"

Steve suddenly felt extremely self conscious. Too much time with the Mr. Coffee manual, he knew.

"The 'Pause 'n Serve'," he said flatly.

"What the hell is that?" she asked.

Steve hesitated and then turned the basket over and showed her a valve on the bottom.

"If the top's not on the pot, then this valve stays closed, see? It gets stuck in 'pause' mode and the coffee backs up and overflows. You just..." he turned from her and spooned the El Pico coffee from the can. "You just need to remember the top; that's all."

"Just tell me one thing," Janet said. "Where'd you learn that high-tech term?"

"Pause 'n Serve?"

"Yeah."

"It's in the book," he said, wiping up the last of the grounds with a yellow sponge. He busied himself because he could feel his face reddening.

"Well," Janet said finally, "I wish you'd read the copier manual. It's pretty damn temperamental too." She walked into her office and collapsed in a chair.

Mary Anne came and stood next to Steve, dumping a Sweet and

Low packet into an empty cup.

"Don't mind her," she said. "She's just mad because she breaks every machine she touches."

"I heard that!" Janet yelled.

Mary Anne shrugged and returned to her desk, where she opened the New York Post and began to read the gossip on "Page Six." Steve studied her over the edge of his own cup. It seemed like such a blatant flaunting of protocol, to read a newspaper on company time. Steve would not have done it. He felt obliged to be poised and ready for work when the clock struck nine. To open some personal reading material and immerse himself in it while he was getting paid seemed unthinkable. But he saw Mary Anne do it every day, and it didn't seem to affect her relationship with Janet. Or anything else, for that matter.

It was payday. On his lunch hour, Steve took his check to a bank a block away and waited on the money card line rather than dealing with a human teller. He added his weekly earnings, which came to $151 and change after taxes, to his account and pressed the "balance inquiry" button. The machine buzzed and coughed out a printed statement. Including today's deposit, he had $19,857 in his account. He folded the paper and stuck it in the watch pocket of his Levis.

Three and a half years earlier, Steve had had just under a hundred thousand dollars. The money was a combination of an inheritance (small) and an insurance settlement (large) that he collected after both his parents were killed in a car accident on an icy road two miles from their home near the Canadian border in upstate New York. The sub-zero temperature and blinding snow effectively cut off a rescue attempt for over three hours. His mother had died instantly on the car's impact with a disabled snowplow abandoned too close to the road, but his father, with multiple fractures and serious contusions, had frozen while bleeding slowly to death.

It had taken the family lawyer, Tom Bource, Jr., the arrogant, affect-ed son of the original family lawyer, Tom Bource Sr., seven weeks to locate Steve, and when he did it had been a lucky fluke. At the time his parents died, Steve had neither seen nor spoken to them for over four years.

He did not make the trip to St. Regis Falls, his hometown, even after he learned that his parents had also left him (their only child) their house. The eight rooms full of knick-knacks, plaster crafts, and Sears furniture held no allure for him. He expected that the local bad boys, for St. Regis Falls was famous for its bad boys and outlaws, had quickly broken in and helped themselves. He didn't care. He had sent Tom power-of-attorney forms and had him wire the money into his account in Long Beach, CA, where he was living at the time. He hadn't even had to sign anything. It had simply appeared one day on a printed money machine receipt. Now he was down to his last twen-ty thousand. It would stretch another year and a half, perhaps a lit-tle more if he held onto the job at *Expression*. Then he would have to do something, make some decisions.

Steve glanced at his watch. With a half hour left on his lunch break, he wandered down First Avenue and stopped to watch some Catholic school kids play kickball. A small-boned Hispanic boy rolled the ball toward home plate and another boy gave it a power-ful smack that sent it flying. It zoomed back toward the pitcher and hit him full in the face.

Jesus, right in the kisser, thought Steve, wincing for the boy.

The ball bounced backward and landed in the teacher's hands. She spun and rolled it toward first base, then went to the Spanish kid, who was screaming and covering his face with his hands. She took a quick look—miraculously, no blood—and then pressed his little head into the comfort of her belly, patting his hair and rubbing his back. Steve felt tears stinging at the edges of his eyes. He stepped abruptly back from the chain-link fence. The pitcher broke away from the woman and reclaimed his place in the pitcher's circle. The other kid had made it to first. The game would go on. Steve brushed his hand across his eyes and returned to *Expression*. He spent the afternoon Xeroxing and answering phones.

When he left work, he went to the gym. He did a slow, systematic workout on the Nautilus machines, skipped the cardio-vascular equipment, and took a lengthy sauna. The dry waves of heat comforted him, a slow, hot caress along the whole length of his body. He adjusted his towel and stretched his legs out, locking and releasing the calf and thigh muscles as he felt himself let go. A cold shower revitalized him, and he decided to walk home.

Steve meandered past City Hall Park and up through Chinatown, where the sidewalks were packed and the sounds and smells reminded him of Olongapo, a filthy, desperate town in the Philippines he'd come to know too well as a machinist's mate, third class, in the U.S. Navy. For three years, he sailed to and from Subic Bay naval base on the U.S.S.Constellation, an aircraft carrier with a staff of five-thousand men. In and out of port, he spent torturous hours working in the unbearable heat and noise of the engine room seven levels below the main deck. Soaked in sweat, he would trace an irregular sound pattern back through the labyrinthine pipes and valves that hissed and rattled in the stagnant air. The massive engines made complete, logical sense to him. He became the ship's mechanical troubleshooter, which gave him a certain cachet in the ranks and a measure of freedom in the engine room. He used this freedom to hide bricks of high-grade heroin, primarily for his own use, though he did make the occasional sale.

Nights he spent with the narrow-hipped bar girls who spoke in sexy broken English and would do anything for a negligible price. He chose one and paid her to live with him in a small, plain apartment in a three-story concrete building on the edge of a section of town that was off limits to American sailors. Steve's coloring—his straight dark hair and eyes and his skin, which turned a deep brown in the sun—seemed to make him invisible to the jeep patrols of armed forces police that swept through the forbidden streets. His girlfriend, Wai Ping, was not loyal but he didn't mind as long as she was home when he was; there, as he tied off his arm and boiled his beige/white dope in a silver spoon; there, when the rush of well-being warmed his blood and finally let his mind cool off; there, when he wanted to reach over and feel her lean body, pull her on top of him and fuck her in the rhythms the dope, not the woman, dictated.

Steve stepped off the curb to avoid a crowd of tourists cackling around a menu posted in the window of a small, bright restaurant on Mott Street. He crossed over and bought three pork buns through the street service window of a steam-table cafeteria and ate them as he strolled north toward 10th Street. He meant nothing by going there, he told himself. It was just more interesting to have a destination.

He finished his last pork bun sitting on the same bench he'd occupied that morning, but now the park was buzzing. Players in a pick-up basketball game pounded back and forth, and along the park, East Village types, dressed for sex, paused to admire the sweetness of the cherry blossoms.

Lights were on on three floors of her building. Steve didn't actually expect to see her. If this were the movies, he thought, she'd suddenly appear in a silk kimono, probably with a cigarette in her hand. He, from the street, would watch the smoke halo around her head and... And what, he wondered. What did he want?

Well, he thought, he wanted to read the letter that had thrown her so off balance in the Stuyvesant Post Office. She had been so vulnerable as her sunglasses clattered to the floor and her usual cool facade cracked and collapsed. He wanted to be her silent port in the storm. He wanted to enter her life, silent and unseen, and help hold her up. In that moment, he admitted what he had unconsciously known ever since he found himself in the ABC Locksmith. He was going in. He just had to plan it, find a way.

The tee-shirt-and-jeans guy from the morning passed by the window on the fourth floor.

He would slowly collect these bits of info and construct a chart, he thought, that would help him locate the woman's apartment. He began to feel a flicker of excitement.

He knew about the old woman with the dog and the guy in the suit. Where were they? Two of the floors were dark now—the second and the fifth. It occurred to him that he could try those doors. He would knock first, and if anyone called through the door, he would run. He rose to his feet and crossed 10th Street. Fumbling in his pocket, he produced his key ring. Looking very carefully up and down the street, he slowly climbed the steps and tried the first key in the door. It didn't fit. He was nervous. Tried the second key. No. He turned it upside down and it slid in. Steve twisted the key and stepped inside. A second door opened with the same key.

A strange, low-pitched rumbling stopped him: the dog, growling behind the door of apartment #2 to his left. It was the only door on the floor.

With no time to waste, he crossed the terrazzo floor and started up the stairs, moving quietly and quickly past apartment #3 on the third floor and #4A and #4B on the fourth. The higher floors had two apartments, he noted as he climbed. The building was quiet; he heard muted music as he passed 4B, but that was all.

Steve felt afraid as he hesitated on the landing of the fifth floor. Light shone in a thin line under the door of the rear apartment. The door to #5A was around the banister, on the opposite wall. He crossed silently and placed his ear to the wooden door. No sounds inside. He pushed the doorbell. A dull buzz echoed, but there was no response. After fifteen seconds, he rang again. Nothing.

The door had a heavy-duty Medeco lock and a smaller one. He chose the round key, the sturdiest of the three he'd copied, and put it into the Medeco. It fit. He caught his breath and turned his wrist. The cylinder clicked. The sound reverberated in the hallway, and Steve cast a quick glance at 5B. No patches of darkness in the line of light under the door indicated that someone was standing there, peering through the peep hole. Steve relocked the door and withdrew the key. There was no reason to test the other lock. He already had what he needed.

Blood pressed against his temples as he ran down the stairs and pulled open the front door. No one had seen him. No one suspected he was there. He dropped the keys back into his pocket and stepped through the outside door, pausing to glance at the name next to her doorbell: C. Timberlake.

Steve casually descended to the street. The moon, half full and beaming in the black sky, seemed centered directly over the park, and the wind coming off the river was cool and pleasant. Steve took the First Avenue bus uptown. C. Timberlake, he thought as he stared absentmindedly out the bus windows. Catherine. Carol. Charlotte. Christine. Cecilia. Carolyn. Crystal. Carrie. Cicely. Caroline. He occupied himself with C names all the way to 64th Street.

3

The logical thing to do was to follow her. To Steve, it was a harmless amusement, a way of occupying his time and his mind. It was like being a spy or an investigative reporter. To observe one human life at close range, he thought, and reconstruct the person living it based on evidence he collected would perhaps reveal some mystery or allow him to reach some understanding that had, so far, escaped him. And it would be a secret. Secrets intensify life, he knew. Having a secret, a big untold story that would widen the eyes of, for example, the most detached shrink, definitely raised the moment-to-moment stakes in life. He knew, because he was a secret keeper. He came from a long line of secret keepers. He had kept secrets until they just deflated and became worthless.

Friday was a busy day at *Expression*, and even busier that Friday because Mary Anne was about to leave the city for a six-week stay in a writers' colony upstate. Janet had agreed to hold Mary Anne's job, but she resented the enormous inconvenience and was determined to make Mary Anne suffer before she left. The office atmosphere was tense, punctuated with short, clipped instructions and loud, disgusted sighs. Steve watched the clock for 4:15, post office time. Before he left, he stood in front of Mary Anne's desk.

"Good luck, Mary Anne," he said tentatively as she looked up. "I mean, with your stories. Up in the colony."

She was surprised; it showed in her eyes.

"Well...thanks, Steve." Then a little louder. "It's nice to get some support from somebody around here."

Steve moved away, toward the door. Mary Anne's attention turned back to him, away from Janet's door, which had been slammed shut an hour before.

"Steve?"

He turned.

"Don't work too hard, huh?"

He smiled and left with his box of "outgoing."

At 4:16, Steve was midway down the second curve of the line, hopeful that he'd be free by 4:30. He planned to tail C. Timberlake until he got tired of it, or the fun leaked out of it, or he hit a dead end. Having this plan, he felt a passing identification with the other people on the line, with their edge of impatient anger and resentment at being under the postal clerk's whimsical control. But all that was for nothing; he made it in time.

She was punctual, as usual. She checked her box, discovered it was empty, and left. Steve followed her from a discreet distance as she walked purposefully toward First Avenue and disappeared down the subway steps. He felt the vibration of the approaching train and quickened his pace. It was pulling into the station just as he hit the top of the last flight of stairs.

He scanned the crowd on the platform and spotted her just a few feet away. Her closeness jolted him as she moved toward the first car and waited outside the middle door. Steve joined the crowd pushing through the first door, wiping his forehead, which had broken out in a sweat. The L train was cool, full but not packed, and the woman dropped into a seat, dug into her bag, pulled out a fat book, and began to read.

Steve held onto the metal pole and positioned himself to study her.

Her long legs were drawn in, knees primly together, and she sat with what he felt was unnatural straightness. Her bag was on her lap and her book rested on top of it. She didn't seem to move at all as she read. Her eyes were invisible behind the dark glasses, and her hair was tied straight back in a thick pony tail that trailed over her left shoulder a good six inches. Even in the light of the subway her skin looked smooth and even-colored. He didn't think she would be considered a beauty by movie-star or even magazine standards. Her lips, for example, were thin and her mouth was small. The combination gave her a severe, somewhat punishing look. And her bones were big, so she looked overlarge, economy sized, despite her slimness. Her clothes fulfilled the fashion requirements of the late nighters of the East Village and were interchangeable with those of any of a number of women in her age group, which he took to be twenty-eight or twenty-nine. In other words, four or five years younger than he was.

C. Timberlake didn't get off or even look up as straphangers appeared and disappeared around her. Except for the systematic turning of the pages, she could have been in a trance. Steve noticed that she wore several silver bracelets that jangled the slightest bit when she moved her arm. One of them had turquoise stones in it. Her skin was light with a tendency toward brown tones rather than pink. Somehow, that made the turquoise bracelet seem out of place, as if it were wrapped around the wrong wrist.

At the last stop, she exited with everybody else and climbed the metal stairs leading to the 14th Street exit. Casually, she stepped around the sprawled out, unconscious winos sleeping shoeless in their own urine on the street. Steve followed her south down Eighth Avenue, but within a few doors she took a right and entered a bar called Skinny's.

Steve stopped. He didn't want to follow her inside, and the concept of skulking around with the drunks on the corner was not appealing. The windows of Skinny's were covered with thick, velvet curtains, complete with fringed tiebacks that had probably been gathering dust for years. A wire of blinking Christmas lights framed the front window, but nothing else was visible from the street.

He noticed a pay phone in the entry vestibule and went inside. As soon as his eyes adjusted to the near darkness, he dialed 411 and asked for his own number, twisting to peer through the glass door into Skinny's. It was empty, except for two old barflies hunched over beer mugs at the end of the bar. The walls were painted black, he noticed: no ferns, no wall glazing, no ceiling fans, no bamboo bar stools. This was the kind of dump you had to live in the city for years to find, a neighborhood bar that probably hadn't added anything new to the jukebox since 1965. There were a few black and white photos, portraits of people, stuck into the metal frame around the mirror above the bar, but Steve couldn't see them clearly.

He stepped a bit closer to the door and saw her sitting at a table against the front window, her jacket gone. She had a cup in front of her, probably coffee. She was laughing and talking. Steve couldn't see who sat across from her, but he experienced a short stab of jealousy. Suddenly she got up and went to the bar. She stepped onto the footrest and leaned way over, straightening a few seconds later with a glass of water. She returned to the table and sat down.

Steve let himself out into the daylight. It was just after five, and the foot traffic along Eighth Avenue was picking up. He was not sure what, if anything, he'd found out. But suddenly he felt an oppressive black mood coming on. These moods hit him quickly, like the rainstorms in the Philippines when it would go from glaring and bright to dark in a matter of minutes, and then it would pour rain so thick he couldn't see through it. He remembered the first time he'd experienced one of these storms. When the sky had opened and the rain beat down, Steve had stood in the doorway of a sari-sari store with a cold beer and felt enormous relief: not from the heat, because it was just as hot during the rain, but from the realization that nature had a built-in pressure valve, something that would automatically release and let the torrent out. This had given him a sense of optimism. It had been cleansing.

Steve headed to St. Vincent's Hospital, where they had a Narcotics Anonymous meeting every afternoon at 5:30. He knew where all the meetings were, all over the city, but this would only be the fourth one he'd attended in his five months in New York. He recognized that black feeling in his heart, and he knew he should short circuit it. No better way, he thought as he zigzagged between the pedestrians on Greenwich Avenue, than to immerse himself in a meeting full of losers, most of whom would never be able to stay clean, even with the help of the N.A. program. As for Steve, he firmly disagreed with the group's basic fundamentals, but he found it comforting anyway.

The antiseptic smell of the hospital nauseated him and he considered leaving, but he forced himself to climb the stairs to the meeting room. He pushed through the swinging doors and settled into a folding chair at the edge of the group, prepared for an hour of pitiful, pathetic stories, the kind that reminded him exactly how oppressed the average narcotics abuser is.

He divided them into three types: those oppressed by their physical, mental, or economic conditions; those oppressed by inner demons who, no matter what the disguise, wanted to see them dead; and those oppressed by boredom, by meaninglessness, by the

Furies he'd read about in his one semester of world literature (which he didn't finish) at Long Beach City College. Of the three kinds of user/losers, he thought only group #3 had a chance. He considered himself a member of that group. He'd seen successes, of course, from groups one and two, but they were usually in the saved-by-religion (usually Jesus) school, and he suspected that, sooner or later, that religious zeal and sense of well being and belonging would wear off and they'd be let down again, more disappointed and more full of rage.

The way Steve saw it, every human being came into life with a certain allotment of raw energy. The healthy personality controlled both the flow of this energy and the places it went. Energy that got channeled into substance abuse was obviously misdirected, so the user had two options: 1) pull the tablecloth out from under it and substitute a new container, like religion or the program, or 2) find a way to lose interest. One thing Steve knew for sure: if the user tried to conquer the habit by will power, he would fail, because all that fighting used up the energy a junkie needed to start over. That was exactly why Steve didn't do the 12 Step Program. He didn't believe in the disease concept: once a junkie, always a junkie, once a drunk, always a drunk. He believed that if a person found a way to drain some of the energy out of the relationship with the substance, he could dabble now and then for fun.

The room was filling up, all kinds of people. Many greeted each other as they spooned Cremora into their instant coffee and sidestepped along the rows to their favorite chairs. A woman smiled at him warmly and he nodded, but they didn't speak. The unwritten rule. People lit cigarettes and held tinfoil ashtrays in their laps. Steve's mind wandered until the stories began. He needed to hear the stories. They proved to him that all people, not just him, are totally alone, and each time he was reminded of this, his own darkness would slowly lighten up.

Steve was so far away, mentally reviewing the concepts of drug addiction he'd formulated during his stint at a drug rehab clinic in California, that he didn't catch the first speaker's name or the beginning of his "sharing." Even the sharing aspect of the 12 Step Program annoyed him because he didn't want anybody else's share of shit, and he sure as hell didn't want to impose his on others. On the one hand, they told you to draw boundaries; on the other, they told you to let every junkie's pain in. He couldn't let it in; he didn't want it. And he couldn't let his out because he immediately lost respect for anyone who'd take it. Taking on someone else: he viewed it as a masochistic act.

The guy talking looked like he'd done some prison time somewhere down the line. He had the jailhouse mustache and the sideburns. His body was tight and muscular and he wore a perfectly white polo shirt and pressed jeans. But a homemade tattoo showed, in part, beneath the short sleeves.

"...now I got a girlfriend...excuse me, woman friend," he was saying. "Last weekend she took me to brunch at her family's place out in Long Island. Two years ago I didn't even know what brunch was." That brought a round of hoots and several people clapped loudly. "So," he continued, "I got 185 days clean and I think I'm getting my life together. I mean, I still wanna use, but...one day at a time, one day at a time." He sat in silence for several beats, staring at the floor, and then looked up and reconnected with the group. "So that's it," he finished, and he slumped in his chair. When no one spoke immediately, he cracked a crooked smile and yelled, "Next!"

"I'll go," said a woman across the room. She was wearing a silk shirt in pale pink and a straight black skirt. An attempt at sophistication, Steve thought, but the gold jewelry and the moussed hair pinned her as a "bridge and tunnel" girl. She started to cry before she even spoke. The group waited silently as she slowly regained control. "I had fifty-two days," she said, "...and then, three days ago, I slipped." The room was quiet. "I just...bought a gram of coke and...you see, my boyfriend, him and me made these plans to take a trip together and..."

...and he fucked up and you took the fall, Steve supplied in his mind. The same old story. He did not dismiss the woman or doubt the pain, but it was all so familiar. Even in this group, collected because their lives were organized around the exact same central theme, he didn't fit in. He had never stood up and shared his story with the group. In fact, he had never felt their problems and his were related. Logic told him that they were, but he didn't see it. He felt he was a one-of-a-kind person with one-of-a-kind problems, and no one knew what to do with him, including the psychiatrist he saw five days a week at the clinic he'd finally checked into a year after his parents' deaths.

"That sounds a bit inflated," Dr. Greene had said at the end of his third session, "to think you're so complex you're beyond under-standing...by anyone."

"I didn't say complex," Steve answered. "I just said different."

"How?"

"I don't know."

"Then how do you know you're different?"

Steve wanted to answer. Some words were trying to form deep inside him. Vowels and consonants were being scraped into a pile, like the dust the Bible's God used to make Adam before he blew the life into him. But somehow the life never got blown into Steve's thoughts, so they couldn't come forth as words. He tried. He waited.

Dr. Greene waited too, leaning slightly forward in his leather chair, his arms resting on his knees and his fingers forming a spider web. The lights in the office were dim.

Think, Steve, he said to himself. He tried to will the words up from the depths.

Nothing.

Steve finally shook his head.

The animation, the pink look of expectancy, left Dr. Greene's face and his shoulders dropped.

"I'm sorry," Steve said flatly. He meant it too. He wanted help but his...what? memory? mind? body? what? would not cooperate. "There's nothing there," he added helplessly.

"Maybe not," Dr. Greene said. "Everyone has his own hell."

It seemed like a strange thing to say, but Steve had found it comforting. They had sat in a painful silence for the rest of the hour. Steve felt the doctor's pervasive sadness as closely as his own. If either of them had been able to put words on it, Steve thought, they would've had to commit suicide together right then.

The N.A. meeting was about to break up. Steve headed toward the door before the recitation of the Serenity Prayer. He hated the words of that prayer, the circle, the hand holding. He slipped into the hall and relocated the exit door. It was Friday night, 6:30. He needed something to do, some place to go. A line was growing outside the movie theater on the corner of Greenwich and West 12th Street; a mindless action movie sure to gross fifty million its first weekend. Steve laid out his $7.50 and walked around the side of the building to join the line. It was warm and the first hints of summer smells hung in the air: blossoms and garbage; pot and rancid falafel oil. Steve didn't think he would last all that long in this city, this huge brain. It seemed too logical to him, too precise for normal life.

The doors to the theater finally opened and they went inside. Steve chose a seat down the right aisle against the wall. He stared at the quizzes being presented via slides on the screen. His knowledge of movie lore was spotty and he couldn't answer any of the questions.

Two hours later Steve was back on the street. The guys with guns in the movie had been mildly entertaining but not engrossing. The usual. He had a slice of pizza next door and then strolled back up the avenue toward Skinny's.

It was much more crowded and the woman whose keys were in his pocket was behind the bar. He hesitated and then took a seat at a small table against the wall. The bar was long and narrow. At the far end there was a raised platform with an upright piano to one side. From the card on the table, Steve learned it was a rhythm and blues joint. The band was about to start a set. Otis Redding wailed on the jukebox as the patrons, a cross section, filled the tables and lined their quarters up on the one pool table.

A waitress appeared at his table.

"A Bud," he said. She vanished toward the service bar. Steve watched C. Timberlake reach below the bar and produce a cold Bud and a frosted beer mug. She seemed different as she sauntered from one end of the bar to the other serving the customers, more animated than he'd ever seen her. She smiled easily and whisked her stray hairs into place. When she wasn't busy, she moved to the music.

The waitress deposited the beer and he paid the $3.50 tab with a ten.

"The bartender," he said as she counted his change, "is her name Catherine?"

"Nope. Christine."

"Oh. I thought I knew her. I guess not." He gave her a dollar tip and poured his drink.

Christine Timberlake, he repeated to himself as Otis's "Love Man" blasted from the speaker above his head. "Which one of you girls wants me to love you?" sang Otis.

Christine.

He stayed for one set, eventually surrendering his table to strangers and leaning against the wall, his beer growing warm in his hand. The band was not bad, though he'd heard better. He stood in the shadows and watched Christine work the bar. She moved fast and took good care of everybody. Her tip cup behind the bar overflowed with bills and she kept stuffing more in. Her face maintained its patina of amusement and availability, but Steve saw nothing to indicate that she had a real friend or lover at the bar.

At 11:40 he left. The place was packed and getting hot. He headed uptown and let himself back into his apartment. Christine Timberlake.

He turned on the TV and watched a movie on HBO. It had been a nice day. He'd learned Christine's first name. And tomorrow, if she was working, he'd go down and check out her apartment on 10th Street. He stripped to his underpants, removed the couch cushions, and pulled out the sofa bed. He tightened the sheets, shut off the light, and fell asleep quickly. He had no nightmares and slept until 9:30. That was a shock because he couldn't even recall the last sunrise he'd missed.

Steve did his morning run, annoyed by the Saturday strollers and the "quality time dads" who overran Carl Shulz Park. The sun was bright and hot and rivulets of sweat ran off his scalp, across his face, down his chest and legs. Running at dawn was better. He liked the ambiguity of the light, the transition period between the two opposite extremes—dark and light, day and night, the time to work and the time to sleep. He felt most at home in the grey dawn when the eye played tricks because the edges of perceptible things shimmered and pulsated. Steve thought, at times, that he could see the molecular level of objects in the dawn, the vibration, all the space in the solid objects around him.

He cleaned up and went down to the corner coffee shop for breakfast. Opening an issue of *Newsweek*, he read a review of the movie he'd seen last night, and checked out the "Newsmakers" column. He lingered over his Spanish omelet and drank three cups of coffee. He wanted to stretch out the day and enjoy each part of it, let the little white glow of anticipation he felt in his chest grow brighter and brighter until that night.

It was as if he had a date, one he waited a long time to get. More correctly, he imagined this was what it felt like to look forward to a date, though he hadn't had one since high school. The women he knew were just around, available; he didn't have to call them up, offer a plan, and wait to see them. Or sleep with them, for that matter. They were the grey-area women, as uninterested as he was in the rules of the ladies-and-men game. If you had money or dope, they found you. If they wanted to fuck, they found you. There was no ceremony, no pretense of relationship and meaning. That was not to say that the time they shared was empty; on the contrary, it was often warm, close, sexy, fun. But it was rooted in the moment only. There were no hopes or future plans built in. Those were pointless. These women always let men down. And men like him always let women down. They were made for each other.

But, of course, he didn't really have a date.

He returned home and spent the early afternoon tidying up. He liked the place to be neat and clean; grime depressed him. He had read somewhere that seventy-five percent of New York City dust was composed of dead skin cells, blown or rubbed off the bodies of the city's eight million inhabitants. He found that to be disgusting. So he scrubbed the kitchen, dusted the tables with a damp cotton rag, and mopped the whole apartment, navy style, with strong smelling disinfectant. Then he did his laundry in the cramped laundromat across the street from his building.

At 3:30, he called Skinny's. First, the sound of the jukebox in the background, and then a woman's voice.

"Skinny's."

Momentary panic. Was it her? He found his voice and spoke.

"I'm...uh, trying to find Christine. Is she working tonight?"

"Yeah, as far as I know. She gets in around five."

"O.K. I'll stop in later."

"You want me to leave her a message?"

"No. I'll see her later. Thanks." He hung up.

O.K., he thought, O.K.

He decided to take a nap. Stretched out on his clean sheets in his clean apartment with the shades pulled against the afternoon sun, Steve felt a familiar tingle deep in his balls. He swept the sheets back and watched as his cock grew, pushing out through the foreskin until its purple head was fully exposed against his stomach. The shape of the head reminded him of a fireman's hat, and he ran his finger up and down the slope, around the edge, until a few crystal drops oozed out. The germ killer, he thought, the pre-cum that exterminates the bacteria in the vagina in preparation for the sperm.

His hand moved downward, around the shaft. He pushed his hips up and examined his erection, propping it straight up with his thumb at the base. It looked strong and angry. His hand closed around it and he let himself sail along on concentric waves of pure pleasure. He did not allow Christine's name or face into his mind until long after he was done.

Steve woke up a few minutes after five, dressed quickly and left his apartment. On the bus downtown, he was agitated and somewhat nervous. The bottom of his left foot itched inside his sneaker. The high school kid who sat down next to him had his Walkman turned up too high. The bus itself seemed too tired and old to make its way down Second Avenue. Steve closed his eyes and tried to block out the distractions. He didn't want to let them spoil his day.

He sat in the park and ate a lime Froze-Fruit. The tension subsided a little. No one came in or out of Christine's building, and he knew she was across town, behind the bar at Skinny's. He dumped his popsicle stick into the trash can and crossed the street. The rims of his ears burned as he climbed the front steps and rang her buzzer. He expected no response, and he got none. His key turned easily in the lock, and he stepped through the street door and ran up to the fifth floor. Quickly Steve undid the two locks, pushed the door open, and entered Christine Timberlake's home.

4

"What're you doing here?" Christine's voice snapped with anger and her hand shook slightly as she took a defensive step backward and put the glass in her hand down.

"What's the matter, Christine? You're not glad to see me?"

"You have no right to come in here."

"Hey...it's a public place." The man climbed onto a barstool. "Gimme a draft, huh?"

Christine didn't move. Her eyes were steady on the man's face and she crossed her arms in a protective gesture.

"I'm not gonna serve you, Parker." Her voice was flat, expressionless. "I want you to leave."

"You know," he said, reaching into his shirt pocket and withdrawing a pack of Benson & Hedges cigarettes, "that has a real familiar ring to it." He lit up, blowing a stream of smoke upward toward the grimy acoustic ceiling tile. "'I want you to leave, Parker.' That's your hit tune." There was a bantering edge in his voice. Teasing.

Christine was silent. She glanced up and down the bar. Two young women chatted together where the bar curved toward the wall and that was it. It was just after five, too early for her Saturday customers. Mike, the sound man, was in the mixer's box, but he was fussing with dials and cords, oblivious to everything else.

"I can't make you go," she said at last, "but I don't have to talk to you." She walked the length of the bar, climbed onto the stool she kept behind the bar during the slow periods, and opened her book.

Parker slowly finished his cigarette, staring at it as he smoked as if it were a mysterious, unfamiliar object. His hands were big and bony, just like the rest of him. He stood 6'3" tall and had the rangy, weathered look of a man born and raised in the southwest, where the sun bakes the skin and turns it tough early in life. His blond hair was pulled into a tight, short pony tail, which revealed a hairline quite receded and a single gold ring in his ear. With his rayon shirt, the sleeves rolled up to show his powerful forearms, and his baggy, pleated pants, he presented a fashionable, GQ-style image. He looked like a man who got attention wherever he went, a man who was used to it and liked it.

One of the two women from farther down the bar crossed toward the vestibule to use the phone. Her friend's eyes wandered and settled momentarily on Parker. He smiled invitingly at her and then stood up and started toward her. Her eyes, a crystal blue, intensified with interest as she watched him slide up next to her at the bar.

"I see you have an untouched glass of water," he said with a stylish smile. "Do you think I could have a sip? You see, I'm very thirsty and the bartender—my wife—refuses to serve me."

Ex-wife, thought Christine, refusing to look up. Ex-wife.

"I don't want to get in the middle of this," the blue-eyed woman said.

"I can't blame you," Parker answered, "but it's only water." He reached over and took the glass and downed the contents. He put the glass on the bar in front of him.

"Christine," he called, "this lady needs another glass of water."

"No, I don't," the woman said in Christine's direction. "We were just leaving." She got up, tossed two dollars on the bar, and quickly departed, pausing to collect her confused friend who was just hanging up the phone.

Parker walked to the opposite end of the bar where Christine sat.

"I need to talk to you, Chris," he said.

"We do our talking through lawyers now, Parker."

"I mean, personally."

She looked up and closed her book, glad to be separated from him by the width of the mahogany bar. She took a breath and tried to stay calm.

"No," she said.

"No what?"

"No personal talk."

Parker sat down on a stool. A bad sign, Christine thought.

"I just thought we ought to discuss—"

"Parker," she interrupted him, "it's over. Get on with your life."

"I can't. Not until—"

"I'm gonna get another restraining order," she said. "If you come here again, I'll call the police."

"Reasonable as ever," he said as he rose and walked back down the bar to collect his cigarettes. "Just remember, a lot can happen before the cops arrive. Right?"

Christine's eyes fluttered to the baseball bat the owner kept below the bar.

"Leave me alone," she said, her voice a low monotone. "I mean it."

"Sure," he answered. "No problem. Whatever Christine wants."

She could feel his eyes on her as he slowly stubbed out his cigarette and casually slid into his jacket. Watching him from the corner of her eye, she continued to turn the pages in her book. "I'll call you, Christine," he called, "later, when you calm down." He crossed to the door, opened it, and disappeared.

Christine realized that her hands were gripping the edge of her stool with so much intensity they actually hurt. She released her fingers and stood up. Parker's reappearance after eight months was very bad. She had only just begun to relax and believe it was over, and here he was again. If she'd had the privacy, she would've cried, but customers would soon come in, and anyway, she'd cried enough to know it didn't help that much.

She pulled a bar rag from the stack, wet it, and wrung it out. Then she removed the glasses from the bar and wiped it down, dumping Parker's cigarette butts into the garbage. How many times had she done that? Cleaned up after him, tried to erase his presence from her life by destroying all signs of it?

The last time he'd passed through New York—or perhaps it was only the last time she knew about—was in October. He'd phoned her at home. "I'm downstairs, on the corner," he said, as her mood, so elevated after a long weekend in Montauk, abruptly sank. It was discouraging but not surprising that he'd found her. "Come on out," he said. "I'll buy you dinner." She had gone because she was afraid he'd get into the building, show up at her door, and cause a disturbance that would anger the other tenants. She had sworn she was quiet and hermit-like when she'd convinced the co-op board to allow her a one year lease on apartment 5A.

She had been nervous to meet the board, even if it was only composed of stylish East Villagers. What could she say to convince them to accept her? She'd only been in New York for three weeks at the time and had just started the job at Skinny's, not because she needed the money but because she needed something to do, and she knew the bar and restaurant business inside out. And she was still sleeping on her friend Patty's futon couch, fresh from a bad marriage and a worse divorce. The court battle over their shared assets—a trendy restaurant called Paco's in the upscale Marin County town of San Anselmo and a condo in San Francisco—had provided a safe place for Christine to attempt to get revenge against Parker. To sign her part over to him would've been easy and perhaps they would have disentangled sooner, but she felt he'd taken enough from her already. She wasn't going to give him her money too. The communal property became the symbol of power, and they both locked their jaws around it and tugged like beasts. And she had come away with a fat check for what was legally hers. And something infinitely more precious too. She was proud because she'd squared off and refused to be intimidated. But outside the court room, it seemed impossible to stand up to him. There was no one to lean on, no one to step behind if the interactions turned ugly.

After Christine had moved to her apartment on 10th Street, she rarely left it. She felt an inner compulsion to stay still, to draw a magic circle around herself and keep the world out of it. She needed to sit quietly and recover, or perhaps create, her equilibrium, somewhat like a war victim for whom the only cure is a long period of uninterrupted peace. She collected her things from storage and placed them carefully in her new home. She had been there eleven months already and was just beginning to feel the outer stillness permeating her inner world.

And now Parker was back. Even if he left the city without contacting her again or showing up at her door, awareness of him would remain with her, like a bad smell that lingers long after the windows are opened and the candles lit. She finished wiping down the bar and put out a few dishes of peanuts.

Mike came out of the sound booth carrying a coiled extension cord in his hand. "Jesus, what's wrong?" he said when he saw her.

"What?" she asked, forcing a smile that felt weak and phony even as it formed.

"You sick or something?"

Christine tried to laugh it off.

"You look green."

She turned to examine herself in the bar mirror. Even in the dim light, her eyes looked hollow and dark, like black mica reflecting out of a deep hole. The edge of her mouth was so pinched that her lips had gone pale, as if the blood had been sucked out of them. And he was right: she did look green. Seasick green. She reached for a piece of ice and ran it along her forehead and behind her neck.

"Watch the bar for me, will you, Mike?" He nodded, looking concerned and somewhat perplexed. Christine walked to the ladies room, wiping the trail of ice water off her skin with a paper bar napkin. Inside, she hiked herself up on the sink shelf and let her body fall forward until her face was between her knees.

Parker had such power over her, she thought, fighting down a white hysteria that made her want to get up, run out of the bar and away from New York to someplace he would never think to look. She wanted desperately to be free of him, permanently, so she could start again.

She sat up and brushed out her hair. Loose, it fell to the bottom edge of her shoulder blades. She left it down, a sexy curtain to hide behind, reapplied her lipstick, and lined the edge of her mouth with a lip pencil. When she reemerged from the bathroom, she felt calmer. There were four people at the bar and a couple had settled into a table right in front of the bandstand.

"Thanks, Mike," she said, redepositing her bag in a cupboard behind the bar.

"All better?"

She nodded.

"What happened?"

"No questions, O.K.?" She averted her eyes, refusing to break the seal she had just placed on her feelings. Mike paused for a few seconds, then shrugged.

"O.K. You got a tab running on Patrick and Jeff. Two Buds." He slipped from behind the bar, lowered the service section of the bar top, and walked to the bandstand where he adjusted the microphones and amplifiers. Billie Holiday's version of "Am I Blue" played on the jukebox, mixing with the smoke and the moods of the people to create the bittersweet atmosphere that Christine felt somehow nursed her slow-healing wounds. Still, she wished she could be home now, listening to Billie in private in her safe little hiding place on East 10th Street.

5

Steve closed the door behind him and locked it. He stood completely still, his eyes closed, until his breathing stretched out and deepened and his heart quieted. Aside from the street sounds five floors below, it was silent. There were no warm cooking smells in her apartment, just the faintest trace of the lilacs he had caught out of the corner of his eye on the table to his left as he locked the door. He felt himself relax. This was not like his adolescent forays into the locked-for-the-season camps of the summer people. He remembered feeling rushed, terrified he would get caught though he knew chances of that were virtually nonexistent. No one was ever caught, and the lakefront camps were routinely hit. Here, he had every chance of getting caught, but he felt easy and safe. He felt at home, as if his intrusion would be tolerated if he were discovered there.

Slowly, he opened his eyes and looked around. Christine's apartment was a palace compared to his dump on 64th Street. He was in the foyer. To his left was a large living room with two windows overlooking the park. The walls were white; the wood floors, pale, bleached out, and varnished to a high gloss. She had a white leather sofa and two space-age chairs composed of gleaming metal and wide leather straps. A tall lacquered bookcase covered the west wall, and a few nondescript tables and an antique trunk were placed here and there around the room.

Steve moved to the center of the room and did a slow turn. The

walls were covered with paintings and artwork, mostly large canvas-
es, except for a grouping of smaller pieces on the wall between the
windows. The paintings were primarily blacks, greys, and dull
shades of off-white. They were abstract and, Steve felt, emotionless.
Their dismal colors and short, tight brush strokes seemed instantly
and enormously depressing to Steve. Plus, there was a regularity to
the display that agitated him as he looked from one room to the
next. The lilacs, placed in a square white vase, provided the only
color in the room.

He sat down in one of the leather chairs. The straps cut into his
back as he leaned into it. Steve let his eyes drift around the room.
Dolls sat in a row on top of the bookcase, dolls that Steve knew had
names though he certainly didn't know them. These were dolls from
long before the Cabbage Patch craze and probably somewhat after
Betsy Wetsy and Barbie. Christine's childhood playmates, he
thought. He scanned the group: dolls with spun-gold hair in permanent ringlets, dolls in cloth dresses and bloomers, Raggedy Ann and
Andy. She had a dozen little people up there on top of the books,
their unblinking plastic eyes staring blankly out into space.

He would've liked to have stretched out on the couch, but the
cushions still retained indentations where Christine had been, and
he planned to be obsessively careful about leaving any sign of his
visit.

He noticed a child's chair in the corner. Magazines were neatly
stacked on it. On the table, a carved wooden box. He lifted the cover
and music played. Inside were old photographs, turning up at the
edges and yellowing. He would take his time with them later or the
next time. He moved to the kitchen, which also overlooked the park.
Against the far wall, a simple metal table with one chair. A noisy old
fridge; a stainless steel sink that looked dirty despite an obviously

good scrubbing out; a small microwave. He opened the refrigerator. She had a pint of Half and Half and a tin of coffee, one carton of blueberry yogurt, two bottles of seltzer, and a dented and shriveled cantaloupe. In the freezer, he found the bottle of Tanqueray. Three inches of ice-flecked gin remained in the bottom. Doing quick mental calculations, he figured she drank six shots a day. More than was good for anybody, he thought, though, of course, she might have shared it with someone.

He walked to the rear of her apartment, stepping softly across the bare floor.

Her bedroom.

Leaning against the door jamb, he looked in. Translucent curtains with a pattern of small flowers blew gently into the room. Again, the walls were white and the floor was bare, except for a straw mat along the side of her bed. The bed was massive, a four poster built of logs. It stood high off the floor. A child would've had to climb up onto it and then been lost in the king-size expanse. The white eyelet bedspread was pulled tight over the mattress and the pillows, four in all, were propped against the pine logs of the headboard. Aside from the art on the walls, grey and muted like the paintings in the living room, the bed was the only thing in the room.

Steve walked to the window and moved the edge of the curtain. The window faced north, and between the safety bars, he saw the Empire State Building and the Chrysler Building silhouetted against the steel blue sky. A fire escape ran along the windows and up to the roof. He dropped the curtain and crossed to the bed. He had to get on tiptoe to sit on it. Impulsively, he kicked off his sneakers and stretched out. The bed was hard but comfortable. It smelled clean. Steve stretched out his arm and felt the raised stitching around each cutout in the eyelet of the bedspread.

Who are you, Christine Timberlake? he asked in his mind. Here you are in this black and white world, your life of greys and whites and muted blues. Her apartment was stylish in a sparse way, but who was she? It looked like neither work nor play took place in this home. No project, half finished, was left abandoned on the living room floor; no stack of books had fallen over by the side of the bed; no tangle of plants grew into a green maze in the windows. The apartment, he realized as he lay there in it, seemed more like an exhibit than a home, like the rooms of a dead person which the family kept dusted and refused to change. "These were Christine's rooms," he imagined them saying, and the visitor would peek in reverently. "She liked art, I see," the visitor would say. But what would he say after that? Of course, Steve knew there was a subsurface world here, the world inside the closets, inside the drawers, inside the antique trunk she was using as a table in the living room. He would enter that world, but he would take his time.

Suddenly he felt drowsy. Perhaps it was the airy coolness of Christine's apartment, the open feeling which was so different from his cramped place on 64th Street. He felt his body begin to drift and he fell asleep with his cheek pressed into a pillow with a pastel blue case on it. Far in the distance, he heard the voices of children playing. Peals of laughter were punctuated by happy shouts. He let himself lie back and float along, nothing above him but the blue sky and the white streaks of shorebirds in flight.

Oh no, Steve thought, the dream. One of the dreams. He hadn't had this one in a long time. He felt his mind split. Part of it remembered Dr. Greene's advice. Stay with the dream; try to watch it like a movie; ask questions; don't wake up. But the larger part of his mind felt the grip of panic as strong fingers closed around his shoulders, pushing him down into the cool blue water. The shadow of the person behind him blocked the sun and the water suddenly turned slate grey and clammy. The fingers dug into the flesh where his neck met his shoulders. They closed around the front and pushed him downward. His vision began to fade at the edges. A black circle developed, as if he were looking through binoculars. The circle got smaller and smaller. The cold grey water snaked into his hair and filled his ears. He opened his mouth to scream. Oily water gushed in.

Who are you, Steve asked in his sleep, watching from a distance but not disconnected, not enough, from the boy in the water. He felt afraid. There was no response, no answer. The boy began to struggle as the black water closed over his little circle of vision and cold, slimy water seeped between his teeth and pushed into his throat.

Steve woke up gasping for breath. The room seemed quiet. He didn't think he had screamed this time. Where was he anyway? His eyes swept over the shapes in the room. It was quite dark. Then he remembered: Christine's. Jesus, what time was it? He stood up and crossed the room, looking for a light switch. It was by the door, of course. He listened for a second and then snapped it on and looked at his watch. 10:20. Careless, he reprimanded himself, very careless.

He went into the bathroom off the bedroom and took a leak. The bathroom was spacious; the tiles were sea-foam green. Bottles of bubble bath and a glass full of bath oil beads were placed on a shelf above the towel rack, and a white terry cloth robe hung on a hook behind the door.

Steve returned to the bedroom and straightened the covers on the bed until the wrinkles disappeared. He turned the pillow over and replaced it on its edge against the headboard. As an after-thought, he reexamined the pillowcase for hair but found none. Then he decided to have a look in the closet.

The door opened into an unexpectedly large walk-in closet. A clothes bar directly opposite stretched a full six feet. Steve pulled the string of a bare overhead light bulb. The room lit up but his first impression was one of darkness because many of Christine Timberlake's clothes were black. Very few colorful garments broke up the dark monotony. He stepped forward to examine the dresses, blouses, and skirts. He did not touch them. She had a lot of clothes, he noted, but most were the same style. His eyes rested on one emerald green floor-length gown in a clear plastic dry-cleaning bag. It seemed out of place, but its presence intrigued him. Where does an East Village type wear something like that? And when?

On the far wall were built-in floor to ceiling shelves on which tee-shirts, jeans, and bed linens were neatly folded and stacked. He assumed the one drawer contained her underwear. It didn't seem right to open it so soon, but he stood in front of the shelves and allowed himself to study the piles of clothes. Almost by chance he noticed three plastic milk crates pushed against the wall behind the winter coats at the very back of the closet. The crates, which were full of books, were stacked one on top of the other.

It seemed odd to him that she had stashed these crates of books. Judging by the display of shelves in the living room, Christine was proud of her books. A collector. Steve carefully moved the coats aside and squatted down to read the titles on the spines of the books.

Confusion and dread enveloped him as his eyes traveled along the rows. Every book was about father/daughter incest. Every one. Steve lost his balance and fell backward against the wall. He felt choked with sadness for her. Of course, he thought as he stood up, this might not necessarily mean anything. But he knew it did. He had entered into a stranger's life and he already knew a huge component of her story. He knew the secret tucked into the closet behind the full-length winter coats. For the first time, he experienced a wave of regret that he'd gotten involved with her, copied her keys, and come in here.

He replaced the coats so they shielded the crates, pulled off the light and left. Standing in the entrance to the living room, he focused on the line of dolls staring blankly into space, with their painted-on smiles; at the child's chair, covered with magazines, but still there, reminding her; at the wooden box full of family photos. He felt angry with Christine. It exploded into a white heat. Why did she hang onto these awful reminders? Why did she clutter her life with objects that tied her to a past with her father in it, the man who'd obviously forced himself into her body and her mind? The images disgusted him and he felt an urge to knock those dolls off their perch and stamp their blank little eyes into oblivion.

But the fire of his rage was suddenly snuffed out by a wave of unbearable sadness. Steve steadied himself against the wall. He looked at his watch. Almost 11:00. He had to leave, but he felt afraid to step backward through the door and pull it shut after him. Afraid to get caught or questioned in the hallway as he made his way down-stairs. Afraid that he would never come back here and afraid that he would. As he reached for the door, the phone rang. It sent a bullet up his spinal column.

An answering machine picked up after the second ring.

He heard her voice.

"This is 555-6039. Leave a message at the sound of the tone. Thanks." A pause. Then the machine beeped.

There was noise in the background as the man spoke.

"Christine...look, I shouldn't've come in and surprised you like that. Sorry. But I do need to speak to you, so gimme a call, will you? I'm at the Carlyle. It's important." The man clicked off. Steve looked around for the phone and found it on the wall in the kitchen. The light on the message machine on the floor blinked once. Steve stooped and pushed the "outgoing message" playback button. He listened, copying her number across the back of his bank receipt.

He left the apartment quickly. No one was in the hall as he descended and no one saw him on the front stairs. Steve walked south along the edge of the park and stopped in a bar for a nice cold drink. He sat at the bar and thought about Christine.

It had become complicated, he thought, as the music of the jazz quartet playing across the room faded somewhat from his conscious mind. Stand face to face with another human, Steve thought, any human, and their overwhelming complexity, the endless number of possible permutations, and the density of the tangents off their central core made it impossible to know them. It made Steve think of a drawing he'd done at the clinic in one of their mandatory "express your feelings" workshops.

He'd felt ridiculous at the communal table with a supply of crayons, colored paper, glue, and scissors at the center. A bunch of adult kindergartners participating in a farce. He'd tried, though. He'd taken a fat multi-colored crayon and made wild, random marks on a white sheet of paper. The colors were blended in the crayon so there was no decision making, but the bright blues and deep scarlets of the sharp-edged cloud he'd created pleased him. Suddenly he drew a stick figure, arms raised to an imaginary sun, in front of it. The little arms looked both pitiful and authoritative to him.

On a whim, as a sort of tongue-in-cheek joke that he thought would amuse Dr. Greene, he block lettered "Me and my unconscious" under the picture. An analyst in training from the graduate program at Antioch was facilitating the group that day. She was the perky type that he would run from after the first psychotherapy session. She passed behind him and stopped to peer over his shoulder.

"Gee," she said cheerfully, "it really pushes you right along, doesn't it?"

He looked again at the picture. To him, the cloud looked threatening, all powerful, ready to crash down on little Stick Man and impersonally crush him, despite his raised arms which desperately tried to channel the energy he needed to live on. Miss Perky had gone on around the table without waiting for his response. If he could've formed the questions, he would've asked her to explain the origin of her happy, optimistic interpretation which had popped out so spontaneously, he believed it was honest. He looked at the picture again. Maybe. Maybe.

But even if you could harness the power of the invisible, subconscious turbo-jet and sail along at a healthy clip, sooner or later you crashed into someone else's storm cloud and it was the simplest, most natural thing in the world to sink. Out of sight. Down, down, down. Gone.

That was exactly how he felt sitting in the bar on Avenue A. He'd sailed his ship into a tornado and found a woman foundering there. He could try to save her, but depending on how panic stricken she was, she might kick and scratch and pull him under. And he was scared too; he was no selfless hero with bulging muscles and an indomitable will to survive.

When you stand at the edge of the abyss of another person, Steve thought, and you make your decision (if you're given that luxury) about whether or not to jump in, it takes enormous faith to believe it'll ultimately work out well. From his own observations, because he wasn't much of a participant in human relationships, most people leaped without looking. The part of it that interested him was why. What ingredients ultimately mixed together to create that compulsion to rush into the dark mystery of another person's life? Miss Perky, Steve thought, would say that it would always lead to self discovery, understanding, and growth. What did quietly backing away from the edge lead to? he wondered.

6

*C*hristine, counting out her tips at the end of the night, wondered what to do about Parker. She uncrumpled the dollar bills from
her tip cup, set the quarters in stacks of ten, and sipped a stiff gin
and tonic: $92.65, plus her $25 shift pay. An average weekend night,
with the average number of belligerent drunks, horny assholes, and
sexual sparks igniting along the sides of the bar. As usual she had
gone on automatic to produce the average number of smiles and the
expected repartee with the horny ones. It was a relief when it was
finally over and José, the Mexican clean up man, turned on the light
and chased out the last of the merrymakers. She changed her money
to bigger bills and cashed out the drawer, locking it into a small safe
in Frank's office behind the bandstand. She collected her denim
jacket from the coat tree there and locked the office behind her.

"Take it easy, José," she called as she left.

"O.K. Bye," he answered, as always. She wasn't sure how much
English he spoke. He came in at 2:30 in the morning, after some
other shift somewhere else, Frank had told her, and swept and
scrubbed for three hours. Then he took the subway home to Queens.

Christine hailed a taxi. It was 3:30 and the streets were still spotted with couples who lingered, singles who moved quickly through
the streets, and the homeless who wandered up and down the
block. At home, she ran up the stairs and fitted her key into the lock.
It was good to be there.

As she stepped inside, something felt off kilter. She hesitated for a second before turning on the light. Everything seemed to be in order, but just to be sure, she made a quick sweep of the place; it was exactly as she'd left it. She kicked off her boots and flopped on the couch. Long night. Long life, she thought as she got up and went to the kitchen to pour herself a wind-down drink. She saw the message light blinking on her answering machine and felt a buzz of uneasiness. She hit the button.

Parker.

His voice reverberated in the quiet room. She reached into the freezer for her bottle of Tanqueray and poured a shot into a crystal snifter, focusing on the way it oozed out of the bottle. You again, she thought, unsure if she meant the booze, the uneasiness in her body, or Parker.

She glanced at her watch. Almost four. Might as well get it over with, she thought as she dialed the Carlyle.

"Parker Horton's room, please."

Parker answered on the first ring. He sounded wide awake, expectant.

"This is Christine," she said formally.

"Good," he answered. "You forgive me." His voice was engaging and flirty.

"It doesn't have anything to do with that, Parker. Let's just get this over with. What do you want?"

"Well…" He hesitated.

"It better be important," she said. She was standing up, tense, in the middle of the kitchen.

"I wanted to tell you that I'm…involved with someone else."

"I feel sorry for her."

He ignored that.

"...and I'm selling the apartment."

"That has nothing to do with me."

"And I'm probably moving to New York with her."

Christine felt her knees go weak.

He knew he had stunned her. "And," he continued with a slight change in his voice, "I hired a detective—supposed to be world class, by the way—to find Petra, and when he finds her I'm gonna take you back to court and this time I'm gonna get custody. Cause you're not doing the job, Christine." He paused expectantly.

So like him, she thought as she fought to get control of her voice.

"Is that it?" she finally said.

"Yeah."

"O.K. You told me." This time she paused. The same old game: who has the upper hand, and for how long. He said nothing, so she continued. "Goodbye, Parker."

"Goodbye, Christine."

They hung up. Christine carried her drink to the living room and collapsed on the couch. She felt whipped, beaten, as if she'd folded up into a little ball and been brutally kicked over and over again. Every part of her body ached—her brain, her teeth, her stomach. Her eyes burned and her skin felt overexposed and tender.

Petra, she thought. Petra.

There had been many times over her eight stormy years with Parker that she had wished for the courage and the wildness to kill him. These thoughts had shocked and terrified her in the beginning, but later she indulged herself with them. She had detailed fantasies about the weapons she might use: her bare hands, a claw hammer, a crowbar. A brick, brass knuckles, a bicycle chain. She favored weapons she could hold in her hands and wield repeatedly until the venom was drained out of her or the possession passed. It was never a gun or a bomb or a severed brake line for Christine. Too removed, too distant, too technical. She had never raised a hand to Parker, except that one time to protect herself, and as time passed in their marriage, she even used words less and less. She swallowed her anger and it boiled inside and poisoned her blood; it mutated and grew out of control, like cancer cells, invading every organ; it contaminated her circulatory system, her nervous system, her digestive system, her respiratory system, her excretory system. She was ill with hatred when she finally got away. Now she wondered if she had gained the strength to fight back and win.

Not to see me now, she realized, coiled up in the fetal position on her white sofa.

She got up and poured another shot. It slid down and calmed her. It pushed back the helpless fear and in the second that her feelings unlocked, she cried, gut-wrenching sobs that would make her sides ache for days afterward.

Crying was relatively recent for Christine. For most of her life, her tears had turned to sand inside her. They built up in her body and made her feel heavy. First her feet and legs seemed weighted, then her hips. She felt trapped in an invisible full-body cast. When the tears had finally loosened and broken free, starting when she'd taken Petra, fled California, and ultimately landed on Patty's couch in New York, the relief had been enormous. She felt the hard, yellow plaster of her invisible cast filling with a grief so deep that merely admitting it cleansed her. Later, when she was able to think again, she meditated on that step from the utter defeat of apathy to the relative freedom of grief. She had wondered, still wondered, what would come next.

There had been no one there as the walls of her defenses rocked and fell. Christine felt compelled to spare her one close friend, Patty, from the shock waves because she feared they would drive Patty away. It would have been inevitable. Patty would have had to run, like all people automatically run before an avalanche or a flow of hot orange lava. "How're you doing?" Patty would ask on the phone, and Christine would feel the tension of keeping the truth back, far back, in her voice. "Oh, pretty good," she would answer. "Just living my life like a living liver." They would laugh. It was a line from one of the poetry readings that had been held during the early days of Paco's, when Christine and Patty had both been waitresses there and Parker had been too busy launching his new enterprise to notice either of them.

That had been nine years ago, when Patty was nineteen and Christine was about to turn twenty-one. For Patty, Paco's had been a summer stop-over job before her freshman year at New York University. She had a plan: college, law school, public service. One by one, she'd checked off her goals, only now, two years into her career, she called it "public disservice" and felt helpless before the bureaucracy, the deals, and the paperwork. For Christine, Paco's had been more. She'd been drifting for over three years, from place to place and job to job. At Paco's, she found a world where she felt she belonged. She fell in love with Parker. They married. Petra was born. They worked hard and built the business together. And then, one by one, those things were yanked away.

When she woke up, still dressed, still on the couch, the bottle of Tanqueray empty and tipped over on the floor beside her, Christine felt calm. It was important not to panic. She listened to the sounds of the Sunday morning soccer game on the court across the street before she got up and went to the window to watch. The two teams hollered and swore at each other in Spanish. They were there every Sunday, all year. They wore sweatshirts and stocking caps in the winter and peeled down by April to shorts and sneakers. She liked to watch the so-called harmless aggression, so full of kicking and insults, from her window five floors up. Men, she thought, were always pounding back and forth, overwhelming in their hugeness. They were thunder and lightning, and she was a skinny, stalky plant, just trying to get ripe. Did she have a chance of making it, with the thunder booming and the rain pouring down? More importantly, did Petra?

Petra, she thought as she puttered with her coffee-bean grinder and her espresso pot in the kitchen. Petra.

Could Parker's world-class detective find her?

No.

She had been careful. More than careful. Obsessively determined, in fact, to erase every possible trace and clip any link. She called the school twice a week, but always from a pay phone, a different pay phone each time, and she always used coins. She wrote and received letters, but she kept neither the letters nor any written record of the school's address. School, she thought, now there was a euphemism. She had collected all the photographs of Petra and put them in a safety deposit box that was inaccessible to anyone but her. The rent on it was paid for ten years. The cash for her daughter's school was carried to its director by a bonded messenger dispatched by Patty from her office. No one could trace it to Christine.

She had not seen her daughter in over a year. Aside from Patty, no one here even knew she had a daughter.

No. Parker would not find her.

But his comment had stung her: "You're not doing the job," he had said. That depended on how you defined the job, she thought. Baking cookies and being there at three o'clock at the nursery school gate—no, she wasn't doing that. But Christine viewed those as the fifties TV sitcom, the fairy tales, of motherhood.

She ran her bath, dropped in a royal blue bath-oil bead that smelled like camphor, and lowered herself into the steamy water, balancing her espresso cup on the corner of the tub.

What exactly was a mother's job?

Who knew, who knew?

The medicinal smell from the water was subtle but it seemed to cool her, despite the steam rising all around, covering the mirror and the faucets with a layer of fog.

Mother, mother, mother, she repeated. What is a mother's job?

Her entire experience, she realized, amounted to a small triangle with Petra on one point, herself on the other, and her own mother, Nina, on the third. Did Nina do the job?

Who knew, who knew?

Evaluations like that, Christine thought, required precision where precision was impossible. Nina had baked the cookies and welcomed little Christine home from school every day. That was good. But she often welcomed her with what she called "a little highball" in her hand, and it was always obvious that the highballs had begun long before school let out. That was bad. And sometimes, Christine would climb the wooden steps to their ranch-style house in Playa del Ray, a worn down, dusty suburb near Los Angeles International Airport, pull the screen door open, and see Nina asleep on the couch. Her mouth would be open, a big noisy O, and she would be covered with pages of the L.A. *Times*, spread over her shoulders. Nina said the newspaper was warm and it saved her dragging a blanket out of the linen cupboard in the hallway. Christine would stand a few feet away and say, "Mom!" in a louder and louder voice until Nina would sputter awake, sitting up in a crackle of newspapers.

"Hi, baby. You home so soon? I just lied down five minutes ago," she would say, pulling Christine close and kissing the top of her head. That was good. But the smell of her breath, that was bad. "Let's rustle you up something to eat," Nina would say, re-folding the newspapers and tapping a Chesterfield out of her pack on the coffee table. Christine would follow her into the kitchen. "Now what do we have on the menu?" Nina would dig through the cupboards, calling out the possibilities: PB&J? Rice Chex? Tomato soup? Butter and sugar sandwich? All that was good. Sitting there in her father's chair, answering Nina's million questions about her day in school, with Nina in a cloud of cigarette smoke, that was good. But as Christine got older, past ten, past eleven, definitely past twelve, the goods had ended and the bads had multiplied. Now it was an effort to remember the goods at all.

Exactly when or how it had changed was impossible for her to pinpoint, but she still felt stunned whenever she remembered one particular July afternoon when she was twelve. She had been playing kickball in a vacant lot between a three-story apartment building and a discount supermarket. The palm trees that marked second and third bases were sticky with the heat, and the sand burned when she slid into home plate. Christine left at the last possible minute to clean up before a baby-sitting job on the next block. She'd taken a fast shower and had barely buttoned her sleeveless shirt when Nina came into the bathroom without knocking. Her eyes were dull, the way they usually were by sundown, and the whiskey smell filled the room. She closed the door behind her. She had something in her hand, down by her side, which Christine couldn't see.

"You're getting older now," her mother slurred, "and you're getting B.O."

Christine, standing at the sink in front of the mirror with the comb in her hand, felt sliced open by Nina's words. They invaded her, like her mother invaded the bathroom: viciously and without apology. Christine turned slightly to face Nina and felt her fingers grip the edge of the sink. Nina started toward her. It took three steps to cross the bathroom. She raised the object in her hand. Christine confusedly saw it was a bottle of Ban roll-on deodorant. The top was off.

For Christine, it seemed to happen in some awful form of slow motion. Nina grabbed her wrist and lifted up her arm. Christine resisted and tried to struggle but her mother pushed her backward against the wall and pinned her there. She rolled the Ban up and down inside the hollow of Christine's armpit. It was cold and thick and the smell was disgusting.

"You need to use this every day," Nina hissed, grabbing Christine's other arm and repeating the application. "B.O. isn't gonna help you, sister." Christine turned her face, away from the smell of booze, smoke, and Ban roll on. She felt ashamed of her body for stinking and ashamed of herself for not pushing her mother back, off her, down onto the cold floor.

"There," Nina finally said, "now let that dry for a minute." She screwed the top on the bottle and pulled open the metal door to the medicine cabinet. "I'll put it in here so you can use it every day." And then she left.

Christine sat down, stunned, on the toilet seat covered with a fuzzy rug in avocado green. She and Nina, she realized, were now going to share the bottle of deodorant. Neither would have B.O. Christine tore off a few squares of toilet paper and pressed them into her eyes, blotting the tears before they could form. She would not allow Nina to make her cry, not before a baby-sitting job. It took several minutes to get control of herself. When she finally stood up, her back was straight and her long spindly legs, banged up and mosquito bitten, carried her out of the house without calling a goodbye.

That was a bad memory, one of the early ones from the time when all the trouble started. Was Nina just doing a mother's job?

Who knew, who knew?

Christine climbed from the tub and toweled herself dry, studying her reflection in the full-length mirror on the back of the bathroom door. Her body amazed her. It was such a hiding place. It stood tall and strong, one continuous smooth unbroken line, curving and stretching, making it easy for her eye to move up one side and down the other. Her shoulders, she thought, were her best feature. Wide and bony but naturally sculpted into shapes that pivoted dramatically when she moved. She draped that body in skin-tight clothes, clothes that said, "I am here; I am not afraid," and she fooled everybody. Her clothes, no matter how flashy they were or how much attention they brought her, were disguises. She knew her body, with a tight skirt stretched around it like a bandage, was a long, hard lie, but it was the kind that short circuited questions and judgments. No one could look at her and see the real Christine. No psychological misalignment, no sad story, presented itself to be read by a passing stranger.

Her face; well, perhaps it was not such a fortress, such a suit of armor. She had the feeling that her face soaked up the gaze of any person who looked at her. It had some crazy similarity to gum on the street, she thought; if you came in contact with it, it held on, spread, stretched to maintain a connection. She was not happy about this. She thought it was her deep sadness that made people look once and want to dive in and save her. She was a dark, cool pool that seemed both serene and terrifying. So she used lipstick and a tinted foundation cream to form an invisible block, and never left the apartment, except in the dark, without her sunglasses.

Christine, she thought, looking into her eyes in the mirror till her nose almost touched it, who are you anyway?

She slipped into her terrycloth robe and went into the kitchen for more coffee. Looking down at the pink blossoms along the park, she dialed Patty's number.

"What're you doing, kiddo?" Christine asked.

"Just sitting here waiting for the new me to arrive," Patty answered.

"Oh yeah? Which one is that?"

"The one that exercises. The one that stops after half a carton of Haagen Daas. The one that's already gone downstairs for the paper."

"Oh, that one," Christine responded. "When is she expected?"

"She's not expected. That's the problem." Patty didn't really sound dejected.

"You want me to bring you the paper?" Christine asked.

"Only if you'll bring some O.J. and some bialies too."

"Done," said Christine. "I'll see you in forty-five minutes."

She stepped into her closet and dressed quickly. She could be out the door in five minutes, easy. Not like when she was married to Parker, when she agonized over what to wear, which colors would please him, and nervously searched his blue eyes for approval. Now she wore uniforms. She stepped into her black tights and pulled a black skirt off the rack.

She walked to Patty's apartment in SoHo. Patty lived on the third floor in a two-room apartment crowded with law books. Christine walked fast, zigzagging down to Houston and over, one block west and one block south. She would not tell Patty about Parker's call, at least not today. But the threat nagged at her, made her feel defensive and somehow misunderstood.

She loved Petra with all her heart, all her senses, all her mind. Depositing her at the Warren School for Girls on Cape Cod and leaving her there tore a wide hole into Christine, as if a grizzly bear's claw had ripped into her chest and pulled out organs that would never stop dripping blood. She had squatted down, tried to see behind her daughter's blank blue eyes. She pulled her into her lap. Petra felt like a giant rag doll. Eight years old and missing already from the cage that was her little body. Petra had escaped. No one knew where she was.

"Petra, sweetie, little love girl," Christine had whispered into Petra's tangled brown hair, cropped off short to keep her from pulling it out. "Mommy loves you; Mommy does." Christine held Petra's hand and stretched out her fingers, one by one. They curled up again the second she let them go, a little fist with the thumb tucked inside. Dirt clumped in a thin line along the crease where the palm of her hand folded over. Christine cradled and rocked her, but Petra remained limp and unaffected. Christine quieted her own breathing and listened for Petra's. She had read that matching the pattern of inhalation and exhalation sometimes built a bridge into a person like Petra. But her daughter's breaths came in no discernible pattern.

Christine had carried her up the marble stairs to her room. Three little beds; three little girls. Pink spreads and colorful animals on the wallpaper. Stuffed tigers and lonely dolls, moved off the pillow by nurses only, never the children. Petra, in the bed. Christine, leaning forward, kissing her forehead, her cheeks, her hair. Standing up. Those blue eyes, blank in the shadows. The walk to the door. The little body, amidst the stuffed animals. The silence. And then, the marble steps. The sharp, concerned eyes of the night nurse, not in a uniform, no, in slacks and a powder blue sweater. Christine had raised her hand and shook her head. She left without one word, one reciprocated human touch. Into the blackest night of her life.

Was she doing the job of a mother?

Who knew, who knew?

Christine followed the smell of warm bread to a bakery on Prince Street.

"What's yours, Miss?" asked a white-haired lady behind the counter.

"Two bialies and two cinnamon bagels." Collecting the little morning picnic would require three separate stops. Christine liked going from place to place, filling her arms with small reminders of how much she loved Patty. She liked delivering the load and seeing Patty in her same old ratty bathrobe, shoving aside the books and papers to clear a spot on the minuscule kitchen table for the Sunday feast. They always separated the paper into stacks: for Patty, the front page, the Week in Review, Arts & Leisure, the Metro Report; for Christine, the Book Review, the Magazine, the Style Section, the Classifieds; for the trash, Sports, Real Estate, TV, Travel, Business. Patty would put on a CD. Lately, it was a ten-year-old Brian Eno record. Space music. And it would feel, to Christine, as if the little apartment was whirling through the solar system with its two oblivious passengers happily along for the ride.

7

*P*arker slept until one in the afternoon. With the heavy drapes pulled across the windows overlooking Madison Avenue, the room was dark and cool, and the shapes of the high-backed chairs and the outline of the fireplace and mantle were barely visible. He pulled himself to the edge of the bed and lowered his feet into the thick green carpet. He fumbled around on the table until he felt his watch, a five-year-old Rolex, and turned the lamp on to its lowest setting; 1:10. Time to get up.

Parker lifted the phone and called the concierge's desk.

"I'll be checking out at four," he said. "I need a limo to J.F.K."

"Yes, sir."

"Can I order some breakfast?"

"I'll connect you with Room Service." The phone was answered immediately. An efficient female voice with the trace of an accent, probably German, Parker thought.

"This is room 623. Can you send up a western omelet, well-cooked, with rye toast and home fries? And a pot of black coffee."

"Right away, sir. Would you like the Times?"

"No."

He hung up without saying goodbye or thanks. For Parker, politeness kicked in after the pot of coffee. He crossed to the bath, half aware of his morning hard-on bobbing gently up and down in front of him as he walked. He was thirty-seven. Too young to be concerned about the day he'd open his eyes to find his penis flopped to one side, limp. But he did think about it once in a while, when he woke up weary for reasons that would not have slowed him in the least a few years back.

He took a quick cool shower and had already combed his hair straight back and pulled on a pair of sweat pants when Room Service knocked on the door and wheeled in a breakfast cart. Parker took three dollars out of the pocket of his trousers, flung over the back of a chair, folded them, and gave them to the waiter without making eye contact. The coffee smelled good, but the size of the cup irritated him. He liked a sturdy mug for coffee, one he didn't have to refill every two minutes. No one drinks coffee in cups like these anymore, he thought, examining the flowers and the silver trim along the rim and turning it upside down to read the trademark. These were for old ladies whose bio-systems had gone fragile, widows who were raised in the pre-World War II days when gluttony was still considered a vice and not a national pastime. The handle was too small to hold comfortably, but he had no alternative; he poured the coffee out of the silver pot into his dainty flowered cup and settled down to eat.

He set the sprig of parsley on the tablecloth and divided his omelet in half with his fork. He was in the business so, of course, he was interested in the food, the table, and the presentation. Paco's was at the opposite end of the continuum, with its deliberately mismatched dishes and its napkins, all hand-stitched from material remnants. Its funky charm delighted the customers and they paid prices that were more or less in the same ball park as the Carlyle's or any other good hotel or restaurant. Of course, his waitresses—young, beautiful, and sexy—helped too. He selected each one himself: looks first; a certain undefinable vibration which he privately called the "possibility factor" second; skill at the job third and last.

Except for Christine, he had never tested the "possibility factor," no matter how tempted. It wasn't worth it. The decline of the relationship and marriage, the public nature of it with its accusations, innuendoes, and lies, had humiliated Parker almost beyond endurance. His face used to burn when he imagined the customers talking about him after he'd led them to a table and pulled out their chairs. But it had ended, at least on the surface. People's memories were short and fickle, and now it felt somewhat normal again.

But it wasn't. Not to Parker. And not to Christine, if her performance during his visit to Skinny's and last night's phone call were any indication. He had known her for a long time, intimately, through many stages and personas. The sweet and vulnerable young Christine, twenty years old to his twenty-seven, who had been too shy and uncomfortable to sit alone with him and have a glass of wine after the restaurant closed. Christine, the bride; grateful, tentative, tender. The pregnant Christine; fearful, angry, given to fits of irrationality and moodiness that made him dread entering their apartment in Pacific Heights. And then, after Petra's birth, the growing, unanchored rage that he couldn't understand. She had everything, he thought, and she wanted to pull it all down, destroy it. Destroy him, specifically. And for what?

Parker thought she had created some imaginary version of him and infused it with so much life that she was no longer able to separate the reality from her fantasy. She had taken his small actions, planted them in the fertile territory of her perceptions, and grown him into a monster. He had felt helpless when he saw himself through her eyes, growing out of all proportion, and he had tried to stop the process. But that had led to more accusations and more charges. And finally he'd gotten fed up and simply returned fire for fire. It escalated. Then she became Christine, the bitch who distorted everything; Christine, who deserved an Oscar for her performance in the courtroom; Christine, who arrived in his life broke and adrift and left with half of everything and exclusive rights to Petra.

The crazy thing was, she still fascinated him. He'd felt pumped up when he left her bar, as if he'd stepped back into a boxing ring for a rematch. He had trained this time and would not be caught unaware again, not like last time. She'd played her hand with her usual cool distance—returning his phone call at four in the morning, for example, blasting him out of a sound sleep—but he knew she was afraid. And for good reason. No matter how long it took and no matter what he had to do, this time he would win. And she knew it.

Parker rejected the last corner of his second piece of toast and placed his napkin alongside his empty plate. He took his suit bag out of the closet and quickly hung a few things in it. He hadn't brought much. He'd made this trip, he felt, for the sole purpose of informing Christine that he was not out of the game. He did it because he wanted to be fair with her. He could've hired Greg Litner, the private investigator, without telling her, but that wasn't his style. He didn't play dirty. Of course, he lied about moving to New York, but it had just come out of his mouth, a surprise to him, and since it had thrown her so off balance, he had decided not to retract it. It would not hurt to have her off balance.

And, he admitted to himself, he wanted to get a look at her, wanted to see those sad dark eyes again with the lines just beginning to form at their edges. And he wanted her to see him, to see how well he looked. Perhaps remind her how easily he moved through the world, how liable he was to show up anywhere, anytime.

He picked up the phone again and called San Francisco.

"Hello." It was a woman's sleepy voice.

"Hi, baby."

"Oh," she said, and it was clear that she was glad to hear his voice, "Parker."

"Did I wake you?"

"No. I'm awake, but I'm still in bed."

"Sounds good."

"I want you to come home," she said. "Leave New York right this minute."

"You miss me?" he asked, lighting his first cigarette of the day with one hand as he leaned back against the headboard.

"Come home," she repeated.

"You're pretty bossy today, Lily," he said with a slow smile. "Pretty mean."

"I'm not mean." She sounded petulant and it made him smile.

"Are you sweet?" he asked.

"You tell me," she answered. "Tell me how sweet I am."

"I'll tell you when I see you. I'll show you." She was silent for a few seconds. "You picking me up?"

"Um-hmmm," she purred.

"You have all the information?"

"Um-hmmm." Her voice was sexy, teasing. It made his dick hard just to hear it.

"O.K. I'll see you tonight."

"Mmmmm."

He dropped the receiver into its cradle and rested his head against the headboard. Lily was young but that made it easier. Things that had nothing to do with an actual relationship passed for the real stuff with her. He could say the words and she would purr. He could do the right things and still have ninety-nine percent of his mind free. He finished his cigarette and put on a shirt.

Greg Litner arrived promptly at 2:15, as scheduled. He had a hel-luva handshake and a military bearing. No bullshit. Parker opened his slim-line briefcase and produced the photos of Christine. Greg sifted through them, studying each one. Greg made notes in a small notebook he kept in the breast pocket of his very expensive suit. Parker found it easy to lay out the job to him. Greg was a pro; he did-n't flinch one bit.

8

$\mathcal{A}$s Parker and Greg were descending from the sixth floor in the meticulously maintained teakwood elevator, Steve in his apartment a few blocks south, was readjusting a noisy table fan, directing the airstream directly into his face as he stared at the TV. The temperature had shot up to ninety-two degrees, turning New York into a steam bath in the course of a few hours. Steve's apartment had no cross ventilation. The bricks absorbed the heat and held it. He gave himself an occasional spritz with a plastic spray bottle. This was just a freak hot spell for May, but in July and August it would be normal and he doubted he could stand it. Too oppressive.

Steve had rented three movies, all spy thrillers. He liked to lie on the couch and observe the movie makers' versions of the secrets of international politics. He viewed them as interesting but totally inaccurate reflections of the way governments actually work. In the movies, smooth, cultured agents who wore clothes well and never experienced fear slipped to the center of espionage rings and pulled the fuses out of time bombs. In reality, loathsome, corrupt human rats, like Richard Nixon, sent bumbling lackeys to steal election strategy secrets and then lied about it and ended up millionaires on the lecture circuit. In the movies, French resistance fighters held clandestine meetings and no one lost his nerve, but in reality, Hitler or the Khmer Rouge or Stalin rose to power and committed mass genocide as all the spies in the world peeked around corners and made notes. All that espionage activity, Steve thought, masked the truth that no human, and therefore no human group, had ever passed square one, which was blatant self interest.

Which brought him to the question of Christine Timberlake.

He was spying on her but the fact that he did it without malice and without any desire for personal gain was, he thought, extremely significant. Whatever the power game in spying was, and he wasn't sure what motivated or constituted it, he wasn't playing it. He just wanted to know one normal person well, someone who was not a junkie, not a prostitute, not a doctor, not a patient. He felt he could know Christine, just a random person, by observing her life and examining the things she valued and displayed and the things she hid. When that was over, nothing more. It was like being an actor, he thought: you're assigned a part and you have to go on stage and find a way to make it real. You had to act as if the situation were upon you, whatever it was, and since you knew the script and therefore you knew the actions that would follow, you had to find a way to make them yours. Well, Steve realized, he was trying to find a way to make life his, to make normal relationships and normal interaction possible.

The problem was, of course, that even though he had already entered her life somewhat, he felt more baffled than ever. He looked around his sublet: it said a few things about its owner, the would-be actress. Her name, a stage name he presumed, was Abby Zane. Everything from A to Z, he'd thought when he met her. The walls were covered with movie posters precariously thumbtacked into the plaster. She had bookshelves full of plays and how-to manuals for actors. In her closet, she had boxes full of hats she'd probably worn in some Off-Off Broadway showcase. She had a complete Tupperware set, mismatched bath towels, and a huge economy size box of laundry detergent. So he had an idea of her interests and her lifestyle, but he was dismayed by the layer of filth on everything, the disgusting putrid-green shag rug in the living room. He understood that for an actress wanna-be, life probably took place in the future, in some indeterminate time when all the hard work finally paid off and her dream came true. Steve understood that if you lived in the future, you became progressively more oblivious to the present. He figured that explained the greasy dust layered along the top of the window casings and the picture frames, the cobwebs in the high corners of the kitchen, the black mold in between the squares of tile on the bathroom walls. So he had learned something about Abby Zane, but she didn't seem particularly normal when all was said and done.

Steve had been raised in a house that smelled like lemons. Twice a week, his mother, Sarah, dragged out the Lemon Pledge and used an old cloth diaper to wipe down the surface of the furniture. Sometimes in the evening, while supposedly relaxing, she would suddenly stand up and grab a broom, energetically poking the straw spokes into the corners and along the tops of the baseboards. Sarah liked a clean house, and she frequently made self-satisfied critiques of women who mistook neat for clean. She had never had a paying job, though she contributed a small portion to the family's upkeep by making and selling plaster crafts and teaching plaster crafts classes. Steve was raised in a house full of meditating Jesus faces, flat on the back and painted with bisque paint to simulate natural skin tones. People liked religiously-oriented plaster crafts, Sarah had told him. Praying hands were popular, as were Jesus faces, bas-relief nativity scenes, and youthful Virgin Marys. He had several of them decorating the wall of his small bedroom, though he never remembered his family going to church or praying before dinner or bed.

His father, Lyle, worked for twenty-three years at the Alcoa aluminum plant outside Massena, New York. The plant was situated, along with two other industrial factories, on the banks of the St. Lawrence River at the edge of a Mohawk Indian reservation that spanned the U.S./Canada border. The smoke poured into the sky and the factories dumped their PCBs into the river. Lyle had driven every day through Akwasasne, the reservation that had been named Hogansburg before the Indians developed what Lyle called a big case of delayed pride and changed it to an Indian name. He worked second shift and rarely saw his son. Lyle liked hunting and fishing and later, just before he died at the age of fifty-six, dirt biking. He liked to be out of the house, alone, tramping in the woods or tearing through it on his bike. He liked beer. But Steve never had a sense that he liked Sarah much, or Steve either. Sarah was his lunch-box packer, his laundress, his reluctant partner at Alcoa's annual picnic. And Steve was "the kid." "Get the kid to do it," Lyle would say when Sarah nagged him to mow the lawn or burn the trash; "he's old enough. Let him take on some of the responsibility around here."

Steve could only remember one time when his father systematically taught him something. Sarah's sister had invited Steve for a long weekend at her place on Long Island. A trip to the ocean was planned. Steve, a boy of nine, had the New York State map out on the dining room table and was searching for Jones Beach. Lyle had stood behind him and pointed it out. Then he said, "I s'pose you know all about undertow."

Steve twisted his head to look up at his father. Was it all right to admit he didn't? He finally shook his head. His father took a thick black pen and drew a rough cross section of a wave.

"This part of the water wants to come into shore," he said, using his pen as a pointer, "but this part wants to go back out to sea. If you're swimming in this part here and this part here rolls over you, it'll carry you back out with it."

Steve was terrified. How did you know what to do? How did you make sure you got in the part of the wave that wanted to go into shore? His eyes were wide with apprehension as he tried to form the questions.

"How do you swim then?" he finally asked.

"You gotta get the feel of it, that's all."

That was the end of the lesson. A week later, Steve stood on the warm tan sand and looked at the huge expanse of salty ocean water rolling in, rolling out. His father's diagram was fixed in his mind and he felt consumed with images of the cold, blue water pulling, pulling, pulling him out so far he'd become a tiny speck, like the birds on the horizon, just before he disappeared. He was too afraid to go in. Finally, Aunt Nancy had taken him by the hand and led him into the sea. She squatted down and took both his hands.

"Feel how the water wants to push you all around?" she asked with a happy giggle. "Doesn't it feel funny?" Steve let his muscles go a bit less rigid. "Now we got three things we can do here," she continued, "jump, dive, or swim." Still holding his hands, they inched, face to face, farther and farther from shore. They tried each option with Nancy calling out the big decision in a loud voice at the last second. After a while, Steve called one. "Dive!" he hollered and they both disappeared under the surface and came up behind the wave, sputtering and laughing. At the end of the weekend he had asked Nancy if he could come and live with her, but her face became a chalk-white mask and she said no. She said her life was too complicated to have a kid in it.

Years later, Steve would stand on the catwalks of the U.S.S. Constellation, just before the Officer of the Deck would announce over the IMC, the loudspeaker to the troops, that the catwalks were closed due to dangerous storm conditions. The carrier would ride the thirty to forty-foot swells and Steve would watch the four acres of flight deck, two inches of solid steel, flex and twist in opposing directions. The cold wind would whip the tops of the swells and the water would sting his face. Steve stepped around the fire hoses rolled up on their drums and the fueling stations for the jets, and he would wonder if perhaps this was the time the lumbering ship would not make it through the storm. He did not feel afraid in moments like those. He felt a cool, calm acceptance and a readiness to let go. He was glad he knew that about himself. It was the cornerstone of his identity. He felt a pang of disappointment when the sailors were ordered back inside the belly of the ship where there were no windows, where his relationship with the elements was severed and the only clue to the storm was the subtle internal shift from feeling weightless to feeling compressed. But in that moment, just before the catwalks closed, Steve often remembered the one lesson he'd learned from his father: to be afraid of the water. Well, he knew the water could and would kill him, and he still wasn't afraid. So much for Dad's wisdom.

Steve believed that children absorbed the personalities of their parents. He knew that each little child embodied the strange combination of one pair of great opposites, the masculine and the feminine, but when he imagined his own parents unconsciously pouring themselves into the big end of the funnel, and himself, coming out the small end, he had to wonder who those tense and joyless people were. Since he was five, they had lived in a small community, but they had no close friends. They owned a home but resented both the financial strain and the time involved to keep it up. In fact, Steve felt the only positive thing they'd ever given him was the death benefits of their insurance policy, and that had come to him more or less by default. There wasn't anyone else to leave it to. Lyle had probably put Steve's name in the beneficiary slot for one reason: to keep the state of New York from getting for free what he'd slaved for.

Thinking about his family gave Steve a nauseous feeling high in his stomach and a sense of heaviness in his chest. The oppressed feeling that resulted from that combination seemed disproportionate, but when it got a foothold it was hard to shake off. It felt as if he had swallowed an all-pervasive restlessness and it was growing inside him, pressing against the barrier of his skin. It was an inescapable, black feeling. In the old days, he would reach for dope. Now, post-cure, and he used that word with smirky cynicism, he reached for the third spy video and shoved it into the VCR. Perhaps a little wine would help. He got up and poured himself a glass of well-chilled Chablis. He had been in this place before, many, many times. The wine would take the edge off and he would make it through. But to what? For what? Those were not the types of questions that got him anywhere.

Steve immersed himself in the movie, this one about an aborted assassination attempt on Charles de Gaulle. Its slow, inevitable pace distracted him a bit. He felt the wine dig into the blackness of his mood, like a good masseuse digs into the pain and stiffness in the muscles and lets it out. To relax and let the cramp go was hard but worth it. By the time Charles de Gaulle did not get assassinated, Steve's inner storm had calmed. The psychological swells it had sent howling to his mind had raged until they wore themselves out, but he was still standing. More correctly, he was about half drunk, lying down, wildly spritzing his face with cool water and letting it dry in the breeze from the fan. But he was not high, not like the days in the past when even a minor storm sent him, shipwrecked, into the big nothingness.

The next day was a work day. Steve arrived precisely on time to find Janet slamming file drawers and disrupting the piles on top of Mary Anne's desk in an exaggerated and, Steve thought, childish display of irritation.

"Six weeks!" Janet was muttering. "This whole office could sink out of sight in six weeks. Jesus H. Christ."

Steve stood to the side. He would've liked to say the right words, but he had no idea what they were, and it didn't seem worth it to be an extra, a bit player with no power to change the story, in Janet's little drama.

"I need the goddamn Federal Express number and do you think it's in my Rolodex? No. That would be too easy. Can you believe she pulled this?" Janet's eyes finally fixed on Steve. He said nothing. "Why don't you say something?" she snapped.

"Because you're not talking to me," he answered. His voice was quiet and expressionless.

Janet dramatically looked to the left and right.

"I'm not? Who'm I talking to then?"

"I'm not sure," Steve said, "but it isn't me." He moved toward the Mr. Coffee.

His response seemed to deflate her. She looked intensely at him through her leopard glasses as she flopped into Mary Anne's swivel chair, lit a cigarette, and took a big drag. She blew the smoke out her nose.

Steve emptied the coffee filter and proceeded to fill the pot. He could feel her eyes on him. "I'm thinking about what you just said," Janet remarked. "It's quite interesting."

Steve knew she was trying to initiate a conversation. He knew it was his turn, but he felt awkward and self-conscious.

"I just don't usually answer people who aren't talking to me."

How could he tell her that, from his observation, most people, himself included, had an unruly inner monologue rolling along at all times. They considered it a conversation if they turned the volume up loud enough for others to hear. There was a big difference between talking to a person or talking at him. Most people pummeled those around them with meaningless words, sentences that meant nothing. Like Janet's ranting. There was no point in pretending that it involved or even interested him. Furthermore, if she considered it worth either communicating or worth listening to, she was wrong. But to say all that, to wrestle it into language and present it to a woman he wasn't even sure he liked was too much to try.

"Well, what constitutes being talked to, for you?" Janet asked.

Oh no, Steve thought, she's going to push it.

"I guess I'd have to feel like part of it," he finally answered. "You want some coffee?"

She nodded. He handed her a cup, black. She was strangely quiet. Then she said, "So Steve, what do you think about Mary Anne taking six weeks off? I really wanna know."

He considered his options, and decided to try the truth as an experiment.

"I think if you couldn't handle it, you should've fired her. But you gave her the time, you know, so you should quit complaining." He almost said "bitching" but managed to replace it at the crucial second. He felt irritated, as if he'd been flung into the midst of a confrontation that wasn't his. Neither Janet nor Mary Anne mattered to him much. But then, once he'd been hooked, he felt his distance and neutrality vanish. He wanted to get Janet straight on this issue, and that seemed odd. Why should she listen? Why should she care? But there she was, sitting at Mary Anne's desk, listening closely. It suddenly hit Steve that merely giving his opinion felt like an aggressive act, as if by simply stating who he was, he was simultaneously attempting to diminish everyone else. That thought formed and flashed through his mind just before Janet spoke.

"You're right, you know. In general, I probably chew a helluva lot more than I bite off," she said. Then she laughed, a small spurt of laughter that sounded almost like a yell, and got up and went to her office. Steve refilled the paper trays on the copy machine, swept up, and began to meter stamp the mail that was piled up in Mary Anne's out basket. Janet's door was closed. Steve felt lonely in the aftermath of their conversation. It was as if a connection had been made and broken before he was able to calm down and experience it. He glanced at his watch: 10:53. He lifted the receiver off the phone on Mary Anne's desk and dialed Christine's number.

The phone rang twice and the answering machine picked up. Steve felt enormously attentive as he listened to her voice. But half way through, the message abruptly stopped and there was a loud click. Christine said, "Hello? I'm here." Steve got an instantaneous mental picture of her standing in her kitchen, her thick dark hair flowing down toward the small of her back. He said nothing. There was nothing to say. "Hello?" she repeated. She waited a few seconds and hung up. Steve slowly replaced the receiver.

She was home now, he thought, stepping away from the phone this very minute, perhaps pausing to look out the kitchen window over the park. The phone call would not have upset her. She would simply assume it was a wrong number or some computerized tele-marketing device that was slowly reprogramming itself. The sound of her voice had warmed him. It gave him some sort of reference point, like the needle pointing north on an old compass.

That night he went to Christine's apartment to search for the let-ter that had upset her so much that day in the post office. First he had strolled by Skinny's and seen her behind the bar, so he knew he wouldn't be caught. He was familiar with her building now and amused himself by counting the stairs to her apartment: sixty-eight. He gave the doorbell a perfunctory jab before he used his keys to casually walk in. But just after he closed the door behind him, before he had even thrown the dead bolt, he heard the door to 5B open and the jangle of Christine's neighbor's keys. Steve spun around to place an eye against the peephole. He could see the entire landing through the fish-eye lens. This must be Sheffield or Benito, he thought. He did not recognize the man, a blond of medium build who adjusted his Walkman and disappeared down the stairs.

Inside Christine's place, Steve locked the door. The near encounter had shaken him. He wasn't, after all, a casual visitor who could come and go. That kind of attitude led to mistakes which he could not permit himself to make. He turned into the apartment. The same. Orderly but cold. Where would Christine place her important papers, he wondered as he did a quick scan of the living room. There was no desk or file cabinet. Steve's eyes stopped on the wooden box full of pictures, and he crossed to it and carried it to the middle of the living room. He sat on the floor and dumped the whole box out, face down, on the shiny bleached wood. He would replace them in their exact order.

In the bottom of the box, under the pictures, was a tiny plastic hospital bracelet, the kind that is attached to the wrist of a newborn in a nursery. It was cut apart and flattened. Steve picked it up and read: Petra Elizabeth Horton. Female. Born 2/12/85. Mother: Christine. Date of admission: 2/11/85. Steve stared at the bracelet. Where was this child? he wondered. Christine seemed so singular and self-contained, it was difficult to imagine such an encumbrance for her. He dropped the bracelet back into the box and turned over the top photos on the pile. None showed Christine with a child or a baby or even a child alone. They were mostly grade-school pictures, the kinds kids exchange after their parents are pressured into buying them, and old black and white pictures of an older-looking couple dressed in 1940s style clothing. They stood smiling in a driveway next to a shiny new car. In another, they stood on a porch behind a hip-high railing, waving. It was a two-story house in a place that looked hilly and cultivated. Not like the wild woods and intensely rugged terrain of his own home in St. Regis Falls.

Steve studied each photo before he replaced it in the box. The old couple appeared again and again. There were also a few pictures of a younger couple whom he assumed, because of a noticeable family resemblance, to be Christine's parents. One photo showed this couple sitting on the concrete steps of a small house. Christine, about ten in the photo, sat down one step with one parent on either side of her. Her father's hand was cupped around her upper arm, just below her right shoulder. Her mother sat slightly apart and her attention seemed to be distracted by something off to the left. Steve raised the photo to eye level to stare at the man who, he knew because of those shelves of books in the closet, had sexually molested his own daughter. He looked like a normal man: short dark hair, black framed glasses, a shirt with a button-down collar. Steve could see the man's penny loafers on the step beside where Christine sat leaning back against his legs. He was looking directly into the camera and smiling. He didn't look like a man with a secret.

Steve's eyes moved to the woman. She was pretty like Christine. Her hair was short and brushed forward into bangs over her forehead. Perhaps it was the way her attention was off somewhere, as if she might've seen or heard something out of the ordinary in the next yard, but Christine's mother looked lonely and isolated in the picture. She touched no one and no one touched her. Steve's eyes moved from point to point on this little family triangle and he was filled with emotions he could not immediately identify. He replaced the photo, thumbed quickly through the rest of the pile, and replaced the box on the table. It was in that second when he put the carved box down that he identified the enormous pity he felt for all of them: the father, the mother, and the innocent little child.

While he was in Christine's apartment, he felt that time became quite skewed. It was like entering a vacuum that was so dense it immediately severed all connections to the outside world, which was fine because her inside world was extremely peaceful and interesting to him. Just moving through her cool private rooms was enough. He felt he was busy doing something just by being there. Having a purpose, like finding the letter, was extraneous; it became a chore. But Steve was used to doing chores, so he went to the closet to find her denim jacket. It was hanging there, but the inside pocket was empty. He looked around and then pulled open the drawer built into the shelving unit. Her underwear, as he had expected.

The drawer was divided into three sections. Panties were piled into one; bras were thrown into the second; and socks, paired and rolled, filled the third. Steve rifled through the socks but felt no letter tucked beneath them. Pawing through the bras gave him a slight pause, but he lifted them in a clump and immediately replaced them when no letter showed itself in the bottom of the drawer. He felt very unsure about touching her panties. They were so absolutely personal. She seemed to favor basic functional cotton bikinis in pastel colors, he noticed, though there was a bit of black lace peeking out of a few places in the pile. Finally he overcame his hesitation. He would simply detach and do the job. He lifted the panties. They felt soft against the skin of his hands. Again, this part of the drawer was empty. He placed the underwear back as it had been and closed the drawer.

Steve reached up and felt along the top of the shelves. Nothing there, not even dust, which didn't surprise him. He checked the pockets in the winter coats, lifted the mattress, and then checked to see if there was something taped to the back of the headboard. Nothing. He returned to the living room and opened the antique truck. It held mostly heavy, folded winter sweaters. He felt around and through them, but there was nothing. That left the wall of books. The letter could be between the pages of any one of them.

He sat down. Perhaps she hadn't kept the letter. There was so little that was personal in her home it seemed odd, even to Steve. It suddenly occurred to him that perhaps that level of anonymity was intentional. Even he had a few items that described him: his DD214 release documentation from the navy, a letter from Dr. Greene that he'd never answered, a homemade syringe in case he ever decided it was worth it to slip. Christine only had her paintings and books.

He got up and stood in front of the bookcase. There was a section on art and design with lots of expensive, illustrated coffee-table-style books in it; two entire shelves of psychology books, from college texts to popular, off-the-drugstore-rack best sellers; the rest were novels and short story collections. He had read some of them, but most of the titles were unfamiliar. The next time he came, he thought, he would choose one and sit down on her couch and read it. Perhaps it would give him something to talk about if he ever had occasion to speak to her. Because he knew in his mind and was ready to accept that he actually wanted to speak to her very much. Crazier things have happened, he thought.

He was falling in love with Christine Timberlake.

What's more, he was doing it clean and often sober, and this one didn't have a built-in end to it the way it did if the woman was a prostitute or a junkie. The last woman Steve had been with was a fellow patient at the detox center. They had not really liked each other, but coming off a big habit, after the initial chills and aches passed, left a huge empty place in your life which you simply had to fill. Sex helped a little, but theirs was troubled sex, brimming with rage and need that were completely out of proportion. Their little affair crashed and burned, but both Steve and Marlene were glad to get out of the briar patch with only a few scratches. That had been more than a year ago. And, he reminded himself, it had been mostly about sex. This thing with Christine didn't start with sex like the interlude with Marlene had: it would end with it. Instead of beginning at the finale, he would start slow and win her, and the sex would be the seal on their secret, private file. Knowing as much about her as he did would give him a slight edge, but he promised himself that he would not get so lost in the game that he would use this information to manipulate her. No. He would stand back and let her be herself and then he would look for the grooves on both of them that would interlock naturally, without force or pressure. He felt like a pioneer. His job was to hack a place out of the woods and keep it clear enough for her to settle down and build a life with him.

This idea filled him with energy and he abruptly decided to leave. He needed a long, fast run. He took his gym clothes from his backpack and changed in the foyer. The night air was cool when he moved to the window and stood there, enjoying the steady breeze and watching the couples, arms around each other's waists, poke along on the street below. The lights down Avenue A looked like irregular silver blotches on a black canvas. It was pretty, he thought, very, very pretty from up here. He crossed the room, flipped off the light, and left.

9

Outside, across the street, Greg Litner watched with interest as Steve moved from the window. He jotted a few words in his small leather notebook and returned it to his shirt pocket. Apparently the ex-Mrs. Horton had a little action going: a guy who came and went with his own keys, who remained alone in her apartment while she tended bar in that shithole on Eighth Avenue. Greg had been around the block a few times and he knew a few things; he knew she didn't belong there. If the ex-husband stayed at the Carlyle and wore Bally tassel loafers without socks, then the ex-wife belonged on a shopping spree, her Balenciaga coat worn carelessly over a tee-shirt. Definitely not behind the bar at Skinny's House of Blues.

Greg recognized Steve when he stepped out the front door of the building, skipped down the steps, and headed east at a fast clip. Greg got up and followed on the other side of the street. He saw Steve cross Avenue B and continue on into the heart of Alphabet City. The people down here were screaming about gentrification, and the legions of homeless who'd been evicted from the park over a year ago still graffittied the neighborhood sidewalks with witticisms like "Mug the rich" or "Die Yuppie Scum." Greg couldn't see many signs of gentrification. Buildings were still boarded up, and vacant lots were filled with lean-to shelters constructed out of cardboard and discarded junk from the streets. As he walked along he passed a beat-out pregnant woman with a tee-shirt stretched across her belly. It said, "Third Street Needle Exchange" in big letters across the front. Beautiful, Greg thought. Your kid really has a chance in life. People like that made him sick. They were useless. They were parasites who leeched off other people. Then, if they finally got caught in the act, they got sent to some jail that was run like a summer camp where they got their teeth fixed and watched cable TV. Three hots and a cot was better than they ever did on their own, by far. And it only cost the taxpayers thirty grand a year per scumbag.

All Greg had to do was look around and his blood pressure rose. Of course, the guy who came out of the ex's apartment wasn't helping much. He was moving along pretty damn fast. Greg was in good shape for a guy his age, but he liked to exert himself on the racquetball court and nowhere else. Sometimes he thought he was getting too old for this stuff. Forty-eight. This kid he was following had fifteen years on him at least.

Steve hit the East River Park and sped up.

Oh shit, we're going jogging, Greg thought. He wasn't dressed for it. Plus it was dark, and he saw no reason to run his aging white ass along the edge of the projects when he could easily pick up on this guy some other time. He wasn't afraid of the hoodlums from the projects, though he knew they were getting crazier in direct proportion to the amount of crack they smoked. He could take care of himself and them too. But it took more than a daily wage to get him to bother. It wasn't like when he was just starting out.

"Expect to get beaten up a couple times a year," his first boss had said, "and if you stay in the business for three years, you'll get stuck bad at least once. Count on it." All that for $7 an hour, no benefits, not even hospitalization. The funny thing was, he'd taken the job, which largely involved skulking around in his beat-up Toyota Tercel with a video camera, filming the moment when the guy in the neck brace tossed it off to play a little baseball with his kid. He was made for the job, and as soon as he saved up enough cash he high-tailed it back to New York, his hometown. Nobody ever knew he got into the P.I. business because he was so broke he was sleeping in the same car he did surveillance from. He never left New York again. Some people fell apart on its streets, and others were made for them. He was in the latter group.

He had rented the second floor of a row house on 45th Avenue in Queens, not far off Northern Boulevard, and had lived there ever since. Last month he'd logged up twenty years there. One wife had come, been driven nuts by the uncertainty and danger of his work, and gone. They'd had no children, though she had four with her second husband, an office supply distributor in Westchester County. Greg still saw Norma for lunch about once a year, and he swore he saw regret in her hazel eyes when they parted at the Metro North Station.

He hailed the first cab he saw and sat back to enjoy the view along the FDR Drive. He liked the way the reflection of the lights shimmered in the dark, dirty water. As the Pakistani cabby made the series of turns to swing onto the 59th Street bridge, Greg closed his eyes and let his head rest back against the seat. The endless construction on the bridge annoyed him. The cab rattled and bumped over all the obstructions and the cabby cursed in English. Greg smiled to himself when he heard it: the first thing they learned when they shook the sand out of their sandals upon arrival in New York, he thought, was how to say, "Fuck you, you stupid asshole" out the window of a taxi.

His neighborhood had changed too, become progressively less Irish and more hispanic and black. It was noisier and his car got broken into more often, but it was essentially still a family neighborhood. He collected a receipt from the cabby, jogged up the single flight of stairs to his apartment, and went inside. As usual, he pulled his clothes off in a trail to the shower, cleaned up, and opened a ginger ale. Greg allowed himself one beer a day from his "International Collection," which he stocked by the week, and he liked to have it later, sitting on the back terrace overlooking the yards and gardens behind the houses.

This Horton case would probably not present much of a challenge. Parker Horton wanted to locate his daughter; once that was done, he wanted evidence assembled that would stand up in court and force some judge somewhere to reverse an earlier decision. Horton had been frank and unapologetic in his explanation of that decision. Christine had systematically distorted the facts, using dramatic, horrible pictures of her battered face and body, so that the one time he had lost control and roughed her up a little appeared to be a regular event. He had trashed the house too, he said, on that one occasion. The reason for the rage, Horton said, was not Greg's business. It was between him and Christine and no matter how it looked or what she said or did, she knew the simple truth, which was that she had set out to destroy him and almost managed to do it. He had never hurt their daughter, he said. Petra was mentally ill and needed a loving, stable environment that Christine could never provide. Horton had written Greg a check for $5,000 and said he expected detailed reports every week.

Yet the man had a slippery side, Greg thought. He could look you dead in the eye and shake your hand like a man with no axe in the world to grind, but when you left—and the good-byes were all very polite—you felt like you'd been given the bum's rush and Parker Horton was already washing his hands in the bathroom sink. Greg had been in the P.I. business a long time, though, and he knew one thing for sure: whether the client was a suit with manners or a slime-ball, they all wanted the same thing—to drive a spike through some-one else's balls and roast them on a spit over a nice hot fire. The civ-ilized veneer didn't fool Greg. He knew that humans were blood-thirsty, wild animals trying to run each other down and have them-selves a feast. He was a good P.I. because he could run right along with the pack, and he definitely knew the thrill of tearing into a fresh carcass.

Of course there were times, when the frenzy passed, when he felt bad about delivering up a carcass to the person who'd paid him, but he'd made a decision starting out and he'd stuck to it his entire career: never turn down a job; just adjust the price according to the likelihood that his conscience would bother him after it was wrapped up. Looking into Parker Horton's eyes as they sat opposite each other in the Queen Anne-style armchairs, Greg figured this case to be at least a six or seven on the Richter Scale of Regret, so he raised his basic daily rate by 35%.

The interesting thing about the case was that his preliminary phone work had produced nothing. Most missing persons' cases could be solved in less than thirty minutes by accessing the big com-puter that had everybody in it—the Big Brother of credit, TRW. After that, phone bills, utility bills, and magazine subscriptions. But when the missing person was a child, all that changed. You looked at bank statements and credit card receipts for regular or frequent pay-ments. Greg had access to all of that, despite the personal identifi-cation numbers and the complete confidentiality that banks promised. All it took was money. His information network, the paper stoolies, he called them, had been in place as long as he'd been in business. It had grown as the information industry grew, and now, if he had a busy month, his informers doubled their salaries from his payoffs. But there turned out to be nothing at all in Christine Timberlake's files except large quarterly cash withdrawals, probably to pay room and board wherever the daughter was. Greg could tell from the amounts that it was the high rent district, but there was no hint as to where. Christine was smart and she was being careful, but she'd slip up eventually, probably sooner than later. They all did, every one.

He opened his fridge and checked out the rack on the door. It was Monday, so his stock was full. Tsing Tao, Dos Equis, Guinness Stout, Beck's Dark, Brooklyn Brown, and a Kingfisher from India. He considered for half a minute and then reached for the Guinness. A wee bit of Ireland, he thought, opening it on the bottle opener mounted on his kitchen cabinet. Then he went outside and parked in a metal chaise lounge with a thick plastic cushion on it. Huge trees lined the inside of the block and the yards and gardens looked like the countryside up in Westchester where Norma lived. He sipped his beer slowly, savoring it as long as possible. He could hear some music, that jungle beat the kids listened to, but it wasn't loud enough to drive him back inside.

In the morning, he thought as he was drifting into a pre-bed snooze, he'd start poking into the Christine Timberlake case in earnest. And before he was through, Parker Horton would have his evidence and the poor kid, God bless her little heart, would be whacked back into Parker's court like a helpless tennis ball.

10

In the week since Parker returned from New York, three things had happened: he'd gotten notice that the IRS was going to audit Paco's; he and Lily rented a medium-sized houseboat in Sausalito where they would officially launch themselves into living together; and Greg Litner reported that Christine had a boyfriend who came and went from her apartment with his own keys. This last bit of information did not surprise Parker: he viewed Christine as the clingy, dependent type who couldn't stand on her own two feet too long without allowing some new guy to sweep her off them. But he still felt somewhat stung, jealous, and displaced.

Irritated, Parker wondered how hard it had been for the new guy. Christine had practically made him get on his knees and beg for the first kiss. She was twenty-years-old then and so wary of sex she belonged in a convent. He'd half expected her to be a virgin but she wasn't, though she refused to discuss her past. She was a question mark, a sad silent beauty set off from all the other girls her age who were nearly salivating to spill their guts to anyone who didn't run away fast enough. Her quietness drew him in. She was a mystery he wanted to solve. Which made him tense. Because Parker knew that he couldn't pry Christine open without showing her who he was too.

To Parker, Christine's presence was a kind of chaos stalking the perimeter of the orderly world he had so carefully planned and executed. He watched her move like hot lava between the tables of

Paco's and felt hypnotized. He grew shy, which was definitely unusual. For Parker, women were easy to get and easy to let go of. He was too busy single-handedly lifting his restaurant off the ground to bother much with romance, but Christine alternately stimulated and soothed him, and he wasn't quite sure what to do about it.

Late one September night, four months after she'd come to work for him, he and Christine closed Paco's together. She had collected the last of the dirty tablecloths and carried them to the laundry bag in the store room. He followed her. When she turned, he was blocking the doorway four feet away.

"Christine," Parker blurted, "I can't...I feel like I'm always standing on the brakes every time I'm near you."

She stood very still.

"You're telling me, Parker," she said in that distant but flirtatious way she had, "you wanna jump my bones?"

"Christ, Christine, no. I'm telling you..." he had fumbled for the right words and then ended up, to his own amazement, finishing with, "...I want to be...careful of you."

He didn't know where it had come from and he felt a hot jet of embarrassment but then her whole face shifted and changed. For a split second, it was like looking through a kaleidoscope. Fragments of her features subtly realigned themselves into a softer, more intimate arrangement. And Parker knew he had her.

It hadn't turned out to be much of a bargain, he thought with a shrug as he pulled off Sir Francis Drake Drive into the parking lot at Paco's and parked his Jeep Wagoneer. The prep staff's cars were already there. Things were running on schedule. Parker wanted that. He liked order and precision and deeply disliked randomness and unpredictability. Without a firm grip on the details of his own life, he would be nothing. The world was full of nothings; all you had to do was turn your head to see them.

He pushed through the door into Paco's kitchen.

"Hey Rafael," he called to the one Mexican working in the kitchen of his Mexican restaurant. Rafael looked up from a huge bowl of avocado.

"Hello Parker," he answered. "The produce delivery was late again. The guy just got here twenty minutes ago. We're way behind."

"Son of a bitch," Parker swore, and Rafael looked down into the bowl of avocado. "I told him I wasn't going to put up with his shit anymore." Parker stormed through the kitchen and disappeared through the swinging doors into the dining room. Rafael exchanged a quick look with the three other men in the kitchen.

"That guy's head's gonna blow off and go into orbit one of these days," said Anthony, a young kid fresh from a two-year course at the San Francisco Culinary Institute, and everybody laughed. Of all the people who worked in the restaurant, only Anthony made snide jokes about the boss, and he only did it when Parker was safely out of range. It wasn't as if Parker forbade a little relaxed bantering. The cooks and the waitresses went at it constantly. But everyone knew that the jokes and comments stopped when it came to Parker and his authority. You accepted it or you didn't, and if you didn't, you moved on. This was not a restaurant where the staff could organize and present the boss with a list of demands; it was a place where you got fired on the spot if you even thought of pulling something like that.

In his office, Parker slammed down the phone and lit a cigarette. Adrenaline fired along his arteries. It felt to him like oil must feel to a rusty old machine. Good. He opened the desk drawer for the ashtray he always stashed there. When he took it out, a framed photo that had sat on his desk for years stared up from the bottom of the drawer. He lifted it out and held it in front of his face: Christine, Petra, and Parker Horton. Mother, child, father. A family.

This was the only evidence of that period he'd been able to squirrel away before Christine went on her rampage and stole all the mementos of their life together. Petra was almost four in this picture. She had on a sleeveless tee-shirt with "Future Heart-breaker" scripted across the front and a short, horizontally striped skirt. They were at Stinson Beach. Christine wore a lime-green string bikini. Her hair, cut short like a boy's, was wet and plastered back from her face. She was kneeling on the blanket behind Petra. Parker lay on his side in a pair of baggy white yoga pants and a loose white shirt. His eyes were hidden by dark glasses but it was clear that they were fixed on Christine. All three were smiling. Patty had taken the picture the summer she'd finished her bachelor's degree.

Petra was normal then, at least she seemed normal. She had always been a reserved, quiet kid, but at that point she was still responsive and aware of her surroundings—and she certainly knew Christine and Parker. Within the year, though, her world crashed in on her like the breakers against the rocks in the background of this photo, and smashed everything.

Parker replaced the photograph and closed the drawer. The energy that had been pumping through him a few minutes before was gone now. With a loud sigh, he got up and re-combed his hair, pulling his ponytail tight and neat, and checked his teeth. He washed his hands in the sink in his small private bathroom and scrubbed his fingernails, though they were already clean. He chose a shirt from the dozen hanging in dry-cleaning bags on the rack behind his office door and put it on. When he stepped into the dining room, he was ready to charm any person who came through the door.

11

*P*etra heard the hum inside her. It was loud, like an old refrigerator's vibration that shakes the floor and rattles the lids on the pots and pans on top of the stove. She could feel it too, buzzing down her arms to her fingertips, around each one, back up her arm, down her side into her leg, around her foot, back up. It was like an electric train chugging along the cliff at the edge of her body. Chug, chug, chug, it went, and the noise got louder until it was all there was. Hummmmmm. Buzzzzzz. The wheels grinding, around and around the edge. Huummmmmm. She stayed still to listen and was familiar with even the slightest alteration in pitch, tone, or volume.

She was sitting amidst the bright blue flowers on the slip cover of an overstuffed couch in the day room. She had been led there, placed there, but she didn't know how or when or by whom. She felt the air brush her skin when she moved through it and she saw blotches of color, flat and runny like paint spilled across a floor, but she did not recognize them or identify them as the couch, the chair, the window, Mrs. Rose. The colors and shapes would pass in front of her and then pass on. Some hung suspended there for a long time. They all meant nothing.

"Oprah" was blaring from the TV. No one watched it but Edna Rose, the afternoon attendant. Cross-dressing was the topic of the day and several men and women sat in the comfortable swivel chairs to tell the story of their oddball obsession. The usual panel of experts stood by to swear that everything they did was normal.

Eight girls, all between five and ten years of age, were around the day room. Of the eight, only one was involved in an activity that could possibly be construed as play. She was seated on the floor holding a soft rubber ball, which she occasionally dropped and then retrieved. A few of the girls stood in the center of the room, their legs spread apart and stiff kneed, and energetically rocked from side to side, as if they were mounted in giant circular rims that never quite tipped over. One reached over the top of her head to touch her opposite ear lobe. Two sucked their thumbs. Several hummed. Two slammed themselves back against their chairs and then forward to their knees.

Only Petra was absolutely motionless and absolutely silent. At least on the outside. Inside, the usual racket. It drew a thick black line around her, a thicker and thicker line that wrapped around her in every direction until she became a living mummy. Her arms and legs were bound tight, her eyes were covered, and inside the machinery cranked and hummed with Petra the only member of its awestruck audience.

Edna Rose sat down beside Petra and placed an arm across her shoulders, gently tipping Petra's body against her side. Petra's cheek pressed into the side of Edna's breast, but neither of them noticed.

"How's my little Petra doing today?" Edna asked as she smoothed Petra's damp hair back from her forehead. "Watching Oprah? What do you think of Oprah?" Her voice was cool and sooth-ing, like alcohol on a sunburn. "You've got your new jeans on Mommy sent you, I see," she continued, "and don't you look grown up. Bet Mommy can't believe you're a size 10 already. That's big for a girl who just turned eight."

Petra caught little tips of the words, little beeps and thuds that slipped over the tops of the mountains and valleys of the buzz inside her body. She felt the warm hand cross her forehead. Like a brief patch of sun that streaked through a big black cloud, it flashed once and disappeared. On the TV, disgruntled audience members with sharp judgmental edges in their voices yelled out questions, and the guests and panel interrupted and tried to out-holler one another in response. Edna stared at the screen. A free for all, she thought. And as usual, if it was free, it wasn't worth much. She sat Petra back up and rubbed her arms. Pretty kid, she thought. What the hell had happened to her?

Edna wasn't trained in psychology or social work. In fact, she'd dropped out of college after one semester to get married and had stayed home till all four of her kids were in school before she applied for this attendant's job. Glorified baby-sitter, really. The little girls could break your heart, though. It made her go back home at four and thank God every day for giving her normal children. Working at the Warren School had changed Edna as a mother. She felt less inclined to focus on the problems the kids created for her and Kevin. Every display of temper, every act of disobedience on the part of the kids was another mile between them and places like the Warren School; she knew it and was grateful. But the real tragedy of it all was that lots of the kids there had started off normal and then something in their system went haywire and all the smart doctors in the world couldn't repair the damage. They couldn't even find it.

Edna loved her little afternoon charges in a confused way: certainly not for their personalities or the cute things they said. Instead, she loved them like you love a puppy—not for what it does but for what it is. Like when a puppy's eyes open and you feel a surge of excitement and pride. It seems wonderful, but it's really only evidence that the pistons are moving up and down in the right rhythm and the sparks are firing on signal. It seems to say that everything is all right, there is order in the world after all, a drum beat or bass line that will always be there, always be reliable.

When one of these little girls did one normal thing, like smile when she saw you or go to the table to eat on her own, hope surged in Edna and she felt full of maybes: maybe the girl would run to her mother on the next visiting day; maybe she would learn to tie her own sneakers. She never mentioned these hopes to the psychologists on staff, not since the first time when she was brand new on the job.

"Don't get your hopes up over something like that," Dr. Sawyer had warned. "Don't see signs where there aren't any." Edna had felt silly and looked down at the floor. "It's just that you'll be disappointed," he said with a fatherly pat on her back. "We have to accept that we don't really know how to help these children. If we get lucky and one goes home, that's great, but don't expect it."

She knew he was trying to protect her, not belittle her for her ignorance, but her cheeks were still hot when he disappeared down the stairs at the end of the corridor. She decided that the day she gave up hope for the girls was the day she'd walk out the door and never come back. So she kept her secret prayers for each one warm, like buns in the oven, just waiting for the right person to open the door and find them.

Like Petra.

That little girl was in there somewhere, and someday she'd surprise them all and come back out. Edna had good reason to believe this because, though Petra was supposed to be completely unresponsive and totally unaware of her surroundings, Edna knew that there was at least one thing Petra singled out to listen to: the fog horn that sat on a buoy between the harbor and the ocean, its low two-tone moan marking the channel past the shoals for the passing boats.

Edna had always lived in Chatham, right on the tip of the Atlantic elbow of Cape Cod, where the land hooked around toward Provincetown. She was born as it was making the transition from year-round fishing village and low-key summer resort to full-time tourist destination and retirement home to New York City executives. Land and housing had gotten so high that many of her friends and their families had to sell out, unable to pay the skyrocketing taxes. Traffic on summer weekends was now so bad the locals refused to leave home, and fudge shops and dim sum restaurants had replaced the hardware stores and five and dimes on Main Street. But through it all, one thing was as constant and predictable as the cold, grey fog, and that was the fog horn.

Growing up, she'd gone through periods where it reminded her of all sorts of things: the rumble in the belly of an old sick cow, a broken New Year's Eve noisemaker, one vibrating string on the world's biggest acoustic bass, some giant saying "aaah" for the doctor. It had depressed her and comforted her, irritated her and driven her mad with its rhythmic intrusion.

She didn't know what it was doing to Petra, but it was surely doing something. Edna had first noticed it eight months before, an almost imperceptible lifting of Petra's chin, a change in the direction of her eyes. It was almost nothing, but it lit a candle in Edna and she'd made a private study of it ever since. When the fog rolled in, if Edna could, she would sit herself down next to Petra and take her hand. Every time the fog horn blew, she would squeeze, not much pressure but enough to feel. She'd only told this to Kevin, her husband, who frequently listened to her long accounts of the girls' behavior.

"You oughta tell Dr. Sawyer," he said. "Maybe this is important."

"What am I gonna say?" she responded, "That I squeeze Petra's hand when the fog horn blows? He'd think I was nuts."

"No, tell him she listens to it," Kevin persisted.

"He could be standing right there and he wouldn't see it," Edna answered. "He sees her, what? Fifteen minutes a week?" She shook her head. "He'd never see it in a million years."

So she sat close to Petra when the fog rolled in, and she waited.

12

*C*hristine felt vulnerable for the two weeks after Parker showed up at Skinny's. He did that to her—took away her confidence and power to control her life. She had assumed that the level of repulsion she felt toward him would create an invisible, impenetrable barrier, one he could never cross again. But when he stood in front of her, he burned straight through her protective membrane and she could not martial the forces needed to toss him out.

How did one person do that to another, Christine wondered as she sat down to write her twice-weekly letter to Petra. She knew the letters did no good. They were read to Petra by a staff member and then added to the stack in the drawer of her night table. Yet Christine felt compelled to write a few lines. "How's Mommy's little girl? Do you know I miss you? Did you get the package I sent you? I love you." Sometimes she'd spontaneously draw a little picture—a stick lady with long, straight hair saying, "Where's Petra?" or a tree full of blossoms dotted in with pink highlighter. Christine wedged these letters into the jaws of her own despair and sent them flying to Petra, never missing a Monday or a Thursday. Petra had over a hundred blue tissue paper envelopes in her drawer now. How many would collect there before Petra recovered or Christine gave up? She wanted to believe that would never happen, but weeds of doubt sometimes took root in her little patch of hope and she had brief but awful visions of herself tangled up in the undergrowth, unable to hack it back.

It was 11:30 in the morning and Christine was sitting at a table in a small cafe on East 7th Street. It had just opened. Christine liked cafes in the off hours when she was out in the world, alone. From her years of working in restaurants and bars, she knew that important things happened when public places were empty. Important conversations took place. She was thinking of a slim Korean student named Shin who'd wandered into Skinny's the day before for a cold beer on a hot afternoon. The happy hour crowd would soon arrive but Shin was alone at the bar when he spread out his assigned reading for the English conversation class he was attending at N.Y.U. He consulted his English dictionary and made notes in Korean in the margins of his homework. Christine, in chatty bartender mode, had asked him what he was reading.

"It is article about happiness," he answered. His sentence sounded hammered out, tap by tap.

"I could use some of that," she answered. "What's it say?"

Shin shifted on his bar stool and took a few seconds to organize himself for a discussion. "Writer says happiness is not possible by formula, but there is formula to obtain contentment."

"Really? What is it?" Christine was half interested in the topic and half interested in observing Shin. Hearing him speak English was like watching a barefoot person cross a vacant lot full of broken glass. He did it carefully, picked his way slowly.

"Writer says, good marriage, good working life, and..." He trailed off to consult his paper. "...and ability to see life as it really is make contentment."

"What if life is bad?" she asked, filling the bar bowls with Spanish peanuts from a huge can. "How could seeing that as it really is lead to contentment?"

"Excuse me, I don't understand," Shin answered.

"Imagine a person whose life is really terrible, and she knows it and sees it as it really is. How could that make her content?" Suddenly a picture she'd seen on the front page of the newspaper flashed into her mind: a grainy photograph of a small boat full of Vietnamese refugees washing up on the shore halfway across the world. "Like...say a Vietnamese boat person. You understand?" He nodded his head. "That person's life is very bad. If he sees it clearly, why would that make him content?"

"Oh," Shin answered immediately, "that person is most content of all."

Christine put down the bowl of peanuts. "Why?"

"Because that person takes a small part of his real life and makes it the whole world."

That idea caught Christine in the heart and sent her reeling.

"I think that person is desperate," she said, "and you think he's optimistic."

"I'm Korean and you're American," Shin answered.

"Maybe I should move," she laughed.

Shin drained the end of his mug of Rolling Rock—Lolling Lock, he had said—and tucked his papers and his dictionary into his briefcase. The first of the post-quitting-time customers emerged through the door and headed for the bar.

"Happiness," Shin announced, "is an absolute. Contentment is a relative value." He smiled then, and this time she saw his small white teeth. His mouth and chin formed a triangle and his eyes almost disappeared. He stood up.

"Well, I hope you find both," Christine said. "Good luck."

"Thank you for opportunity for conversation," Shin replied. He backed away from the bar a few steps and moved through the door on his way to school. As Christine pulled draft beers and slid them across the bar to the happy hour set, the exchange with Shin kept replaying in her head. She had a mental image of a little circle of optimism; nearby someone with a bicycle tire pump inflated it till it was big enough to launch like a raft into the sea. How exactly, she wondered, did you pump up an optimistic image and climb in? Just by believing in it? And which came first, the optimism itself or the hard work of pumping? Or was it just the willingness to take the chance and launch into the sea?

When the bar slowed down around 8:30, Christine took a minute to call Patty.

"Would you say I'm an optimistic person?" she asked. "I mean, in general?"

Patty hesitated. "Is this a trick question?"

"No. I'm just curious about how you see me."

"Well," Patty began, "I think you have a lot of courage and I think you try really hard."

"But what about optimistic?" Christine persisted.

"Shit, I don't know," Patty answered, "but I guess I'd have to say no. You treat everything like a moral obligation or some kind of duty. You're always facing a firing squad, you know? But you have to, so you do."

Christine tried to process what Patty was saying. "Well, thanks, I guess," she said.

"What's this all about anyway? Did you sign up for EST or something?"

Christine laughed. "Not hardly."

"So," Patty began after a second's pause, "do you think I'm optimistic?"

"Are you kidding? You're carrying the Olympic torch," said

Christine, noticing that a customer stood waiting at the bar, money in hand. "Gotta go. I'm at work."

"O.K. Talk to you soon," Patty answered and then added, "Christine? Don't worry; be happy." She pronounced it "hoppy" like in the song that'd shot off the charts a few years back.

"Right." They hung up. Maybe Patty was right. Maybe Christine did approach life through a haze of dread, as if she expected something bad to happen. But so many bad things did happen. Still, she hoped she'd yanked the steering wheel into her own hands over the past few years. She wanted to believe she'd found the exit ramp and was leaving her old landscapes behind.

Yet her hopes had dissolved in a second when Parker waltzed in. Even if she remained calm on the outside and said the words that made him collect his pack of cigarettes off the bar and leave, she still felt she was being slowly peeled, round and round, like the jagged red skin peels in one long piece off an apple, provided the right person wielded the knife. And Parker knew exactly where to place the edge of his knife; he knew exactly how to cut her to the core.

What had started it? What prompted Parker to pull his knife, sharpened by his easy way with words and his cool intellect, and slash her until, in desperation, she'd finally fought back? That depended on whose version you believed. But in both their versions, it had started at the same time: when Petra suddenly withdrew and then slowly began to disappear. They couldn't blame Petra, so they blamed each other; it was that simple. And as Petra got worse, her parents' attacks on each other got uglier, until at times they were so vicious they barely noticed Petra, left alone in her peculiar darkness.

Marriage problems like theirs, Christine believed, were like lethal viruses: random, opportunistic infections that impersonally destroyed their hosts. She knew her marriage to Parker had started off healthy. She had trusted that it was solid and sturdy, a huge ship that would always slice cleanly through the waves, no matter how turbulent the seas. From the beginning, when Parker had followed her into the stockroom at Paco's, she'd felt instinctively safe with him, a rare experience for her. It was partially because he hadn't moved toward her or crowded her. His hands had been loose at his sides, not reaching or clutching.

"Parker," she said, her voice thin and throaty, "I can't."

"You don't like me?" he asked, his body leaning against the door jamb. The only part of him that moved was his eyes, and they didn't exactly move: they got bluer.

"I do like you, but..." Her voice faded.

"You don't feel the...desire between us?" he asked.

She did. She had felt it pressing down hard on her nerves for weeks. Sometimes when she got home after a long day near him in the restaurant, she felt she could wring their desire out of her hair it was so thick.

"Yes...but I was hoping we'd just ignore it until it went away."

"Is there someone else?" he asked.

"No." She wondered if she shouted it. "It's not that." It was very quiet in the tiny store room. Christine could hear the blood in her head as it circulated past her eardrums. Finally she whispered, "I just can't."

"Why not?" His voice was gentle.

Should she tell him? Suddenly she felt a wild compulsion to blurt out that she was constitutionally unable to breeze into a relationship with him or anyone else. She was not normal. But she couldn't possibly say that. Not yet.

"I just can't," she repeated. She tried to smile but she could tell from the strange sensations in her face, in the way her skin stretched out of shape and her mouth felt lopsided, that it wasn't very convincing. She saw Parker straighten up and come toward her.

His bony hand circled behind her and landed lightly on the small of her back. And then it dropped down below the curve of her ass. She could feel the vapor in his breath and see the tiny flecks of green in the blue of his eyes. She knew she wasn't breathing, that her throat had sealed off after her last breath, that she was waiting for his tongue to open it up again. In that moment, when she wanted him to unlock her, he stepped back, away. His hand fell from her body. It made her trust him more.

"God," he said, "you make me ache." And she had known it was true because she could see the pain in his eyes. He looked like a lonely person staring through the bright window of a big old house at a happy family. Something deep inside her calmed. Her lips parted as she moved toward him.

The next day Christine called in sick and Parker showed up at her door in the middle of the lunch hour while back in the restaurant the other waitresses and the cooks nodded at one another knowingly and said they'd seen it coming for months. All except Patty, who wondered how Christine could've kept such a huge and important secret from her. By the time Patty arrived at Christine's above-the-garage apartment behind a big house a mile from Paco's, Parker was drinking iced coffee with his feet up on the railing of the tiny deck, and both of them looked pink, like newborns, against the green backdrop of the enormous trees all down the hillside. Three weeks later, Patty was the witness in their civil wedding ceremony. No one else attended the wedding or for that matter was even invited. Parker and Christine honeymooned in the little garage apartment and then moved her things to his condominium in San Francisco.

They were happy. Christine considered it a real life miracle, what had happened between her and Parker. She had been frozen and he had melted her. She felt dizzy with luck and determined to please him always.

And for the first four years, she had. Her marriage put a strong fence around her, and she could finally come slowly out of her hiding place and sun herself like a snake on the rocks. Little by little, late at night in their big bed in a room full of windows overlooking San Francisco Bay, Christine told Parker her secrets, about a childhood spent hiding in the basement of her mother's house, stretched out on top of an old deep-freeze, a book in her hand and her head resting on Brown Berty, a ratty stuffed dog that had been abandoned by a neighbor child who had grown up. She had promised Brown Berty that she would never leave him and never grow up. So when the first dark pubic hairs pushed through the creamy pinkness of her skin "down there," she closed the bathroom door and leaned against it and cut them off with Nina's razor. It felt like a slaughter to Christine and she was happy to do it. It made her feel young and safe, and she closed her eyes and let denial warm her. But they came back, scratchy and strong, and more hair grew as she looked on in helpless outrage. Christine considered adulthood an invasion by an enemy, a strong enemy that would always overpower her and leave her crushed.

She told Parker that she had learned then, at age twelve, that she would always lose the important fights. She saw herself as an unwilling soldier, a draftee who wanted to be anywhere but in this army of crazy adults, marching along unknown roads in some awful place. She knew she would see things that would sicken her and do things that would shame her, and each one would be another part of the horrible initiation that began with the red blood in her underpants and the black, unruly hairs spreading across her body like a blight, under her arms, across her crotch, down her thighs.

She cried back then until the tears that rolled off her neck soaked Brown Berty and turned his pale brown fur to the color of the bitter chocolate squares that Nina used for making fudge. She cried because she didn't want to go forward into life and she couldn't go backward or stand still. She cried as she told Parker that she still felt that way, as if each new phase of her life would unveil a new set of horrors, a new set of unimaginable unknowns that she would not have the nerve to face. She felt weak and self-conscious revealing all this to Parker. When she looked around at the people in the world and considered all the awful possibilities, she felt she hadn't been hit all that hard by life. But it had still been too much for her. It paralyzed her, and she was deeply ashamed.

Parker listened. "You're like a lion that's been beaten," he said, patting her head and tucking her close against him, "but you're safe now." So she told him more, as if bits and pieces that she had hidden from every other person in her life had loosened from some inner wall and were crashing down around her. She felt compelled to label these old feelings. No matter how painful, she wanted him to know her. So she told him how she felt about sex in her teens, how the world of kissing, fondling, and fucking with boys gave her a sick feeling in her stomach. It wasn't the boys themselves that made her feel that way, she said; it was the state you had to be in to do it: mouth open, body exposed. It was the concept of being entered in so many ways and so many places at once.

"I knew there was a point to sex," she whispered, propped up on an elbow and staring into the blue of his eyes, "that it was somehow a great experience and people would kill or die for it. Or feel they'd gone to heaven. Or hell. Or been transported to some place where usually only the gods are allowed. But I couldn't feel it." The idea of being smothered, entered, pushed into, forced open; the idea of another person's spit in her mouth, his fingers in her most private parts; the idea of his mindless frenzy and the semen, thick and white and warm, left inside her like garbage, as if she needed it, as if it were the order of things that she would be penetrated and fertilized like some dimwitted cow in a field—all of that was too much. Christine had felt it physically when her connection to the possibility snapped and broke off.

And then, in the middle of her confession, she would notice the incredible kindness deep in Parker's eyes. She knew that he cared, that he understood, that he suffered with her in his silent listening. And then the need to express it all would disappear. She didn't know why. It was like being on a fast train that had just switched tracks and was barreling along toward somewhere else. Only she didn't know where. And she would feel hot and giddy and lost inside, and her fingers would slide down past his belly, and her gaze would fixate on the pink edges of his lips. Onward she would go. With Parker, she let herself fall blindly, certain that he would always be there to catch her.

And then, after Petra's problems escalated, he used her every secret against her.

Every one.

Christine glanced at the clock on the wall above the cappuccino machine. It was 12:15. Several customers were perusing menus in the cafe. They had entered and sat down while she was lost in space, her favorite pastime. She signaled for her check and took out a few dollars and a book of postage stamps, tearing off one for Petra's letter. Hank Williams's face was printed on the stamp. Did you ever see a robin weep, Hank? she asked in her mind as she placed the stamp on the blue envelope, piled some cash on top of the bill, and left.

The city was hazy. As she turned up Second Avenue she stopped to look far north where the brownish yellow smog seemed to hang low and dark between the buildings. It was bad, but not as bad as Los Angeles, she thought, where the Hollywood Hills completely vanished several days a week. It amazed Christine to realize that she was actually living in this city, a place that provided so few of the things that soothed her. No sun baked the mountain tops; no shady bicycle paths where the eucalyptus leaves brushed her shoulders as she pedaled by; no view of the San Francisco Bay with the ships docked along the harbor.

But it was the perfect place to be anonymous and Christine needed that. She needed to relearn who she was, from the inside out, not the outside in, and New York was helping her because it was huge and impersonal and no one here was interested in her. It gave her the freedom to lie on the couch and let her mind be blank. At times, she considered herself to be in the wide awake version of a deep coma. Her world was quiet and isolated. Yet she believed that somewhere deep inside the pieces of her life would suddenly snap into place and she would know what to do next. But until then, she was under the surface where things were too murky to tell a good decision from a bad one, so she had to wait a little longer. That was difficult with Parker's menacing words ringing in her ears. Maybe she should take Petra and run. But where?

She started walking north, back toward 10th Street.

"Coke. Crack," a voice hissed in her ear as she waited for the traffic light to change. Same thing day after day: young black men standing on the corner, hustling drugs. Everyone knew the corners, but no one stopped them. Periodically, the cops shuffled them around, drove them off to establish new temporary headquarters, but that was all. She dropped Petra's letter into a mailbox on the corner and turned right. She would climb her stairs and lock the world out. Flop on her couch with a fat book. She was going through several a week, compulsively turning pages as imaginary characters dug themselves into deeper and deeper holes and then found a way out.

It would happen to her.

She knew it would.

13

*A*t 4:55, Steve finished sweeping up the *Expression* office and put the broom and dustpan away. Janet had calmed down a bit about Mary Anne's departure. Steve answered the phone more and arranged the bills for payment, and John came in two extra hours a day for word processing. Janet was swamped but she was stoic in the face of it. He stood at her office door.

"Janet? I'm leaving. See you tomorrow."

She glanced in his direction and waved him off.

"O.K. Steve. Thanks. See you in the morning."

He put the trash outside the door and took the stairs slowly. He had formulated a strange plan and decided to go ahead with it despite his misgivings. At the street door, he stepped over the stoop sitter. He turned to him.

"You want a beer?" Steve said. "I'm buying."

"What?"

"I said I'd buy you a beer."

"You some kind of faggot?" the stoop sitter demanded. Steve had expected some display of attitude and paid no attention.

"I got a business proposition I wanna make. Come on."

The stoop sitter got to his feet in a jangle of chains and creaking leather and fell into step next to Steve.

"What kind of business proposition?"

"I'll tell you when we sit down. Let's go over to the Blue Lagoon."

That involved walking one block to Second Avenue and then downtown a few doors. Steve felt like he was in a movie, him in his slip-on Keds and a well-pressed shirt and the punk flying his colors along beside him.

"What's your name?" Steve asked.

"Alex," the stoop sitter answered.

"Steve," Steve said, and to his astonishment, Alex said, "Nice to meet you." It sounded bizarre coming from the pierced and be-ringed lips, like vestigial words from some early moment in Alex's evolution. They continued on to Second Avenue in silence, though Alex's boots made a loud clump with each step.

Long ago, the Blue Lagoon had launched some of the blues greats and now primarily launched great price tags for cheap beers. The dingy bar was more than half empty. A pale, aging, white woman placed two sweaty drafts in front of them and returned to the opposite end of the bar to continue a conversation with an old black man in a red beret.

"So what's the deal?" Alex asked.

Steve hesitated.

"I want you to get something for me," he said.

"You mean fucking steal something, right?" Alex's grey eyes were more than a little challenging. "What makes you think I'd be interested?" Steve didn't answer. "What is it anyway?" Alex asked.

"This was a stupid idea. Forget it," Steve said.

"No man, I'll do it. What is it?"

"I wanna find out who's writing letters that are upsetting my girl-friend," Steve said. "She won't tell me and I can't find the envelopes."

"What're you gonna do? Kill the guy?" Alex asked with a smile that revealed a greenish coating on his teeth at the gum line. The smile faded when he saw Steve's reaction.

"No," Steve finally said. "I just wanna know who it is." His voice was cold.

Alex drained his glass and raised it to Steve like a child asking for more milk. Steve nodded and Alex yelled, "Hey baby, one more down here, huh?" Then he turned back to Steve.

"Why me?" he asked.

"Cause she doesn't know you."

Alex considered this. "How much?

"Hundred bucks."

"Shit," Alex said. "When?"

This was risky and Steve felt uncomfortable.

"She gets her mail at the post office," Steve said, "and she stands there and reads it. Then she rips it up. All you have to do is grab the envelope before she tears it up and get outta there. Not the letter, just the envelope."

"Why not the letter, man?"

"Because," Steve said, "that's her personal business. I just want the return address."

"You're fucking crazy, man. You should find out what the fuck is saying to her."

"That's her business," Steve said again, and Alex just shook his head.

"O.K., man," he said.

"You think you can do this without getting caught?" Steve asked.

"Abso-fucking-lutely," Alex answered.

"Cause I don't want any trouble from this. I just want the information."

"Don't worry. I'll handle it." Alex hesitated. "So when do I get the bread?"

"Twenty-five now and the rest when I get the envelope."

"Deal." Alex extended his grimy hand, half covered by a ratty glove with the fingers cut off, and Steve shook it. He pulled out his wallet and passed a twenty and a five to Alex.

"By the way," Steve said, "I wouldn't want you to get the idea that you have anything on me cause you're doing this for me."

Alex looked over. "I read you, man," he said. "Loud and clear."

"We understand each other?" Steve asked quietly.

"Yeah. No problem."

"O.K." Steve laid some cash on the bar and got up. "I'll come down about 4:25 tomorrow. I'll show you who she is. She doesn't get a letter every day, so you might have to watch for a couple days."

Alex nodded.

"I'm heading out," Steve said.

"I'm gonna stick for a minute," Alex said with a gesture that took in the dirty walls and the battered bar stools. "Nice joint."

"Right. See you." Steve pushed through the street door, out of the stale, sour smell and into the noise of the rush hour traffic heading down Second Avenue. He walked south toward Jack LaLanne's. He was agitated, a combination of anticipation and inevitability that didn't mix well. It was, he mused, sort of like the old movies he'd loved as a kid where the cowboys had to transport a vial of nitro-glycerin across the prairie in a stage coach. You had to believe you'd make it, but at the same time you knew your chances were slim. So you gained something and you lost something with each step. You gained the euphoria of negotiating yourself safely through the maze, but you lost your belief in a happy outcome as the odds stacked up higher against you. His goal was to pick his way to Christine without tripping off an explosion. He did not want to become visible in the glare.

He was being extremely careful, of course, and he had thought this through, point by point. But no one could foresee all the possible permutations, and any one of them could happen. No one had ever seen him in Christine's building, or even near it; that he was sure of. No one knew he had her keys. He was certain she'd never noticed him at the post office, though the past two weeks it had been difficult to keep from staring at her when she came in. A powerful attraction, he thought as he cut over to the Bowery and crossed the busy intersection at Houston Street, is a very unmanageable thing. Your common sense departs and leaves you stupid. You feel filled with grace, like the beatific faces on his mother's plaster crafts, but at the same time your own emptiness is so complete and pervasive that you feel the sticky, black despair right around your edges all the time. So if you looked at a stranger, even a theoretical stranger like Christine was to him, with all that intensity, you'd naturally expect her to feel it, to look up and notice you. But she didn't. She just went on her way, oblivious. And for now that was fine.

Until Alex handed him the envelope that would yield the next clue to Christine's melancholy, Steve thought, he would delay his trips to the post office. With Janet so distracted, it would be easy to wait until 4:45, when Christine had left, before he headed down the block with the outgoing mail. He knew that it would be a bad idea to be in the post office with both Christine and Alex. Alex would question why Steve didn't speak to his girlfriend. He could not afford to make Alex suspicious. Who knew what a guy like that would do?

The next afternoon, Steve met Alex and they sat in the window of a donut shop next to the post office and waited. It was Friday. Christine rounded the corner as usual at 4:30.

"There she is," said Steve, indicating out the window. "The tall woman in the sunglasses."

Alex shot him a look. "That's your girlfriend? She's hot."

"Yeah, well you get used to the way your girlfriend looks."

Alex slid along the vinyl seat and left. As he passed in front of the window, he had pulled on a baseball cap and was in the process of removing his leather jacket. Precautions, thought Steve, and he was impressed, though he was sure that Christine would never get a close enough look at Alex to identify or even recognize him. When she read her letters, she was lost in them. By the time she realized what had happened, Alex would be history.

Steve nervously sipped his coffee, his Boston cream donut forgotten on its waxed paper square on the table. Within two minutes, Alex was back. He shrugged his shoulders as he rejoined Steve in the booth.

"She didn't get no mail," he said.

"Try tomorrow."

"All right," Alex said, licking his finger and running it through the sugar that had fallen off his jelly donut onto the paper, "but this ain't gonna go on forever, y'know. If she don't get a letter soon, the deal's gotta be discussed."

Steve's blood thickened, as if he'd been swimming and had just hit a cold spot.

"You giving me attitude, Alex? Right now, on the first day?"

Alex looked up sharply. "Nah, I'm just conversating."

"Good," Steve answered. "I'm going back to the office. Catch you tomorrow." As he walked along 14th Street, Steve felt icy fingers jab into the muscles along his shoulders. He was angry. That was how anger felt to him: not hot and red, but cold and grey, as if each cell had been blasted with dry ice until the activity in it stopped. That period afterward, when they thawed, hurt. That was why he hated to get pissed, because it hurt so much to get over it. It felt as if he was losing something, sacrificing something important and he didn't feel inclined to be that generous. He had been over and over this turf with Dr. Greene back at the detox clinic.

"So you feel diminished by letting go of your anger?" Dr. Greene had probed. "Do you think that makes sense?"

"I guess not," Steve had dutifully responded.

"I think it makes a lot of sense," Dr. Greene stated in a matter-of-fact voice. Steve had looked up from his hands, folded in his lap.

"Why?" he asked.

"Sometimes anger's all a person's got to glue himself together. He'd fall apart without it."

Dr. Greene rocked back and forth in his high-backed swivel chair and waited. Steve considered his words.

"I don't feel angry," Steve said.

Dr. Greene laughed loudly and leaned forward. "Steve," he said, "you're the angriest person I know."

"The angriest person you know," Steve repeated, incredulous. "You're kidding."

"No, I'm not," Dr. Greene said. He glanced at his watch. "That's it for today, Steve." He swiveled toward the table where he kept his file folders. It was a dismissive gesture that usually amused Steve with its frankness. Today, though, he wanted to stay and grill Dr. Greene, but just then there was a tap on the door and Steve realized the next patient was about to come in. He rose quickly and left, avoiding eye contact with a woman who'd only been at the clinic a few days. She was hollow-eyed and dazed as she passed in front of Steve, leaving him to close the door behind her.

He went back to his room and lay down on the bed. The shades were pulled to keep the sunlight out.

He had never thought of himself as an angry man. Angry men

smashed things, picked fights, snarled, taunted, yelled. He had seen his shipmates flood into bars and tear things apart, trash hotel rooms, go after each other with broken bottles or any board they could pry loose. But not him. Their rage was free floating, ready to anchor itself to anyone or anything. When it lashed out, loose, his impulse was to quietly return to wherever he was currently pretending was home, and stay there.

Then he would reach for his works and watch the dope bubble in the spoon as he heated it. Tying off his arm, he'd pull his belt with his teeth and hold it while he waited for the veins to pop up, ready. He would tap the needle through his skin and boot the blood in and out of his makeshift syringe, all the better to send it firing into his bloodstream. And the whole world would back off and become a stage set: two dimensional, flat, the background. And under the warm spotlight, center stage, he would feel alive, more sensitive than a thousand nerves. Hot shivers of pure, seductive pleasure would brush his body, opening every pore, every cell, and filling them with great surges of peace. Junkies weren't angry, Steve thought; they wanted pure, unmitigated peace, the kind that paralyzes you with contentment.

Dr. Greene had said that anger was the glue that kept angry people intact. What kept him in one piece, he wondered. What glued him into a recognizable unit that had managed, to one degree or another, to function for three decades? It wasn't anger, he was certain. Dr. Greene was wrong this time. If expressing rage was a ten on a scale of ten and merely showing irritation was a one, then Steve was a minus seven.

But all that analysis had taken place before they stepped him down off his heroin habit by putting him on methadone and lowering the dosage in five-milligram increments. By the time he was on twenty milligrams, then fifteen, then ten, then five, then off, he was enraged, all right. Furious. He wanted to knock Dr. Greene's front teeth down his throat, maybe break some bottles over his head. There was too much pain and discomfort without the dope, too many things to feel. Steve worried that his skin would split and yellow-green bile would splatter the walls. The world seemed hateful and ugly, full of maggots and the smell of rot. And in the midst of it, he had one small moment of clarity and he realized he was indeed angry and hurt, hurt and angry, tired of being so drugged he couldn't feel it anymore. He didn't know if he would survive his feelings. They were like a hurricane with gale force winds pounding down on him. He held tight and tried to recall how it had started.

In the liquor cabinet, aged eleven. Watering down the vodka so his parents wouldn't know and feeling the relief, the great relief, that day, every day since. He sat with Dr. Greene and he tried to remember why he started it. And there was nothing there. Just cold, pitch black darkness in his memory.

So being angry at Alex was fine. It was normal. He had had a feeling; he had done nothing but say a few words in a retaliatory tone and Alex had backed off. It was over. But for Steve, things took so damn long to be over. He considered this a major flaw in his character. Even when he'd been smacked no harder than the next guy, it took him longer to get back on his feet, and, bottom line, he didn't want to start slugging it out again until even the memory of the bruises was gone. Life never gave you that much time. It trampled you if you didn't get back up fast enough.

Steve took the office steps three at a time. He'd skipped lunch that day, explaining to Janet that he needed thirty minutes for personal business in the late afternoon.

"Sure," she said, and then added, "What makes it personal?" She smiled but he could see that she was curious.

"If I told you, it wouldn't be personal," he answered. His voice tone was light and joking, as hers had been, but Steve felt the inflexibility and determination beneath their words. The boundaries were drawn: He had said, "Here's a fence." She had stood on top of it and said, ""Let me in. Do you mind if I jump over?" He had said yes. It was almost as if the scene had subtitles.

"The man of mystery," Janet sighed. "I swear to God, sometimes I'm afraid I'm gonna read about you in the *Post*. Like they'll find you on top of the Empire State Building with a string of hot dogs tied around your waist, threatening to blow it up."

Steve laughed, a big laugh that started deep inside his belly.

"Hot dogs," he repeated, "that's great."

"You know, like you think they're dynamite."

"Yeah, I got it. You must think I'm a lot more nuts than I am."

"Still waters run deep," she said. "I know that much."

As he turned the doorknob and entered the *Expression* office, he wondered if Janet would still be curious. She had probably forgotten all about it. Their moment that morning had probably not meant enough to stick in her mind, whereas he had rerun it several times.

"It's me," he called as he went in. "I'm gonna run the mail down to the post office."

He lifted the box just as Janet appeared in the doorway of her office.

"Mission accomplished?" she asked.

"Yep," he answered, feeling somewhat rewarded. She remembered.

"That's all I get, huh? Yep?"

Steve smiled at her. It felt warm on his face. "That's it, Janet." He reached for the door. "See you Monday."

"Yeah, have a good weekend."

As Steve carried the heavy box down the steps, he wondered what Janet would think if she knew the truth: his so-called personal business amounted to sitting in a donut shop with Alex, waiting for Christine Timberlake to saunter around the corner. What were the chances Janet would or even could understand what he was doing? If she knew, she would shrink back and plaster herself against the wall, her eyes darting from his face to the door and back again. Maybe she was right. Maybe he did have a crazy streak after all. But he was definitely not dangerous. No.

Steve spent a pleasant, quiet weekend. A photography exhibit at the Met. A revival movie at Theatre 80, downtown. Two long, exhausting workouts. He rented two videos and read a magazine and on a whim bought a battered jigsaw puzzle depicting Big Ben for ninety-nine cents at a rummage sale on his block. The idea that he might assemble nine-hundred ninety-nine of the one thousand pieces and find the last one missing amused him more than actually building the puzzle. He constructed the outer edge, lost interest, dumped all the pieces back in the box, and threw the box in the garbage. He did not visit Christine's nor pass by Skinny's to see her there behind the bar. He was in some sort of holding pattern with her, not sure of the next move and not willing to make one until he was.

The next work week plodded by in a similar way, surface calm with a rumble buried deep, deep down. On Wednesday night, he stopped by Christine's apartment on his way home from the gym. It was almost nine when he hit the stairs and started to count, starting at sixty-eight and chopping one off for each one he ascended. But as he climbed, voices and music got louder. From the bottom of the last flight he could see that there was activity, probably a small party going on, in 5B. The door was ajar to help cool off the place and two men sat close to each other on the top step, smoking. Each held a plastic glass full of white wine.

Steve stepped back quickly, out of visual range, and then retraced his steps down and out the front door. His heart felt huge in his chest. He walked west to First Avenue and caught the bus uptown. He did not notice the big man who rose abruptly from the bench by the basketball court and got on the same bus. Steve was so involved in his own thoughts that he didn't see that same man get off at his stop too, and follow him all the way to 64th Street.

On Friday, everything changed.

Steve came down the stairs from *Expression* at 4:50. Alex was standing inside the street door, his back to the glass. He held a white envelope, tapping it triumphantly off the fingers of his other hand. He smiled his green smile as Steve appeared at the top of the stairs.

"I got it, man."

Steve hurried down and placed his box of mail on the floor while he reached into his pocket for his wallet. He counted out seventy-five dollars.

"Man, she freaked!" Alex said. "Started screaming and shit."

Steve felt like he'd just been stabbed. He handed the money to Alex, who continued on, oblivious. He was charged by the hunt, and his words tumbled out.

"See, I made like I had a box, y'know? Then I fucking yanked the envelope off her and took off. She didn't get it right away, but then she starts fucking yelling, 'No, no.' I was out the door, man. I took off down that alley next to the drugstore and hid in a fucking dumpster, man." He handed Steve the envelope. "It's from a fucking school, man. Hey!" he gave Steve a playful punch on the arm. "Maybe it's her fucking report card." Alex shoved the money into his pocket. "I'm gonna stay off the block for a while, man. I'll be around the park if you need me again." And he disappeared through the door.

Steve held the envelope in his hand and read: The Warren School for Girls. 167 Shoreline Drive. Chatham, Mass. 02168. He had the address. A girls' school, he thought, remembering the baby bracelet in Christine's box of pictures. He even remembered the details: Petra Elizabeth Horton. Born 2/12/85.

He pushed through the door and slowly made his way down the block. It didn't feel as good as he expected he would. He had the address, but he had done something that made Christine scream. That definitely did not feel right. No way.

14

It had cost Greg fifty bucks to get Steve's name out of the super.

The ex's new squeeze turned out to be a legal sublettor who had filled out the standard application form required by the rental agency. He had paid a three-month security deposit in lieu of a work reference, and aside from the fact that he worked and he jogged, the super knew zilch about Steve Dant. Greg flashed a picture of Christine. Had the super ever seen her?

"No," said the super, "what is he? A serial killer?"

"Not hardly."

"I know. Child support, right?" The super was in his late thirties, an Italian-stallion type gone to seed. He still wore the sleeveless tee-shirt and the fat gold chain, but he needed more room across the ass of his basketball shorts.

"Not even that exciting," Greg replied. He took a business card out of his wallet. "If you see anything out of the ordinary, gimme a call. It'll be worth it."

The super propped the card up against the salt and pepper shakers on his kitchen table and rocked back till his chair hit the wall. His feet, in his pump-up Reeboks like the kids wear, dangled in the air. "I know the girl down the rental agency. What if I got her to give me his social security number. Y'know, from the credit check."

"That'll be worth another fifty," Greg said, rising. "You have my number."

He let himself out the front door. The hallway smelled like pine, chemically produced, of course. It was sickening. So was human nature, Greg thought. Dangle a few bucks in front of the average guy and he'd sell out his own mother. They never asked why; they only asked how much. They never said, What'm I doing? They said, What's in it for me? As a rule, women were different. Who are you? they asked; why should I tell you anything? He'd take a man any day of the week if he needed information.

As it turned out, he didn't need the super anyway. Steve Dant had a phone in his name, and Greg had long-standing connections at the phone company. Within two hours of getting the guy's name, Greg had printouts of his credit history, bank accounts, and addresses for the past five years. The guy moved around a lot, but that didn't automatically make him a suspicious character. Greg knew better than that. He knew some people are naturally planted and some are naturally movers. There were stand-up individuals in each group. The interesting thing, Greg mused, was when a stayer picked up and took off, or a mover dropped down some roots. That told you a few things.

Steve's profile was average for a mover. In the past five years, he'd had five different addresses: Long Beach, San Luis Obispo, and Monterey, California; a short stint in Denver, Colorado; and then New York. Comparing the addresses with the check record, it appeared the San Luis Obispo address was a clinic for substance abusers where Steve had spent over six months. That Greg found interesting. That was the kind of habit that showed up beautiful on the witness stand, provided, of course, you were trying to punch a few big holes in that person's character. Greg found no record of a motor vehicle, though Steve Dant's California license was still current. No tickets on it. No criminal record of any sort.

Greg placed all the information on Steve in a manila folder and put it in an accordion-style master file marked "Horton." He was meticulous about record keeping, and he forced himself to keep up with the latest office technology, though he felt more and more invaded by electronics as time went by. In his two-room office above a Yemenite restaurant on Queens Boulevard, he now had an IBM computer with a printer, a modem, a phone and fax machine, and a personal copier. He still typed by the hunt-and-peck method, but it took a fraction of the time it did in the old days before spell-check. It was important to him that his reports were professional and literate, and he'd suffered through two years of grammar and composition classes at LaGuardia Community College to make sure they were. He had never hired a secretary, never felt he needed one bad enough to offset the intrusion of another human being into his thinking space.

He stared out his picture window at the usual traffic jam, backed up for blocks due to the construction. Three lanes of Manhattan-bound traffic tried to funnel into a one lane on-ramp onto the bridge. Greg studied it in a detached way. Cars tried to butch in front of each other, horns blared, and drivers shot each other the bird, while overhead the #7 train screeched by, in and out of the el station. He found it peaceful. The racket went on and the tempers snapped, but sooner or later everybody got where they were going and all the pissing and moaning in the world made not one bit of difference. He untied his shoes and placed them neatly under the desk, then stretched out on his office couch. His feet, in their thin brown socks, hung over the arm a bit. He fussed with the throw pillow until it braced up his neck at the exact right angle.

It was time to think.

A dozen years back, when he'd just married Norma, she'd strolled into the office late one afternoon and found him sprawled out on this very couch, though it was new then and still smelled of the anti-staining treatment he'd paid an extra thirty bucks for.

"You call this working?" she had laughed, collapsing into his desk chair and giving him her famous "what a load of bullshit" look.

"Yes," he answered, feeling a bit offended. "I do."

"Well, what're you doing?"

"I'm thinking something through."

"How do you do that? Think through a case?"

That was what he loved about her: her crazy questions.

"You mean, how do I think?" he asked.

"Yeah."

It was an interesting question. She waited quietly while he fished around for the answer.

"Well, first I lie down here, right? And I either look at the cracks on the wall or I stare out at the el tracks, and I get a case in my mind, and..." His voice trailed off. A slight smile appeared on her pretty pink lips.

"Yeah?" she prompted.

He stared at a dark crack in the plaster. It had a dozen tributaries off it, like a giant broken blood vessel.

"I guess I don't think," he said finally. "I just BOING! Get a thought."

"Just...BOING!" she said, nodding her head up and down like a spastic jack-in-the-box.

"Yeah. BOING! Complete thought. I guess I don't really think it. It comes to me already formed."

"O.K. baby," she said, her voice skeptical and teasing, "I believe you."

He felt irritated though he didn't know why. What did she mean asking him how he thought? How did anybody think? What was thinking anyway? Ninety-nine percent of it took place below the surface and then the final product was delivered up, like a telegram from the unconscious. As a private detective, Greg knew the value of putting the information into order and adding it up, but all the so-called thinking he'd done about all the cases he'd solved, he'd never been able to explain or define that last little leap, the one that happened after all the thinking was done, that got you to the other side of the ravine. You built your case and then waited for the gust of wind that'd carry you clear to the answer. Would Norma understand that?

He glanced over. Her curly strawberry-blonde hair spiraled down to her shoulders like a mop. The sun, coming in the window, made it gleam all sorts of pretty colors. She had on a red sweater and a pair of tight blue jeans. Her legs were parted, and, from his position on the couch, her fleshy thighs made a big beautiful V. He stared there, between her legs, and then up to her face. Her coffee-brown eyes were fixed on his. He felt it in his dick. It was already hard.

"BOINNNGGG!" he whispered in a breathless kind of way.

"You're not thinking," she said, opening her legs just a little more.

"How do you know?"

"You got that dumb look on your face."

"Come here."

She did as she was told, and the rest was X-rated.

Oh Norma, he thought remembering that afternoon, you were one hot ticket. And I let you get away.

He reached into the Horton file, standing by the edge of the couch, and withdrew a photograph of Christine. It was recent. He had taken it ten days ago with a telephoto lens as she came down the steps of her apartment. Did Parker Horton regret letting her get away?

He probably did, he thought, but Greg had seen Parker's type before. They kept throwing punches long after the bell had rung. It didn't even matter who'd won. They just had to drive the last couple home. It wasn't exactly clear to Greg how the kid figured in it. That wasn't for him to decide. Some judge would do that. All Greg would provide would be the truth. Pictures and facts didn't lie, after all. And as far as finding the girl, hell, a father had a right to know where his own daughter was, no matter what.

But so far, there were no pictures and no facts.

It was odd. He hadn't even seen Steve and Christine together. And there sure as hell was no sign of Petra.

Lying there on his Naugahyde couch, it became pretty clear that he was gonna have to go into her apartment and look around. Maybe a phone tap or a bug. He decided to rest for a while, and then he'd put his equipment together and go over to Manhattan.

He looked at the clock. It was 6:10. Friday night.

He'd rest a while first.

He slipped Christine's picture back into the file and closed his eyes.

15

Steve went directly home from the post office. The envelope which he'd folded into his back pocket felt like a weight, tugging his spirits down, down, down into hell. He had done something that had made Christine cry out in pain. The word "no" was so pathetic, so powerless.

Looking backward, he was astonished that he'd hired Alex to grab that envelope. He had thought about the end and examined the means, but somehow he'd short-circuited when it came to effect. That was one of the things he'd noticed about other junkies. They didn't see the relationship between cause and effect. Or perhaps they recognized the effect but they could never connect it back to themselves as the cause. It was always "the dope made me do it" or "the guy talked me into it, man."

That was part of what set him apart from the rest of the dope fiends. No matter what, he had the honor to stand up and say, "It was me. I'm responsible. I did it." And because he had this character trait, he had to be careful about what he did. Until now, he had been. He had never robbed anyone to get dope; he had monitored his habit and kept it within his version of reason; he had never given anyone their first taste. And now, this.

It crossed Steve's mind that perhaps his honor was all twisted in with using, like some hellish Mobius strip. Maybe being so anti-social on the one hand inspired his sense of honor on the other.

Without the one, he had neither. This possibility terrified him.

He pulled his highway atlas from the magazine rack and turned to the Massachusetts page. Chatham turned out to be on the Atlantic coast of Cape Cod. About four or five hours away by car. He looked at the nearby points on the map: Hyannisport, Provincetown, Nantucket Island. Images of the Kennedy clan and their family football games flashed in his mind. The whole Cape was probably full of rich people. Was Christine rich, he wondered? Was the Warren School for Girls some kind of ritzy boarding school where kids got trained to keep their families on the top of the economic heap for yet another generation? Was the missing daughter there?

On an impulse, he called directory assistance and got the number.

"The Warren School for Girls," a female voice answered.

Steve paused. Now that he was through the door, he wasn't sure which way to turn.

"Do you have...a brochure or some information about the school?" he asked. "I'm considering it for my...daughter."

"I can fax you a description of services and a rate sheet," she said in a business-like tone. It sounded silent behind her. Apparently no girls at the Warren School were running wild in the halls, having a hilarious game of slide-down-the-banister, like they did in the Hayley Mills movie reruns he'd seen as a kid.

"That would be fine," he said.

"The number?"

Steve rattled off the fax number at *Expression*. His mind was several stops ahead of the conversation. He could collect the fax from the machine on Monday. Janet never bothered with them until they appeared in a neat stack on her desk.

"Thank you, sir. That'll go right out."

"Thank you very much." He hung up, closed the atlas, and went into the kitchen to start a bath. He felt he had some amends to make to Christine, and he was going to do it. He would get cleaned up and head downtown to Skinny's. He was going to sit at the bar, introduce himself, make small talk with her. There would be a way to make her smile and forget the unpleasantness at the post office. He owed it to her.

He finished dressing at 6:45 and was en route downtown ten minutes later. He felt nervous, like the first time he'd put his arm around a girl in the back row of a movie theater and then tried to kiss her. Just like then, he wasn't exactly sure what to do, step by step, but he had muddled through the first kiss and he would find the route to square number two with Christine before the night was over. As the number 6 train sped downtown, Steve caught glimpses of himself reflected in the window across the car. In his new black shirt and jeans, he looked as handsome as he was ever going to. If this didn't work out, he'd go back to his corner and wait for the next round to start. He switched to the cross-town train and pushed through the door to Skinny's at 7:20. The place was full but not packed. He settled onto a bar stool, letting his eyes travel the length of the bar to Christine. His heart pounded and he had a passing concern that his voice would crack when he spoke.

But Christine wasn't there. Instead, a man with horn-rimmed glasses and a leather vest was reaching into the cooler to produce a few beers. A very bad feeling hit Steve in the stomach. This definitely did not feel right.

It took the bartender five minutes to get to him.

"Sorry to keep you waiting, man. We're a little short-handed here."

"It's O.K. I'll have a Bud," Steve answered. When the bartender put it down in front of him, Steve gave him a five. "Where's Christine? She off tonight?"

"We'd like to know, believe me. No call, nothing. She just didn't show." He hesitated and then added an afterthought. "I'm really the sound man. The owner's coming in though." He turned away to make change and his voice trailed off.

"Did you call her at home?" Steve asked when the bartender returned.

"Yeah. No answer. You know her?"

"She's a friend."

"Give her a call. Maybe she'll pick up if it's not work."

"I'll do that." Steve took a quarter off the bar and headed to the phone in the foyer. He dialed Christine's number. The machine picked up after the second ring. He didn't expect her to answer and he obviously couldn't leave a message. He hung up and returned to the bar. The beer felt cool as he poured it down his throat. A minute later, the bartender caught his eye.

"Any luck?"

Steve shook his head.

"I hope she's O.K. It's not like her just not to show up, y'know?"

Steve didn't know but he nodded his head and the sound man continued on down the bar to serve another customer. It was 7:30. She was two and a half hours late and she didn't answer her phone. Steve felt responsible. Three hours before, Alex had yanked the Warren School envelope from Christine's hands, and three hours later she was missing. He finished his beer and stepped outside, hailing the first cab that came down Eighth Avenue.

"Tenth and A," he said to the cabby.

As the taxi swerved its way across lower Manhattan, Steve noticed that his teeth were clenched so tight his jaw ached. It was something he'd done all his life. As a kid in school, he'd stick a pencil in his mouth as he read silently or took a test. When he took it out, deep dents from his teeth cut into the yellow paint on the wood. And when the family cat rolled onto his back, his black and white belly exposed for a vigorous rubbing, little Steve would sit back on his heels and use both hands for Boots' massage. The whole time his two rows of baby teeth would be clamped together, so locked that his lips would drain white and his face would take on the lines of an exaggerated grimace. His father laughed about it. "Look at that mad face," he'd say, pointing his strong finger at Steve. "What'd Boots do to make you so damn pissed off?"

The answer was simple. It hurt to care.

About anything.

And for some reason, he cared a whole lot about Christine Timberlake. He stared out the window of the cab and willed it to get to 10th Street faster.

16

When Christine had squatted down and seen the weekly report from the Warren School in her mailbox, she was feeling quite balanced and content. There had been no further word from Parker and no reason to believe his world-class detective had been able to locate Petra. Christine was on her way to work, a job that was fine for now, and she had been sleeping better lately and felt more rested and able to contend with living in the world. She collected her letter and opened it. Petra's condition was the same, it said. They were running preliminary tests for a drug called clomipramine. It was normally prescribed for obsessive compulsive disorders, but...

And then, from nowhere, a man, a kid really, who was standing near her reached over, ripped the envelope out of her hands, and bolted for the door. She had been stunned by his viciousness, the piercing violation of having her little world yanked away by a passing stranger. Time simply collapsed, and in the crumpled vacuum that resulted she moved out of her body and saw herself leaning against the wall, confident and optimistic, reading her letter. And then it mutated, became its own negative, and all the horrible elements of the dark world pressed in to reshape her life. In that awful flash, she saw her flesh melting, as if her concentrated resistance to the inevitable cycles of death and putrefaction had stalled and the destruction had been instantaneously initiated. And then she heard a voice screaming, "No! No!" and she realized it was hers.

The man in the baseball cap was already at the main door before her brain telegraphed the message to speak and to move. It must have been a few seconds, but since time had unhinged and skewed itself, she saw in slow motion a tall black man with a shaved head raise his eyes from the Express Mail form he was completing. "What'd he get?" this man demanded. His voice was huge and angry and he wheeled around as if he was going to take off after him. "My envelope," Christine cried, and the black man's face switched tracks and dropped downward into a smile and then he just said "Shit" with a snorting laugh and returned to his form. Christine was running toward the door. Heads were turning and people were laughing and backing up as she pushed out into the street. It was bustling and confusing, but Christine was sure she saw the man in the baseball cap turn into the alley by the drugstore and she ran there and looked in. It was narrow and flooded, as if the storm drains had been clogged for decades. Black plastic bags of garbage were piled outside the doors of the brick buildings and rows of concertina wire protected the second-floor windows. It was dark, like the passage to a dungeon in a medieval castle, as it continued behind the drugstore and disappeared.

She was afraid to step inside. It was like crossing the river Styx to enter the underworld, knowing that the chances of re-emerging into the light of day were minimal. She was alone, and the walls were high and cold. The shadows were thick and menacing, yet she knew she had to go in to find the man because that was his world.

And she did not have the courage.

Christine shrunk back from the mouth of the alley and circled backwards until her spine rested against the building. Then she slumped down, till she felt the hot pavement beneath her backside. Her head fell forward over her knees, which were drawn up close, and her hair tumbled down, forming a thick drape that no one could see through. Her breaths were tiny gasps, the kind baby birds might make, and she expected tears, but they did not come. They hardened inside her, like concrete that cures quickly due to some added chemical agent.

Parker, she thought. It had to be Parker and his world-class detective. Surely the kid in the post office was not the detective, but he must've been an assistant or whomever detectives hire to do their dirty work. She would've expected something smoother from a professional. Why have an expensive private investigator if ultimately he conked the victim over the head in full view of a post office full of people? But the kid hadn't conked her over the head, and the people had done nothing but smirk and chuckle cynically at her helplessness.

How long would it take Parker to get to Petra now? He had reappeared in her life a few short weeks ago, and now all her careful planning just evaporated into nothingness. She had already done everything she was capable of doing, thought of everything she could think of. What else could she possibly do?

"Nice pussy." She heard those words close, right next to her ear. She could even feel the heat of the breath that spat them out. Her head shot up and there was a face, a man's face, right next to hers. He was dark skinned and had gold rims in his teeth. His rich brown eyes seemed to float in a yellow puddle and grey stubble poked through bumps in his skin. "I dig the way you wanna show it," he said.

"Leave me alone," she said, managing to climb back to her feet. Her voice cut like a scalpel into his yellow gaze. "Fuck off!"

"You spread your legs, you get what you ask for," he whispered. He remained squatting near her, and when Christine stood up and tugged at her short skirt, she saw him try to look up under it. She wanted to kick his face with her heavy boots, smash the yellow of his eyes until they bled orange and then red onto the pavement, but she couldn't. She was afraid. She pivoted away and ran, ran all the way to Avenue C, until the stitch in her side forced her to bend over and press her fingers into her waist. When she straightened up again, she saw a phone booth and she yanked the receiver off the hook and pounded in the numbers of the phone at Paco's.

"Please enter your Foncard number now," said a robot voice. Somehow she remembered it and then the phone was ringing.

"Paco's. Good afternoon."

"Parker Horton, please."

"May I say who's calling?"

"Just get him!" Christine yelled into the phone.

The woman clicked off and baroque harpsichord music filled the phone line. More than a minute went by and then the music cut off.

"Parker Horton speaking." His voice.

"You bastard. You son of a bitch," she whispered. She felt like she was choking. Parker was silent. "I can't believe...even you... would..."

"Christine?" he interrupted. His voice was calm, questioning.

"Did you hear from your detective yet?" she spit out.

"No. What're you...what's going on?"

"I hate you, Parker. I'll always hate you." She slammed the phone down.

She did hate him, and all the poison that hatred produces over-whelmed her and for a split second she was back in their bedroom. White fog pressed against the windows, as if the apartment had been shoved into a huge cotton ball, and it seemed silent, as if no one else was alive in the world. They were in bed, supposedly trying to talk. But it wasn't talk. In fact, Christine had just shouted out the words that had slowly been building for months inside her. She didn't see Parker move, but suddenly, he cracked her in the side of her head with such force that she flew off the bed, hit the wall, and slumped into a pile in the corner. She raised her fingers to her ears, which were stinging and echoing in a strange way, and tried to stand up. But Parker pounced off the bed and yanked her to her feet and she could tell, even in her confusion, that he was wild. Bloodthirsty. Frantically, she tried to fend him off. She couldn't. He was too big, too strong, too angry. He hit her with his fists, dragging her out of the bedroom, all through the apartment. It seemed forever until the dim pounding started on the door and the strange chant of "Police! Open up!" distracted him. And the last thing she saw before her eyes finally sealed shut with blood was the door to Petra's bedroom, ajar, and Petra's vacant eyes looking right past her to Parker. And now, two years later, here he was again, poisoning her with pure hatred and destroying her all over again.

The corner looked unfamiliar to her, though she'd been there before, had even purchased a bag from the two tiny Indian women, dressed in their bright Guatemalan colors, who sold their handicrafts from a card table on the sidewalk. She could hardly get her bearings; the brick buildings of Stuyvesant Town seemed like a huge blockade, so she turned south and walked through the broken bottles and the trash on the sidewalk. Latin music from the bodegas poured from each doorway. She passed a woman standing on a stoop with a cigarette hanging loosely from her lips. In her hand was a lighter with the flame burning high. The woman, in a junkie nod with her eyes way below half mast, remembered neither the cigarette nor the lighter.

Christine turned into a liquor store and bought a half-gallon bottle of cheap gin. She needed a drink. Very badly, she realized. The music was loud in the store so she had to yell over it; she wanted to scream her head off, nonsense words, until the transaction was completed. The gin bottle had a handle molded into the plastic, so she held it down and it banged into her leg as she walked along 10th Street toward home.

But the thought of climbing the stairs into her safe world that wasn't safe anymore seemed awful and, no, she didn't want to go there. No. She walked into the park at Avenue B, around the gently twisting paths and sat on a bench along the fence of the dog run. Normally, she faced the run and watched the ragtag herd of city dogs stampede back and forth across the dust and the dirt. Normally, she smiled at the adorable animals and their colorful owners, all chatting on the benches inside, their dog leashes temporarily wrapped around their hands. But she didn't care about the dogs or their colorful owners today. She wanted to be numb, to be far away, where the dogs ran free, not inside a wrought iron fence with wire trash cans full of plastic bags of dog shit, collected out of the dust by dutiful dog owners who knew their dog's shitting habits intimately. No.

She uncapped the bottle in its brown paper bag and raised it to her lips. It was warm. It was hot, and it burned her throat and made her cough.

Parker had the name of the Warren School, she thought. He knew the address. Now he would go there and she was helpless to stop him. He had won. She lifted the bottle again, swallowed the warm gin down in three, four, five, long gulps. She was a bartender and a New Yorker: she saw drunks, oblivious to their own degradation, unconscious in puddles of piss on the sidewalk, every single day. She saw the quart bottles of beer that had rolled just past their dirty fingertips and the way they stuck their fingers into the waist bands of their dirty pants and slept so deeply that nothing could disturb them. It had looked awful, but now it looked good, good to be so gone, and she raised the bottle again and swallowed until her veins turned red with warmth and the knot in her stomach slowly began to untie itself. She drank as the sun moved across the sky and left her bench in the shade, and then she drank more. She drank until the trees on the perimeter of the park started to spin slowly in a clockwise direction, revealing and blocking a patch of blue sky, like a giant strobe light.

Christine was sick. She was very sick. She stood up and the trees turned faster. She reached for the iron fence to steady herself and began to walk along it. Vaguely, in the back of her mind, she knew which way her apartment was, but when the fence curved around the dog run and she had to negotiate the open space, with the roller bladers flying by and the noisy people calling back and forth to each other, her legs began to buckle and the paved path seemed steeply banked against her. Suddenly the trees seemed to be growing side-ways. She started to slip. Then she felt an arm, a strong arm around her waist, and she was lifted upright, vertical again, and she leaned against a big man. He was smiling down, but she couldn't make out the features on his face.

"You need some help, Miss?"

She knew her words would be slurry and inarticulate. "Are you a policeman?"

"Sure I am," he laughed. "Undercover. Do you want to sit down?"

She tried to organize her speech into clear sounds in a recogniz-able pattern. "Could you take me home?" She spoke slowly.

"Where's that?"

She wanted to look up into his face, but it was better if she kept looking down where the colors weren't so vivid.

"Tenth Street, by Avenue A," she said. He took the bottle from her hand. A few inches sloshed in the bottom.

"Did you drink the rest of this?"

"Yes," she admitted, contrite.

"You're gonna have one bad headache in the morning."

His arm around her waist steadied her. Maybe he was carrying her, she thought. Her feet seemed to be scraping along the ground, not holding her up in the least. God, she thought, I am so fucking drunk, so stinking drunk. Her brain floated in gin. It could not formulate a thought except the words, Where can I lie down? God, I'm sick, God, I'm sick.

"Which way from here?" the man asked.

"Where are we?" she asked. It made her weak to open her eyes.

"Where do you live, Miss? What's your address?"

She recited the numbers like a kindergarten student, and then they were off again, crossing 10th Street and up the steps to the front door.

"I better take you up," he said. Somehow she still had her bag, its thick strap across her chest, bandolier style. She slid it around to the front and reached her hand inside, miraculously coming up with her set of keys. But she couldn't get them in the slot on the door. It seemed to move around as she aimed her key toward it, so she handed the keys over to the policeman and he opened the door and half carried her all the way to the top and inside. She felt the cool white leather against her cheek as he deposited her on the couch. She closed her eyes and tried to will the room to stop spinning.

She lay there without moving, barely breathing, the fleshy smell of the leather creating little tornadoes of nausea that she desperately tried to ignore. In the distance, far away, she heard crashes, things falling and perhaps breaking, but that did not matter. What mattered was riding the waves tossing the white couch round and round the living room in big, awful, sweeping circles. But she couldn't will the waves away, and she felt sick, very sick, and she knew she needed to get to the bathroom to talk on the porcelain telephone, as her mother used to say, so she opened her eyes and tried to sit up and that's when she saw that her apartment was trashed.

Her purse was emptied on the floor. Her library and video rental cards were there, but her credit cards weren't. Her lipstick had rolled off a ways and her wallet was open and empty. Drawers were pulled from the tables along the opposite wall and her box of pictures was tipped over on the floor, its contents puked out like hers would be if she could get to the bathroom, which she had to do. She stood up, weaving her way across the living room to the bedroom door. The bed was torn apart and the paintings had fallen to the floor. She could hear someone crashing around in the closet.

She covered her mouth and ran to the toilet, dropped to her knees and heaved from the bottom of her stomach. She didn't know what was happening. Couldn't think. Couldn't remember how she got here. Or what was happening now. She flushed the rancid filth away and struggled to her feet, pulling the metal medicine cabinet open and looking for something that would help, anything. The sleeping pills. Just a few, just enough to let her sleep, get over this terrible drunkenness, where nothing was clear anymore, where her head felt underwater, held underwater so long she could not breathe any-more. She had trouble lining the arrows up on the childproof cap, but she pried it open and some red capsules tumbled into her hand. She put them all into her mouth and swallowed.

Christine wanted to lie down again on her big bed with the little blue flowers on the sheets. She stepped into her bedroom and there were those sounds again, the crashing in the closet. She made her way to the door and looked in. A man was on his knees in there, pulling her drawers out.

"Who are you?" she slurred. He snapped around and stood up.

"You got jewelry?" he demanded as he came toward her. His face was green in the light, and his eyes were angry, darting and wild.

"You're not a policeman," she said. It was the only thing she could think to say. It was as if a tiny flame of memory was burning, and in its light she saw backward to the park and she knew she had been fooled. He moved toward her.

"I want your money and your jewelry."

"No," she said, and then his hand shot out, connected hard with her jaw, and sent her reeling, out of the closet onto the bedroom floor. She felt her cheekbone hit the log post of her bed.

"I don't have anything," she said. He stood over her.

"You sure, bitch?" His hand was clenched into a fist. She had seen that before. It scared her, made her weak. She tried to pull her body away.

"I have a ring," she whispered.

"Get it," he hissed.

She crawled to the closet. He looked so big standing there above her. She reached for her old cowboy boots and dumped the ring out. Her wedding ring. Her beautiful wedding ring, with its sparkling diamond baguettes, side by side, pressed against each other like dancers in a kick line.

The last of Parker.

She picked it up off the floor and he grabbed it.

"You keep your fucking mouth shut till I get out of here," he said and disappeared from the doorway.

Christine tasted blood in her mouth. She put her fingers to her face and looked at them. Bloody.

The door shut and she thought she heard footsteps running down the stairs. She got up, unsteady, and went to the door and turned the lock. Amazingly, she felt very calm.

He had her ring. It had been an expensive ring, too expensive for Parker to buy her nine years ago. She had saved it and hidden it in her boot, thinking that one day she would sell it or have it reset and give it to Petra if she ever got better. Now it was gone. Like Parker. Like Petra. And there was nothing she could do about it. Her mind was dark with clouds that blotted out thought, but even in that damp, suffocating fog, Christine prayed that the man from the park had not taken the only thing in her apartment that mattered to her, the only thing of value. The letter.

Panicky, she stumbled to the pile of stuff that he'd dumped out of her bag and reached for the book she'd been reading. In it was a carefully folded letter from the Warren School. Christine had cut the return address off the top of the page, cut the signature off the bottom. How many times had she read this in the three weeks since she got it? A half million? A million? The print was blurry and even the paper seemed heavy. She braced herself against the couch and tried harder to focus on the words.

The weekly report was written in long hand with a fountain pen by the psychologist personally assigned to Petra. Christine knew the letter by heart, but she found it comforting to read the words, the proof, the evidence.

Her eyes moved to the middle of the page across the lines that blurred and faded even as she read. "The night nurse reported a disturbance in the room Petra shared with two roommates. It is not something for you to get your hopes up about, but sometimes in a case like your daughter's, any sign of self-expression, anything at all, is encouraging. The nurse, Mrs. Wilson, heard yelling and she went up to investigate. It was Petra. She was asleep. Mrs. Wilson had never heard her voice before. She cried out three different times. Each time, she yelled 'Mommy!'"

"Mommy," Christine repeated and she held the letter close to her heart. The blood from her mouth had dripped down onto her chest, onto her jacket. She relaxed and felt her body slide down a few inches. The darkness at the edge of her eyes closed in. She slumped sideways. The gash in her chin pressed into the white leather of the couch and reopened. Blood oozed out, bright red against the white.

17

Parker slowly hung up the phone. Christine's final words reverberated in his head. "I hate you," she had said. "I'll always hate you." This was no surprise to Parker; he had heard it often enough in the last few years of their marriage. But it hurt then, every time she said it, and it hurt now. To be hated on first sight or hated for what you stood for, those were somehow forthright and acceptable. But to be hated for what you were, by someone who got to know you over time, especially if that someone began by loving you, that was very painful. Parker pressed his fingers against his right temple and began to rub in slow, small circles. Once Christine had loved him; now she didn't. How did it happen?

He hesitated for a second, then thumbed through his Rolodex until he located Greg Litner's business card. Christine had ranted about the detective and Parker was curious. He looked at his watch. Just after two; just after five in New York. He dialed Greg's number. Busy. He'd try again later.

Paco's was still hopping. The late lunch crowd wouldn't noticeably thin for about another thirty minutes. Parker felt he should go back out and make like the host, but he didn't feel like it. Christine's crazy phone call had upset him, made him feel both restless and melancholy. It was the oldest story in the book. Love and marriage; divorce and hatred; distance, regret, resentment; and then the appearance of that pinpoint of insight, like a tiny star in a black,

black night that slowly grew brighter, and you actually began to understand something. Too late, of course, way too late. But whenever you replayed the memories after that, you saw them in a different way and it hurt that you could not go back and do it all over again.

Except in Parker's case, he thought, he'd have to go all the way back, long before Christine entered the picture, and do it all differently, starting with being born into a different family in a different place at a different time. He was pushing forty, and he wasn't the type to whine about the past, but when he thought about Christine and the mess they'd made of their marriage, he couldn't help but place a part of the blame on his own parents: his father, so-called, who took a permanent hike before Parker was even born; his mother, so-called, who dumped him at age five on his grandmother in a crummy apartment in Cincinnati, where he grew up in the way, sleeping on the couch and using up too much of the meager supply of food and money. What did he know about maneuvering himself or his marriage through rough times? From what he'd observed as a child, when the flame got turned up under the frying pan you hopped out and disappeared.

Which was exactly what Christine had done.

He couldn't forgive her for that.

That would require that he forgive everyone else in his past too, and Parker couldn't do that. If he did, he might slide backward and end up nothing but Joe Ostrobsky, the person he'd been at birth, the identity he'd still have if he hadn't fled from it, down the scuffed stairs from his grandmother's apartment on the third floor.

Joe Ostrobsky. He could barely pronounce it. It stuck like putty in his throat. He had always hated the name; he had even hated forming the letters in it when he was first learning to print in school. It was a brand burned into him by the stranger who fathered him, and it made him ashamed and angry. So, on his way to California, a man of twenty-five, he did what all the famous movie stars and celebrities were doing: he re-invented himself. Under the narrow beam of the reading light in the economy section of the overnight "red-eye" flight, he'd practiced his new signature. Parker Horton. It was a name with brains, he thought. A name with some respectable family history automatically attached. Later, he'd chosen San Anselmo for his restaurant because it was expensive and full of people like Parker Horton, people who maintained themselves in the same focused way that they maintained the art objects they collected for their million-dollar *Architectural Digest* homes.

What no one knew, of course, not even Christine, was that the fashionable Mr. Horton had opened Paco's with a bankroll gleaned from eight well planned and highly successful robberies, all pharmacies within a twelve-mile radius of Cincinnati. Doing them had shaved, he was certain, at least ten years off his life span. But Joe Ostrobsky did what he had to do and didn't look back. He figured the losers who bought the pharmaceutical-grade narcotics and amphetamines from him deserved them. As for Parker Horton, he had never broken the law like that, nor would he. He didn't have the nerve for it.

Yet he had beaten Christine, and that had been a crime. He didn't kid himself about it; he just accepted it. Like all men, he thought, if he was pushed far enough, he snapped. And Christine had pushed him that far. And that was a shame, because she was the one, of all the people, that he had never wanted to hurt.

But all that was moot. They'd done what they'd done, and neither of them could file and forget it. Even now, she probably thought that his determination to get Petra back was just another aggressive act, orchestrated to hurt her. It wasn't. He just wanted to know his own daughter, regardless of the shape she was in. He didn't want to abandon his own child, like his parents had. He wanted that cycle to stop with him.

And besides, he felt responsible for Petra, for what had happened to her, whatever it was. He wanted to make it up to her. If Christine felt driven to plant herself in his way, he would have to plow her under. Petra was that important to him. He could not bear the way Christine had taken her and hidden her somewhere, with strangers who didn't love her.

To Parker, it seemed that Petra had stepped through some hellish mirror four years ago and gotten trapped on the other side. She'd had a loving, doting Mom and Dad, and she'd progressed through the adorable stages of baby and early childhood. And then suddenly, four years old, her smile became a grimace, her laughter became blank silence, and her constant commentary on the big beautiful world became a dry riverbed where all the fish had died and turned to skeletons. It hurt Parker. Oh, it hurt him. And it was no secret that Christine blamed him for it, and that hurt even more.

Parker sat in his antique wooden swivel chair and reached into the desk drawer for his ashtray. He lit a cigarette and sucked the warm smoke into his throat. It was not a habit he was proud of, but it helped him sit still. Parker was not built to be idle. It made him uncomfortable. A cigarette break, ten minutes with an activity incorporated into it, was perfect for him. Still, it disturbed him to think of all of this.

Parker on the witness stand: "Did you or did you not beat your wife so badly that she had to be rushed to San Francisco General Hospital where she remained for eight days?" "I did." "Do you care, Mr. Horton, to inform the court why you made such a vicious attack on your wife?" "We were having an argument." "Really? Really? Is this the normal outcome, do you think, Mr. Horton, of a normal argument between two normal married people?" "No." "Well then, what was so special about this particular argument?" "That's...our business." "No, Mr. Horton, that's the court's business. What was the argument about?" "I don't remember." "You don't remember. How...convenient."

It was an odd and depressing thing, Parker thought, to sit in a courtroom and suddenly realize that the gulf between you and your judges is simply too wide to bridge. Perhaps with a great orator for a lawyer or a great actor to stand in for you, you could recreate the pain of your life and elicit sympathy and understanding. But if it was just you, Parker "the Wife Beater" Horton, Joe Ostrobsky in disguise, you didn't have a chance on earth. So he had given up, right then and there. But at least he'd refused to describe that fight with Christine. He would never discuss it in public and though he'd told Lily, he would probably never discuss it again in private either. He was ashamed of hurting his wife and he was deeply sorry that he'd done it, but his sorrow didn't matter in court and he couldn't turn back time, so he gave up.

In private, though, he sometimes reviewed it all just to remind himself that he was sane.

He had known from the beginning that Christine was misaligned in some basic way. She was timid and vulnerable yet standoffish and self-contained, a sort of Marilyn Monroe, he thought at the time, without the patina of neediness. Yet from the moment she'd let him in, he felt, paradoxically, that he was drowning in her needs. If it wasn't her need for space, it was her need for intimacy. If it wasn't her need to feel independent, it was her need to feel protected. Her mood shifted so fast Parker could barely keep up with her, but it seemed so whimsical and feminine that he'd accepted it and loved her more for it. He was deeply pleased about this. For the first time, he stopped focusing on what other people, or even life in general, had not given him and began to focus on what he could give to someone else. It warmed him, made him feel whole. He gave her everything he could afford and lots of things he couldn't—like the diamond wedding ring that had cost $3500, which, at the time, was slightly more than his whole life savings.

And then he gave her Petra and it all exploded. Not at first, of course. At first, they were the beautiful San Anselmo couple with the beautiful baby daughter. Parker's attachment to Petra was deep, intense, and strangely exclusive. He knew Christine was jealous but he didn't take it seriously. But later, when Petra began to withdraw, she seemed to have reserved her last little bits of communication just for him. Not that it was much, but a tiny smile, the whispered word "Daddy," the hug before bed—these things suddenly became precious. And they were all his. It enraged Christine, made her crazy.

And then Petra lost her grip and sailed away to No Man's Land and Christine blamed him for it. No one knew why it happened: not the doctors they took her to, not Parker, not Christine. But when the human mind is faced with arbitrary chaos, Parker knew, especially in the form of a sick child, it seeks to place the blame. It manufactures pseudo-logic that seems real. Christine filled her mind with this garbage and convinced herself that it was true.

That was when she accused him of the unspeakable, of pushing his penis into his own daughter's mouth, of fondling her like a lover. Outraged, he went for her and then the screen went white and hot and he beat her bloody for what she'd said and for all the things she'd done, step by step after Petra got sick, to take a perfectly feasible marriage and drive it into the slime. Of course, he regretted it.

He was not a bad man. But she had wronged him very deeply and he had snapped.

Afterward he had to live with what he'd done, and that was awful. He was ashamed. But the worst part was sitting in the judge's chambers, signing away his rights to his daughter because Christine's lawyer had made it clear that she would make her sick suspicions public if he fought her. It was terrible to be so powerless, worse to be so helpless, and worst of all to be so afraid of losing what he'd built that he simply let her have it all. It was humiliating almost past endurance, and he loathed himself for his defeat.

It had taken time, but he had more or less forgiven her. There was something wrong with Christine. She was a cracked vessel. Pour all the love in the world into her and it bled out through the cracks and collected into a puddle at her feet. Away from her for so long now, he felt sorry for her. In her way, she was just as sick as Petra.

His cigarette had burned out in the ashtray. He felt drained, exhausted. He picked up the phone and dialed Greg's number again. The answering machine picked up on the first ring. It was Friday, pushing toward seven in New York. Too late for a detective to keep office hours. Parker left a message, tightened up his appearance, and returned, smiling, to the paying customers right outside his office door.

18

When the cab pulled up in front of Christine's building, Steve saw that the lights were on in her apartment. That disturbed him. He went directly to the phone booth on the corner of Avenue A and dialed her number. No answer, just the machine. He climbed the front steps and rang her doorbell, a long relentless ring that would send the average New Yorker flying to the buzzer if only to curse out the visitor. There was no response.

Steve reached in his pocket and pulled out his keys. He entered with an apprehensive feeling deep in his stomach. Then, midway up the second flight, down comes Christine's next door neighbor, the guy with the Walkman. They passed close to each other, nodding a hello, but the guy scrutinized him. Steve knew that was normal in a small building like this. It was only the city version of nosy country neighbors. Still, it made him even more nervous.

Outside her apartment, Steve rang the bell again and pressed his ear close to the door. He heard nothing. He knocked. Still no response. He inserted the key into the Medeco and turned it. Quickly, he reached for the door knob, pushed the door open and stepped inside.

Amazingly, the first thing he noticed was the way the rosy tint of the sunset lit the living room. It glowed in a soft, delicate way, like the light in the paintings by Vermeer he'd seen in the Frick Collection on 70th Street. But then his eyes began to register the rest of the room, and Vermeer's gentle world was ripped away, replaced by a familiar modern landscape: burglary, breaking and entering, who knew what else.

"Christine!" he cried. In that instant Steve had a terrifying vision of her dead in her bed, her tongue swollen, her eyes bugged out, and a stocking wrapped around her long, slender neck. He rushed into the bedroom. It was tossed, but there was no sign of Christine. He checked the bathroom. A few red capsules—he recognized them as sleeping pills—were scattered around the floor, but otherwise it was in order. His pulse raced as he checked her closet. A mess. All the drawers were pulled out and the stacks of clothes had tumbled onto the floor. He ran to the living room.

"Oh God, no," he whispered as he came around the front of the sofa and saw her lying there, propped back against the couch with her head pushed against the white leather at a crazy angle, and all the brown-red blood, on her face, on her clothes, smeared across the white sofa.

He dropped to his knees and reached for her wrist. Good. She had a pulse. She was breathing. She was not dead. He shoved the sofa backwards and sat down, resting her head in his lap. Her face, even with the dried blood, looked calm and at peace. It frightened him.

"Christine," he said in a loud, authoritative tone. "Christine, wake up." He patted her cheeks, hard, like they do in the movies when they want someone to snap out of it, and to his utter happiness, she stirred very slightly, though she didn't open her eyes. Steve laid her down gently and ran to the kitchen where he yanked open the freezer and grabbed some ice cubes out of the plastic bag. In the midst of it, he experienced a searing bolt of terror. Was he doing the right thing? He would call the ambulance in a second, but now he had to at least try to bring her back. He rubbed the ice across her forehead and over her neck. It left little beads of water. "Christine," he said, over and over as he held the ice on her wrist.

She opened her eyes. They were glassy and unfocused. He could not tell if she saw him or not.

"Christine," he said, as he cradled her head in his arms, "who did this, baby? Who hurt you?"

She looked as if she were trying to sweep her thoughts into a big enough pile to express but, of course, he didn't know that for sure. He felt helpless and held her close. "Christine, you've been hurt. I'm going to call an ambulance."

Somehow she managed to form the only coherent thought, the only sentence that was imprinted on her mind, and her voice erupted, strange and loud. "He's after Petra. He's gonna get Petra," she said, and her fingernails dug into Steve's arm, deep, and then relaxed and she passed out again. Steve looked around, at the mess in the apartment, and back at Christine. The guy who did this was after her daughter? Why?

"Christine, come back, honey," he said, but she was far away. He got up and ran to the phone to dial 911. "There's a woman hurt. She's been attacked and needs an ambulance. Hurry." He gave the address and hung up, despite the operator's demand for his name, the circumstances surrounding the attack, more information. He needed to think clearly; he only had a few minutes and he needed to make some decisions. He went to the bedroom and untangled the bedspread from under the mattress and brought it to the living room to cover Christine. Her eyebrows were knit together in what Steve called the New York Pinch. She'd said someone was after Petra. The words echoed in his mind as he pulled the cover over her shoulders.

And in that instant, he knew what he was going to do, what he had to do. After all, he knew where Petra was, at least he did if he'd put two and two together correctly, and if the man who did this to Christine was after her daughter for some sick reason, there was no time to waste. She had been terrified when she spoke. It was as if she'd emerged from a near comatose state to deliver that one important message. He felt duty-bound to act on her behalf. More than anything, he wanted to do something right for Christine. He could go to the Warren School, just to make sure Petra was all right. He noticed a notepad on the floor where her purse had been dumped out. He tore out a sheet and wrote, "Christine, Gone to check on Petra. Don't worry." He folded it into quarters and slid it into the pocket of her black skirt. His fingers bumped up over her hipbone as he pushed it in.

The doorbell rang. Steve crossed to the window and saw an ambulance double parked in front, its red lights flashing. He buzzed the downstairs door open, and with one last glance at Christine, he took off up the stairs, slid the bolt back on the door, and emerged onto the roof of her building. As he was closing the door, he could hear the voices of the medics. "It had to be a walk up, y'know?" a male voice complained, to which a female voice responded, "At this point, all we can do is hope she's ambulatory." "Fat chance," the man said as Steve stepped back from the door as quietly as he could.

His eyes scanned the perimeter for the fire escape. He needed to get down fast and get the hell out of there before the police arrived. Things were escalating fast, too fast. He ran across the building and swung himself down onto the rickety metal fire escape stairs. He did not like heights, did not want to look down through the metal gridwork that formed each step and landing. He knew he was right on the rim of personal disaster. If the police arrived and caught him coming down, he'd be arrested for sure. He took the stairs three at a time, hanging onto the metal railings with both hands, and jumped from the first-floor landing rather than cause the final flight to come noisily creaking down. He found himself in a narrow alley that ran behind the houses on Christine's block, probably a service road from a century ago when this had been called Doctor's Row. Six buildings past hers, the alley curved around and ended with a chain-link gate. Steve squeezed himself between the post and the building and emerged onto 10th Street. Little jolts of electrical current kept shooting up his spine and hitting the base of his skull.

Down the block he saw that a small crowd had collected around the bottom of the stairs to Christine's building. A police car had pulled up behind the ambulance and its passenger door was wide open. Steve walked slowly toward the group and fell in at the edge, his eyes fastened on the door where the medics emerged with Christine strapped into a carry-chair between them. They rushed her down the steps. Steve's eyes were riveted on her face, which looked pale and wan against the stiff material of the chair. On the ground, the medics released a few levers. The chair flattened out and they whisked her into the back of the ambulance and slammed the doors.

Steve felt a pain in his chest and he thought for a second that he was going to break down crying. He clamped his jaw tight and took a breath. The siren cranked up and the ambulance pulled away, west on 10th Street, and ran the red light on the corner. Steve's eyes followed it. Christine was in capable hands, he told himself, and he had a mission to complete for her. He shook off his boyish fears. The crowd was dispersing, and Steve had a strange, paranoid sensation that someone was staring at him. He scanned the people on the sidewalk as he took his first few steps toward Avenue A. It turned out he was right. A big man, nicely dressed and going grey at the temples, stood off to the side, back against the building. He looked straight at Steve and his eyes seemed to be adding something up, putting some puzzle together. He averted his eyes and turned when Steve returned his stare. Steve needed to get away. He walked quickly to the corner and hailed a cab uptown.

He couldn't gauge how much of a head start the man who beat Christine had, but he knew he had to get organized and get going. That meant stopping at his apartment to pick up a few things, and being on the next shuttle plane to Boston. He would rent a car at Logan Airport, drive to Chatham, and find the Warren School. After that, it was anybody's guess what to do. He had to believe he would know his next move when it needed to be made. In Steve's experience that was usually the way it happened, moment by moment. Like with racehorses. They got shuffled here and there, and some vet was always prying open their mouths to stare inside, but periodically, at the chosen moment, the gate opened in front of them and all they had to do was run. Steve felt Christine had somehow opened his gate, and he would run to the ends of the earth for her if necessary. It didn't have to make sense; it just had to feel right. So he had to believe that something would open up and feel right when he finally arrived on Cape Cod.

Here he was, he thought, bumping in a cab over the potholes on a summer night, heading north with a Rasta-man at the wheel. The story of his life. It was even funny if you didn't take it personally. He had always felt swept along. In fact, the concept of being in control of your own life made him suspicious. That was why he watched those "I'm running the show here" types so carefully. He just didn't believe their confidence was real. Take Janet: she drove her little *Expression* chariot around all the curves at breakneck speed, but throw one stone in her path, like Mary Anne's trip to that writer's colony, and Janet's chariot tipped and rolled and left her crying. Or

Dr. Greene. There was a man who believed he had a calling. He said that every conscious act of his life, from adolescence on, had been directed toward becoming a psychiatrist. Then he ended up trying to patch up junkies and coke freaks who didn't have a snowball's chance in hell of staying clean. Was Dr. Greene in control of his life? Was he kidding? Steve, on the other hand, knew his life was totally out of control, random, and chaotic. He expected no sense and he got none.

The cab pulled up in front of his building. Steve paid and started up the stairs. Since he left Long Beach, he'd traveled with one piece of luggage: a folding nylon garment bag with big pockets which, packed correctly, held everything he owned or needed. He spread it out on the metal bathtub cover and then, to his surprise, he began to collect all his belongings and put them in. There wasn't that much. He would've made a good 60s radical on the lam like Abbie Hoffman, he thought, but he didn't believe in anything enough to hold a radical stance either for or against it. He washed the last cup in the sink and placed it upside down in the dish drainer. He snapped his overnight bag shut, put it by the door, and took a short walk through the apartment. Aside from the fact that it was cleaner, it looked as if he'd never been there.

He caught a cab to LaGuardia, missing the ten o'clock shuttle to Boston by two minutes. He withdrew four-hundred dollars from a cash machine and settled down to wait twenty-eight minutes. The terminal seemed incredibly noisy to him, full of people determined to be somewhere else. He felt antsy, and after ten minutes he got up and roamed the corridors in search of a yellow pages phone book. When he finally found one, chained to a row of public phones, he swung it upward from the rack, thumbed through to the letter H and ripped out the pages that listed all the hospitals in New York City.

He returned to the lounge and began to check the names of the hospitals in proximity to Christine's apartment. If he knew hospitals like he thought he did, it was much too early to call. The sheaves of paperwork would not have been completed and no one would've ever heard of Christine Timberlake. Later, he would call them all and find out where she was. He put the list in his shirt pocket just as the crowd surged forward to board the plane. He waited until it thinned a bit before he got up. The plane taxied down the runway and rose into the dark sky. The city looked beautiful all lit up, black and white, just like Christine's apartment before the red blood had been added.

It was a short hop and the passengers were pushing into the aisles and dragging their bags out of the overhead compartments before Steve even finished his honey-roasted peanuts and his beer. He waited until the crowd in the tiny center aisle moved on and then collected his bag and left the aircraft. A clerk at an all-night State Traveler's Aid desk booked him into a motel in Chatham, amidst a peppy chorus of "You don't know how lucky you are to get a room at the last minute on a weekend!" The proprietor there gave him the room number and said the door would be open and not to dare to disturb him when he arrived.

He found an available car at the second rental desk and as soon as it was brought around to the front of the terminal, he slid in and took off. Within minutes he passed through the Callahan Tunnel and was on his way past another well-lit city, reflecting itself in the serene, silent waters of yet another filthy river.

Steve was good at deciphering highway signs and following maps, and he sailed toward Chatham at sixty-five miles per hour. He turned the radio up loud and settled back in the comfortable bucket seat. This was a top-of-the-line car, an Acura Legend, that rented for more than twice the daily rate of the sub-compacts, but it was all there was. It was a nice ride that went by fast. Before he knew it, he was up over the Sagamor Bridge and onto the mid-Cape highway. Chatham was sixty miles out.

When Steve pulled up in front of the gate to the Warren School, it was after two. The school was dark, of course, and peaceful. There was no trouble here. Now that it was located in his mind he felt free to find his room and sleep. Maybe his next move would be clear in the morning. He backtracked to the highway cutoff, found the motel, and fell into a deep sleep as soon as he flopped onto the bed. He slept in his clothes without even moving.

19

When Greg saw Steve come strolling up 10th Street only to stand passively by as his girlfriend got carted out of her building on a stretcher, he knew there was something seriously amiss. That didn't take a genius. As the medics loaded Christine into the ambulance, Greg took the opportunity to use his tiny, new thirty-five millimeter camera to take a few shots of Steve. It had been safely replaced in his bag when Steve finally looked up and saw him. Greg had quickly turned away, but he'd been made and he knew it. Not that Steve knew who he was or why he was interested, but he'd recognize him for sure if he saw him later, so Greg knew he had to be more careful from here on in.

He'd seen Steve take off and hail a cab. Greg was tempted to follow him but his radar told him it'd be more beneficial to get inside the building if he could. After all, he knew where Steve lived, even had a paid informer on the premises.

The cops had stuck a wedge in the front door and in the general confusion right after the ambulance left, Greg slipped in and climbed the stairs. Tenants on the other floors had their doors open and were standing in each other's foyers looking terrified. That happened to people, Greg had noticed over the years. Let a crime, particularly a violent crime, happen in any building anywhere, and all the other tenants started hearing voices that said, "You're next." And it took a long time for the voices to go away.

Climbing the stairs was no picnic. When he got to the top, a couple of young cops stood leaning against the doorway, smoking and tapping the ashes onto the terrazzo hallway floor. Greg started toward them.

"Greg Litner," he said, "Private investigator. I'm on a case involving Miss Timberlake here." The two cops looked over at him without interest.

"They just took her out," the young one said. He looked fifteen to Greg. "Unconscious," he added.

"I saw. I got here along with the ambulance. How bad is she?"

"Didn't look too bad to me. She'll come out of it." He turned his back slightly toward Greg as if to dismiss him and took another drag on his cigarette.

Punk, Greg thought. "Mind if I look around?"

Babyface shrugged. This wasn't a homicide. Most likely it'd just get buried in a file.

"The Crime Unit guys are in there. Don't touch nothing."

"Don't worry," Greg replied, and the two rookies smirked at each other. He stepped into the ex's apartment. Somebody had obviously been looking for something. Probably something small, considering it was mainly the drawers that were pulled out and dumped. The furniture wasn't tipped over or cut up. Looked like a routine B&E, but then Steve Dant, the boyfriend, standing by cool as a cucumber when she was brought out didn't figure. He knew something about this, Greg was positive.

A cop was on his knees dusting the edge of the purse for fingerprints.

"What d'ya got?" Greg asked. The cop looked up at him, mildly interested. He probably figured Greg was a police detective.

"Couple sets of prints so far. That's about it."

"How 'bout the girl?"

"What do I know? Looked like an O.D. to me, but she'd been knocked around too. Weird thing though..." His voice trailed off as he concentrated on lifting the print. Greg waited patiently until he realized that the Crime Unit guy had lost his train of thought.

"What was weird?"

"Huh?"

"You started to say something. You said, 'Weird thing' and then you stopped."

"Oh yeah. Looks like the perp called it in—even hung around to buzz the front door. Went out the roof after the ambulance got here. Took a chance, y'know?"

Greg nodded his head. "I'm gonna take a look around, O.K.?"

"Sure."

Greg stepped into the bedroom and took his camera out of his shoulder bag. It wouldn't hurt to have a few pictures of this, though he had no business being in here. The pills were still on the floor of the bathroom. He shot that, then one more of the living room from the foyer. He called a thank you to the Crime Unit guy and stepped back into the hallway and headed for the stairs.

"Yo, Sherlock Holmes," said Babyface, "find anything you wanna tell us about?"

Greg's spine stiffened as he did an about face. He didn't feel particularly mad because he'd long ago learned to consider the source before he let himself get heated up. But this kid needed somebody to give him a set of brains. It was for his own good and a public service too. He retraced the steps he'd taken and stood directly in front of the kid. He had to get that close to read the kid's name plate without his glasses.

"Officer Burke, do you see my shoes?" Burke's eyes dropped

down for a second.

"Yeah."

"These shoes are custom made, for me, for $450 a pair."

"So?"

"So I don't think you should disrespect an honest working man in a pair of $450 shoes. It makes you look arrogant and stupid." He poked his finger once into Burke's chest. "There. I taught you something." Burke's eyes were wary and his chin was pulled back in, as if to ward off Greg's words, but he said nothing. Greg turned and went down the stairs. Halfway down he heard Burke whisper "Old fart" in a low voice, but Greg could tell his heart wasn't really in it. Greg believed that everybody in the world, on one level or another, would get receptive, even if he didn't seem to on the surface, if he thought he was gonna learn something useful. So the trick was to engage that part of the jerk's personality. Burke probably wasn't a bad kid, Greg thought as he rounded the corner and started down the last flight of stairs. He was on his way to have a little conversation with Steve Dant. If it turned out that NYPD needed to be informed of anything, Greg decided, he'd phone it in to Officer Burke.

He got in a cab on the corner. What Steve Dant did to Christine Timberlake was really none of his business. If it didn't help Horton's case, it was of no interest to him. But Greg smelled a rat and that made him curious. One thing he'd noticed over and over in his years of doing investigations: you take an event, any event, and once you started digging into it, it became like a spider web. It clung to everything and stretched thin and far, and once you got any part of it on you, you couldn't shake it off. But the patterns were also delicate and you had to be careful not to tear any part before you saw the whole design. He knew he had to be careful when he talked to Dant. He didn't want to poke a stick in the web and then not be able to reconstruct it.

He asked the cabby to wait while he checked to see if Steve was home. He rang the super to get in. The building was old and the intercom system hadn't been upgraded, so there was no way for the super to check on who was buzzing. The lock clicked and Greg stepped inside. The super's apartment was in the back on the ground floor behind the stairs. Greg walked quickly back to his door. He needed to get the super out of the way first. He was already standing in the doorway anyway.

"Oh," he said, "it's you. I don't got nothing for you."

"O.K." Greg answered. "I was just in the neighborhood so I thought I'd check back."

"That girl in the office, she wouldn't give me nothing."

"That's the way it goes sometimes. Thanks anyway."

"Yeah," the super said. "Catch you later." He stepped back inside and closed his door. Good, thought Greg, that had worked out fine. He started for the stairs but heard footsteps coming down and instinctively drew back in under the staircase. Steve Dant. He had a suitcase, one of those expensive garment bags, slung over his shoulder. Leaving town all of a sudden? Two possibilities presented themselves: step out and confront him, or follow him. He glanced at his watch. Ten after nine. What the hell, he thought, he'd follow him. Might be interesting.

Steve disappeared through the front door and walked toward Greg's cab waiting in front. Greg cracked the door enough to hear him say, "LaGuardia?" to which the driver responded, "I'm hired, buddy." Steve took off toward First Avenue. Greg let him get down the block a ways before he stepped out of the building and climbed into the back seat.

"See that guy with the suitcase?" Greg asked. "He's gonna get a cab and I want you to stick to him."

"I already know where's he going. LaGuardia," said the driver.

"So stick to him all the way there, all right?"

"It's your money, man."

"Twenty-five buck tip if you don't lose him."

The driver inched toward the corner in time to see Steve climb into a yellow cab. The taxi light on its roof went off and the cab started to move into the traffic with Greg's cab right behind it. Greg kept his eye on Steve's cab for a few blocks but it soon became clear that his driver had the situation covered so Greg relaxed. It had taken him a long time to learn to relax and hand the responsibility over to someone else if it was in any way possible. A few minutes of peace kept you much sharper in the long run. He was interested to see where Steve Dant was heading. If it wasn't too far, Greg thought, he'd go along for the ride.

It wasn't far at all. When he saw Steve buy a ticket for the shuttle, Greg bought one too. He made himself scarce in the waiting area and then boarded in the first crush. He would take a seat as far back as possible, counting on Steve to drop into one farther up. This tail job had some fun built into it because he was sure Steve would recognize him if he saw him. That made it challenging, because at 6'2" tall, he was way too big to sneak around.

But Steve made it easy for him. As soon as they landed, he'd stopped at the Traveler's Aid desk and made a motel reservation. Greg planted himself at a phone, too close to the desk, but he had to take the chance. He kept his back turned and only caught the words "Crow's Nest Motel." He waited until Steve moved off to the car rental desk and then approached the girl at Traveler's Aid. She was youngish, maybe thirty-five, dyed blonde hair, pudgy.

"Excuse me, Miss," Greg began, "I was on the phone over there and I heard you mention the Crow's Nest Motel. I stayed there what? Twenty years ago? It's still there, huh? In Revere Beach?"

"No, this one's in Chatham," she said with a smile.

"That near Revere?"

"No, it's out on the Cape."

"Oh well...another place. Funny though, it really struck a chord, hearing that name. I had a great time when I stayed there."

A bigger smile lifted the edges of her bright red lips. "You wanna tell me all about it?"

The flirty edge in her voice made him feel good. "It's not for young ears," he said with a wink. Another time, he thought, when he wasn't working, he would've made a play for her. A chatty lady working the graveyard shift, she had to be single. He picked up a road map of Massachusetts and said a tender goodbye.

Since he knew where Steve Dant would end up, Greg felt no pressure to dog him every step of the way. The farther back he stayed, the less chance he'd be seen. He watched Steve rent a car from Hertz. He'd used a credit card, of course. If he made a habit of that, it would be easy to keep track of him. He waited until Steve had gone out of the terminal to wait for his car before he stepped up to the desk. Hertz could accommodate him if he was willing to take a luxury model.

"What else?" he asked, and the clerk started in on the paperwork. He folded the receipt and tucked it into his shoulder bag. These bills would go directly to Parker Horton, just as soon as he got back to the city.

It didn't take Greg long to get the feel of the Chrysler New Yorker he rented though he had never driven one before. He had a low-end Ford at home that was much more likely to get passed over by the car thieves of the five boroughs. Besides, when he needed a car for surveillance work, the last thing he wanted was to draw attention because his ride was too nice. Tonight, though, he was on his way to a seaside resort where this car would probably fit in very well. It was, by far, a superior driving experience. Positioned at a slight angle with his back pressed against the corner of the door and his right arm stretched out over the back of the seat, he rocketed over the highway toward Chatham in a happy trance. It was late, there was no traffic, and every time Greg glanced at the speedometer, the white needle hovered around eighty-five. It felt like he was doing thirty.

He liked driving on the open road. The dotted white line mesmerized him, and he felt suspended in a time and a place where everything was perfect. Human beings, he thought, always want to go someplace fast. If you looked at the history of the world, people were always piling into ships or covered wagons, trains or space shuttles, and taking off for parts unknown. But why? There were three distinct possibilities, Greg mused: first, the place where the people were was God-awful and they wanted to get away; second, they believed in the "grass is always greener" concept and were searching for the perfect place to stop and rest; or third, the desire to hit the road and go was built in, part of the genes and the DNA. The first group's motivation was related to the present, he thought. The second's to the future, and the third's to the past. That brought up an issue that boggled Greg's mind: time. He knew that the present was the only thing that was real, at least it seemed so in the present moment, but what created it? The past or the future? If it was the past, he thought, then the present was like the top row of bricks on a high brick wall; on the other hand, if the future created the present, then we were all scrambling to color in some abstract idea, trying to catch up to something we didn't even know about yet.

That was what was on his mind—time—when he pulled into the

passing lane and whipped by the car Steve Dant was driving. Oh shit, how stupid could you get, thought Greg as he snapped out of his trance. He was already slightly past the car when Steve's face had registered on him. Very, very sloppy. He'd been dreaming, and if you dreamed while working in the detective business, you could count on a rude awakening.

He knew better than to slow down and try to get back in behind him. Besides, there wasn't much of a point because where could he be going but the Crow's Nest Motel? It was almost two in the morning, after all. Five minutes later, the Chatham exit came up and Greg turned off. He followed the signs toward town and hadn't gone more than a half a mile when he saw the Crow's Nest on the left. Across from the driveway was a garden shop, empty and dark. He pulled into the back of the parking lot and turned off his lights. Might as well put Steve to bed, he thought. The silver Acura appeared, slowing down to a near stop at the Crow's Nest as Steve checked it out. But then he cranked it up again and continued on toward the town.

This guy's full of surprises, thought Greg. He liked that. It made the game a whole lot more interesting. He let Steve get several hundred feet down the road and pulled out after him. Steve seemed to be following the signs to the beach; when he got there, he took a left onto Shoreline Drive, drove a quarter block, and made a U-ey. Greg hung back until it was clear the U-turns were over; then he followed. Steve drove along for about two miles, then pulled over to the side in front of what appeared to be the gates of a huge private house or mansion at the end of a long, straight driveway. Greg parked and sunk low in his seat. His adrenaline was pumping little telegrams to him: he was definitely on to something.

Steve stayed there five minutes, then did a three-point turn and disappeared back down the same road. Greg waited until the tail lights were gone, and then put the car in gear and drove the last three-quarters of a block to the gate. Off to the side, a sign read "The Warren School for Girls."

Bingo, he thought.

Bingo.

He looked at the digital clock on the dashboard: 2:03. That would make it 11:00 in California. "Now, where am I gonna find a phone in this one-horse town?" he asked himself out loud, into the air that smelled of the sea. It was time to call Parker Horton with an update. Greg circled back around and followed the "business district" signs. Every motel had a neon "no vacancy" light flashing, and he found no all-night diners. When he saw a pay phone along side the drugstore, he pulled up and dug Parker's telephone numbers out of his notebook.

The restaurant was still busy because when the hostess picked up there was quite a racket in the background. While he waited for her to locate Parker, Greg gazed up and down the streets of Chatham, Mass. A cute, sleepy town. Lots of cedar shakes and front porches with rocking chairs. Finally Parker picked up, probably in the office because it was dead quiet in the background.

"Hi Greg," he said, "what'cha got?"

Right to the point, thought Greg. No polite chit-chat.

"There's a couple things I think we oughta talk about."

"Shoot."

"Your ex-wife's...in the hospital."

"What happened to her?" There was real concern in Parker's voice. "She called me this afternoon. She was...she sounded irrational. What happened?"

"None of this is completely clear right now. I'm trying to unravel it, but I thought I should keep you apprised."

"Go ahead."

"Her apartment got tossed and it looks like she got in the way and got assaulted. But..."

"But what?"

"I think it was her boyfriend who did it."

"Did you tell the police?"

"No. I wasn't positive and...I don't run my theories by them, y'know?"

"Why do you think it was the boyfriend?"

"Because I saw him there, acting like he didn't know her. But that's not everything. When he took off, I followed him. He left town immediately. I'm up on Cape Cod with him right now. I...I think I know where your daughter is."

"Petra? Really? God, that's great. It's—"

"It's not so great, Parker. The boyfriend is here and I watched him case the place. I think he's gonna try to grab her."

"What? Are you sure about this?"

"No, I'm calling you because I've got a feeling."

"Jesus," Parker said. "I don't know what to think." He was silent for a minute. "What hospital is Christine in? I should talk to her."

"I haven't found out yet. I've been on the road since this whole thing went down."

"Look, Greg, I don't want to insult you...but how accurate are you when you get a feeling. Usually, I mean."

"Dead accurate."

"All right. Where are you? I'll get on the first flight out."

That made sense to Greg. "It's a town called Chatham in Massachusetts. On Cape Cod. You should fly into Boston. It's ninety miles from there."

"Gimme the information on the school. I'm gonna call them."

Greg read the name and address of the Warren School out of his notebook. Then he added, "I think you should just tell them that your wife's been hurt and you're coming to get your daughter. I wouldn't mention the stalker."

"Stalker?" Parker's voice was thoroughly alarmed.

"I shouldn't've used that word," Greg said. He knew it was laden with connotations and every one of them was correct, but it scared the hell out of people. "People lose their cool, y'know? They go crazy if there's a threat like that. I checked this guy out. He doesn't have a criminal record. I know where he lives, and I know where he's staying tonight. I think it would be better if you just sat on this until you get here and get your little girl." He hesitated. "See, we have absolutely nothing on this guy. You understand that? Nothing. The cops would need something before they could move on him."

"Well, are you gonna watch him? What's his name anyway?"

"Steve Dant. I'm gonna stick to him like glue till you get here."

"How will I find you?"

"Don't worry about finding me. Just go to the school and get your daughter."

"O.K. I'll be on the first flight out, but I don't know when I'll get there. Probably around noon if I'm lucky, with the time change and all."

"Whenever."

"I'm on my way." There was a slight hesitation. "Thank you, Greg."

"You'll be getting my bill, Parker."

They both hung up.

Greg needed to get some sleep. He could only afford a couple hours. If Dant was gonna make a move in the dark, he would've done it already. Obviously, he needed rest. Greg had misgivings about parking in the garden shop lot, being the only car there, but he overcame them because it was after two in the morning and he was dog tired. He set the alarm on his wristwatch for 5:30, climbed into the back seat, which wasn't too bad considering his height, and conked out, knowing full well that Steve Dant, whoever and whatever he was, was one-hundred feet away in a nice, comfy queen-size bed.

20

Steve slept flat on his back with his mouth open, a deep satisfying sleep until the dream started. He called this his "nothing dream." In it, he was in his childhood bedroom in St. Regis Falls. It was dark, but he recognized the shapes of the furniture and the eerie shadows of the huge maple trees right outside the window. He thought he was a small boy in the dream, but he had no evidence of that. He did know that he'd had this particular dream many times, starting when he was a kid, but no matter how often it recurred it was always debilitating and horrifying.

It started with a sense of floating. All of a sudden there was a loud sucking sound and then everything was lost in a purple-blue indigo haze. There was nothing there. No sound, no light, nothing to touch or feel, no smells. There was no air, nothing to breathe, and there was no time to move forward and carry him out of it. Then the skin that covered him and formed him into something began to split and pull apart. And then there was no Steve either. Just nothing. Thick, awful nothing. He felt his heart give up and stop and he opened his eyes in terror that felt just as real this time as it had the first time, when he'd been eight or nine. Then he had screamed, and, after a while, his mother threw the bedroom door open and spoke from the threshold.

"What're you screaming for, Steve?"

"Nothing," he gasped. "There was just...nothing."

His mother was silent for a few beats. "Well, if it's nothing, go back to sleep." She closed the door and he heard her footsteps creaking the boards on the way to her room. He had sat up in bed, his eyes wide and terrified, holding the sheets twisted in his little fingers, and waited for the dawn to come creeping through the maple trees.

He woke up. It was long past dawn now, though, as one glance at his watch told him. In fact, it was almost eleven which, according to the signs posted in three obvious locations in the room, was check out time. He called the desk and asked if he could book the room for another night.

"You're in luck," the woman answered. "It's the last room we got. Now, would you like your continental breakfast brought over? It's free and we stop serving at eleven."

"Thanks, yeah," he said and got up and went to the bathroom. The nothing dream had set his nerves on edge. His whole body felt like his teeth did if he unintentionally bit down on a piece of tinfoil he hadn't quite scraped off a baked potato. The perfect thing to pour coffee on top of, he thought as he waited for breakfast to arrive.

There was a knock on the door and a teenage girl with braces and too much pink lipstick passed him a plastic tray with a dented crois-sant and a large Styrofoam cup of coffee. Packets of sugar and non-dairy creamer were tucked under the paper plate. She obviously was not expecting a tip because she took off as soon as she handed him the tray. Steve paused for a few seconds in the doorway. The day was bright and sunny and the sky was a pretty shade of blue with no clouds anywhere. Even this far from the beach, the salty smell of the Atlantic was in the air. Not a smell he particularly liked after four years on an aircraft carrier. He closed the door and the room seemed dark and depressing. He sat down and opened the coffee. After the first few swallows, he unfolded his New York yellow pages and began to call the hospitals.

"Patient information, please."

"One moment."

"I'm calling to inquire about the condition of Christine Timberlake."

Pause.

"I'm sorry, sir. We have no patient listed with the last name of Timberlake."

"Thank you."

Beekman Downtown, Bellevue, Beth Israel, on through the alphabet he called, and finally found her under "S." St. Vincent's.

"Ms. Timberlake is listed in stable condition. Shall I ring you through to her room?"

"Ummm...no, not right now. Could you tell me her extension, though?"

"Certainly, sir. Extension five one five."

"Thank you."

"You're welcome."

Steve replaced the receiver and lifted his legs up onto the bed. Stable. A comforting word, despite the fact that he wasn't the least bit sure what it meant. From what point did the medical profession measure a stable condition? Still, the word relieved him. Some of the immediacy drained off the situation, though he still felt he owed Christine a trip to the Warren School. With the light of day it seemed unlikely that whoever had beaten Christine would have come this far to find a harmless eight-year-old.

But that perception altered one-hundred eighty degrees when he caught sight of the man he'd seen outside Christine's apartment in New York City just after she was carried out to the ambulance last night. Steve had just carried his bag out to the car to stow it in the trunk, just in case he didn't need to return to the motel. He noticed that the garden shop across the road was doing a booming summer business. Couples with babies in strollers were bent over the boxes of seedlings out front and weekend farmers with city haircuts were testing wheelbarrows and rakes. As Steve closed the trunk, he stopped for a second to watch. It was such an all-American picture with the flowers blooming and the little kids being pulled along by their parents, up and down the rows of plants. Then he'd noticed the man at the soft drink machine back against the building. He was tall and big and somehow familiar. It was the color of his shirt, a cool shade of mint green, that caught Steve's attention. When the man collected his can of Coke and started back across the lot, Steve knew he'd seen him somewhere. The military haircut, the temples gone grey. And then he remembered. He'd seen him outside Christine's apartment last night.

Steve went quickly to his room and stood to the side of the window to peer through the slats of the blinds. His heart pounded as the man got into a black New Yorker at the very edge of the parking lot and popped the top on his can of soda. Steve knew he had to move fast, but what was he supposed to do? He stepped onto the terrace that overlooked a cranberry bog behind the motel, climbed over the wrought iron railing, and dropped down the six feet to the ground. He moved along the back of the motel, then behind the real estate office next door, and then behind the Chatham Rug and Tile Center. He crossed the road beyond the fifteen-foot cedar hedge that lined the edge of the garden shop's parking lot. He had to slow this man down, get to the school before him. He could warn the staff, convince them to call the police or at least to take Petra somewhere safe. He had to do something.

He didn't want a confrontation. The man was older but bigger, and he obviously had some axe to grind with Christine, which probably made him dangerous. A few minutes lead was all Steve need-ed. He walked along the opposite side of the hedge from where the man's car was parked and then squatted down and pushed his way through. The branches were thick and scratched his arms as he sep-arated them. He squirmed through, emerging just behind the New Yorker. Staying low, he moved toward the rear tire and opened the Swiss army knife he'd carried with him since high school. He punc-tured the tire in three places, deep slices that he hoped would buy him the time he needed to get to the Warren School. It seemed like such a flaccid, pitiful gesture, pushing through a thick hedge to punc-ture a tire with a yuppie knife, but it was all he could think to do. Two years of obsessively watching spy movies, he thought, obviously hadn't turned him into James Bond.

He crawled back through the hedge and crossed the road. He doubted if the man would recognize him but he couldn't take a chance. Retracing his steps to the motel, he followed the sidewalk to the office, paid for his room with a credit card and climbed into his car and left. The man across the road was still sipping from his can of Coke. It was so strange, felt so off, Steve thought as he pulled into the steady stream of traffic into town. Beach traffic in the summer.

In his rearview mirror, he saw the New Yorker at the garden shop's exit, nosing out into the traffic. Jesus, he thought, he had barely made it. Now the man from Christine's was behind him, perhaps a dozen cars back. But it was at least three and a half miles to the school. That tire would fold up somewhere along the way.

Steve felt the edges of depression closing in on him as he crept along toward the beach. Finding himself in a crowd of too many peo-ple trying to do the same thing always had this effect on him. People were no more than ants, marching in orderly lines toward the sea. And the beaches were policed once you got there anyway. You couldn't build a fire to toast your marshmallows or swim where there wasn't a lifeguard or even eat the clams you might collect. It made him feel bad, like everything was over and nobody had figured it out yet. Between glances in the rearview mirror, he tried to focus on the sights of Chatham just to keep himself from sinking into the suffocating vacuum of depression. He noticed the road to the airport to the left—there was an exhibition of antique planes today, a sign said. The high school kids were having a car wash in the lot of the A&P. The man from New York was still behind him. He hadn't had to pull off the road with a flat yet.

Steve made the right onto Shoreline Drive. He could feel the incredible tension in his hands on the wheel, in his neck and shoulders. The Warren School was getting closer, the New Yorker was still creeping along behind him, and he still had no idea what to do. A little over a mile from the school, the New Yorker edged to the side, and Steve saw the door fly open and the man shoot out, around the back of the car. He relaxed a bit. He would have the time he needed after all.

The school's gate was open. Steve drove up the long driveway and parked directly in front. He ran up the steps and into the foyer, which functioned as a reception area. A woman sat behind an antique desk. The telephone switchboard and the computer terminal looked out of place on it.

"I'd like to speak to the director, please," Steve said, "about Petra..." He hesitated. Should he use the name on the baby bracelet or Christine's last name? He didn't have to make the decision because the woman stood up.

"Mr. Horton? Thank God. You got here so fast." She came around the desk. "We were so concerned when we got your message. Petra is packed and ready to go." She indicated two suitcases standing next to the wall. "I'll call Mrs. Rose and ask her to bring Petra down." The receptionist punched a button on the switchboard and said, "Edna? Mr. Horton's here. Can you bring Petra down?" She looked at Steve and lowered her voice. "I'm so glad you're taking her away till they catch this....whatever he is. It's hard to believe anybody would..."

Steve half listened. He tried to put it together. Obviously, they thought he was Petra's father. Somehow they knew the man who hurt Christine was after her daughter. They took it seriously enough to want her taken safely away until the guy was caught. What they didn't know, of course, was that he would show up any second at the door. What shook him even more was their willingness to turn Petra over to him, a man they'd never even seen before. It was clear to Steve that Petra was not safe here. But none of that mattered much because the little charade would end as soon as Petra arrived from wherever she was and announced that Steve wasn't Daddy. What would happen then? Thoughts slamdanced in his head but he remained externally calm. Christine's daughter was all right. He had slowed the New York man down and arrived here first.

The door opened and a woman stepped through, gently pulling a young girl behind her. Petra. She wore a pair of blue jeans, red sneakers, and a white tee-shirt with the Ninja Turtles on the front. Her dark hair, like Christine's, was cut short and she was pale, as if it weren't summer and she wasn't a kid who played outside. But then, that was obvious. She was clearly not normal.

He dropped down to her level and his eyes filled with unexpected tears. So this was Christine's daughter. "Petra," he said, and his voice cracked. Edna led her over and for some reason Steve hugged her tight. She was so tiny and frail. And when he released her and saw how helpless she was, he knew exactly what to do. He was going to get her out of this place before the man from New York arrived. He'd hide her until Christine could care for her.

He stood up.

"I'd like to go right away. Now."

"Certainly," said the secretary. "Could you just sign the release form?" She handed him a pen and indicated a blank line at the bottom. Under it, neatly typed, was the name Parker Horton. Steve scrawled it, picked up Petra's bags, and followed Edna out the front door. He put the bags away as Edna buckled Petra into the front seat. Steve shut the trunk and walked to the driver's door.

"Mr. Horton?" Edna called. Steve stopped as she came around to his side. "I...I just don't want Petra to leave unless I tell you. I think— the doctors don't think so, I know, but I think she listens to the fog horn when it blows. I think she pays attention to it."

Steve had no idea what she was talking about, but he took her hand and thanked her. Then he climbed into the car, started it, and took off down the driveway. Petra sat small and still, her eyes distant and unfocused.

"Petra?" Steve said, "Petra, if you can hear me, I want you to know that everything's O.K. Don't worry."

He didn't want to turn back the way he'd come for fear of seeing the man again, so he pulled into the traffic and continued on. Heading away from the beach, the traffic moved quickly. He glanced at his watch. He'd spent exactly five minutes at the Warren School. Steve put the pieces together in his mind. Petra's father would show up at the school sometime soon and all hell would break loose. Clearly, he couldn't sit in the notorious mid-Cape highway traffic. He took the first left that looked like more than a neighborhood street and hooked onto the road leading to the airport. He parked the car, collected his bag and both of Petra's from the trunk, and opened

Petra's door.

"Come on, Petra," he said. She didn't move. He dropped the bag, undid the seatbelt Edna had stretched across her, and led Petra from the car. The airport was tiny. The landing strip was just long enough to accommodate the private Cessnas and Beechcrafts that lined its edge. Inside the terminal, he sat Petra in a chair and went to the information desk.

"Can I get a shuttle to Logan from here?"

"Sure," said the clerk, a man in his late forties with a pot belly. "Next one leaves in ninety minutes."

"I have an emergency," Steve said, pausing for a second. "Is there a charter I could book?"

"How many passengers?"

"Two. Me and...my daughter."

"Lemme see who's around," the man said. "There's normally a couple guys who don't mind making a few extra bucks."

"I'm in a real hurry," Steve said. "I'll pay double."

The clerk got up and disappeared through a door marked private. Steve glanced at Petra, who sat like a statue in the chair where he'd placed her. A minute later, the clerk came through the door with another man.

"You looking for a pilot?" said the man with a smile, "'cause I'm looking for a man who wants to take a ride to Boston. Jim Kelleher." He extended his hand and Steve shook it.

"Parker Horton," he said.

"You got bags?" Jim asked.

"Yeah, right here." Steve led him to the seat where Petra was.

"Well, well, is this my other passenger?" Jim asked, but his face changed when he realized Petra was not responding.

"She's deaf and dumb," Steve nervously explained. "And she's currently mad at me too. She doesn't want to go back home." Jim nodded and reached for Petra's bags. Steve slung his over his shoulder and lifted Petra to his hip. He carried her out of the terminal and into the plane. He felt wired, though he knew Jim Kelleher would chalk it up to fear of flying in a four-seater. He sat in the back and kept a protective hand on Petra's shoulder.

"It's a short hop to Logan," Jim said. "Let's hope we can get landing clearance quick."

"Yeah."

"You live in Boston?"

"No," Steve said. "Just over the state line in Maine."

"On the coast?"

"Nearby."

"Pretty country," Jim said.

"We like it," Steve answered.

"Wicked in the winter, though," Jim added, and then he fell silent and concentrated on negotiating the tiny plane through the air currents and sky traffic. Thirty minutes later they touched down. Steve paid Jim in cash and thanked him.

"You need a hand?" Jim asked.

"I'll manage O.K.," Steve said, hefting one bag under his arm so he'd have a free hand for Petra. "Thanks anyway."

Inside the airport, Steve dropped the keys to the rental car at the desk and told them where it was. "We'll have to send a driver out there, sir, and charge you for the extra day." "That's fine," Steve said, signing the papers.

He led Petra toward the line for the New York shuttle. Half way there, though, he abruptly changed his mind. Christine might remain in the hospital for several days. What would he do with Petra in his little apartment on 64th Street? It wouldn't be good for her and he would surely go crazy cooped up with her. He studied the departure board. Planes were due to leave for Montreal, Baltimore, Washington, Burlington, Albany, and Syracuse. And then he knew what to do.

He would go to St. Regis Falls. After all, he owned a house there, though he hadn't seen it in seven years and for all he knew it was stripped, burned, gone. Still, it seemed like a good idea. He could plan his next move in privacy and Petra would be safe. He withdrew more money from the NYCE machine and paid cash for two tickets to Syracuse under an invented name. They had just enough time to board the plane and then they were airborne. The flight would take sixty-five minutes. Steve ordered a beer from the flight attendant and got an orange juice for Petra, though she didn't even touch it. Looking at her, small and motionless in her seat by the window, the hugeness of what he had done finally hit him. Impersonation, kidnapping, crossing state lines with a minor. Plus, his fingerprints were all over Christine's apartment and if her stable condition worsened, and God forbid, she died, the cops and the FBI would soon be on his ass. Who would believe his crazy story? He had done this for Christine, a woman he'd never met but felt he loved. Petra's eyes were closed and her little fists, with the thumb tucked in, rested on her thighs. Steve took her hand and unfolded the fingers.

"What 'cha got there, Petra?" he asked. "Nothing? You sure hang onto it tight."

She closed her hand again with his finger held inside. He did not want to pull it away. He turned his mind off. What was done, was done. He could not change it. He needed to contact Christine and keep Petra safe until she came for her. That was all. And the little girl's sturdy grip on his index finger provided plenty of motivation to go that far. It made him feel good about himself: life had passed him the baton, and he had run with it as hard and as fast as he could. Steve figured that things like this didn't happen very often, so when they did, they had to be respected. It was like the Bible story about walking on water. If you questioned it in the middle, you sunk clear out of sight. He would do his questioning later. He probably would have plenty of time to go over it step by step, he thought with a little jolt of humor, particularly if he got caught.

In Syracuse, Steve took a cab to Rent-A-Wreck. He left Petra sitting in an old bucket seat propped against the trailer that served as an office and toured the row of rusted, dented cars with the owner, a skinny, frenetic guy with a red beard. Steve settled on an 84 Escort. The body was outrageously rotted, but the engine sounded strong.

"That one's fifty a week, " said the owner.

"What if I gave you five-hundred bucks and we just skip the paperwork," Steve said.

The owner looked at the car, his mental calculations casting shadows over his face. "How 'bout six?"

"No," Steve replied, "it's not worth five, but I'm in a hurry. Take it or leave it."

"Shit, I'll take it and go home," the owner smiled. His teeth looked very grey in his pink mouth. "How you wanna work this? You wanna send me back my plates after you get it registered or what?"

Steve hesitated. "I'd like you not to get concerned for a month."

"Well, I gotta carry insurance if the plates are registered to me. That costs me."

"Fifty'll cover it for a month, right? I'll give you that," Steve said. "At the end of the month, I'll send you the plates and you send me the bill of sale. Report it stolen if you don't hear from me."

"Fair enough."

Even when all the negotiations were outside the rules, Steve noticed, people were always concerned about fair. Of course, the direct translation was "I'm not getting screwed here" which was a long way from fair. Steve opened his wallet and handed the man the five hundred fifty bucks. He dropped the keys in Steve's hand.

"You made my day, man. Now I can go home and watch the game with a clear conscience."

"Well good," Steve said, climbing into the car. He drove it to the office, threw the bags in the back seat, and buckled Petra into the front. The man with the red beard stood at the gate, ready to swing it shut after them. Steve tried to give him the two-beep thank you on the horn, but it didn't work, so he just waved as he pulled out into the street. It was an industrial section where the road maintenance was minimal, so Steve picked his way carefully through the potholes. The car didn't feel half bad. He turned on the radio. It worked. Around the corner he saw a gas station where he filled up and got a road map. He knew the big towns he would pass through along the way to St. Regis Falls: Watertown, Canton, Potsdam. He had a three, three and a half hour drive ahead of him. It was almost five. Five and a half hours since he'd shown up at the Warren School and ended up acquiring a daughter. He glanced over at Petra. She was sitting with her head bent forward, as if she were seriously studying something in her lap. He reached over and rubbed the back of her neck and her shoulders. Her bones felt tiny and fragile under the skin.

"My name is Steve," he said, because it suddenly occurred to him that he had never told her. "Your mom asked me to go get you and in a little while, I'm gonna take you to her in New York. Everything is O.K." And in his heart, he had to believe that.

He pulled onto Interstate 80. Top forty tunes played through the static as Steve and Petra headed northeast toward St. Regis Falls, to the very house he'd hated ever since he could remember.

21

There were several reasons why Steve Dant got away with Petra Horton, and none of them was any good. Each was a personal insult to Greg Litner. He did not like the taste or smell of humble pie. It stuck in his throat and gave him a belly ache. And in the last twenty-four hours, he made all three meals, five courses each, on it.

Sitting in Logan Airport, waiting the two hours for the next flight to Syracuse, he went over it in his mind for the umpteenth time. Mistake #1: he should never have told Parker Horton he suspected a stalker. Greg knew better. Parker, panic stricken, had left a message—a fucking message!—on the school's answering machine at four a.m., eastern time, when he'd changed planes in Denver. The director was away for the weekend, unavailable by phone, and the staff had acted out of the panic Parker planted in them, as Greg had known they would. They hadn't even asked for I.D.

Mistake #2: He'd underestimated Steve Dant. The guy was slick, very slick. He'd made Greg, all right. Strolled over and punctured his tire without Greg suspecting a stinking thing. Of course, there was the off chance that he didn't do it. But...no. He did it, and then he had the balls to drive along to the Warren School and watch in the rearview mirror while Greg's car crapped out.

Mistake #3: Greg hung his head in total shame about mistake #3. It was a whole humble pie in the face. He hadn't messed with the flat. As soon as he saw it, he'd taken off at a dead run toward the school. He watched for a phone, for a cop, for anything, but there was nothing and nobody. He'd charged up that driveway, but the calm face of the receptionist as she examined his P.I.'s license calmed him. She said, "Petra's father already arrived, Mr. Litner, and he took her away. Why? Has the stalker been seen in the vicinity?" Alarm colored her face a watery shade of pink. The blood from running a mile in his good shoes must've clogged his head or the lack of sleep had dulled his wits, that was all he could think, because the only other explanation was that he was losing it as a detective and he could not face that. But for some stupid, unexplainable reason, he'd accepted the pink cheeked receptionist at her word. Perhaps because he remembered his own words to Parker: "Don't worry about finding me. Just get your daughter and take her someplace safe."

He had felt relieved. In a way, his case was closed. Getting herself beaten up and setting a stalker loose on her sick kid would make Christine look like Lizzie Borden in court. Parker Horton would get his custody rights restored. Petra was found and back with her father. Steve Dant was gone, but Greg knew he could find him again if Parker wanted to press charges. So, in a way, he'd stamped the case closed and sealed the file in his mind, which was another bad sign. If you looked forward to the end, saw it when it wasn't even there, then you definitely were losing your edge.

He'd taken a look around the grounds and felt better. The Acura wasn't parked anywhere in the vicinity. Probably Greg had scared him off after all. He'd used the school phone to call Triple A to fix the flat and accepted the receptionist's offer of a cup of hot coffee while he waited for the guy from the garage to pick him up. She'd taken him to a small staff lounge that overlooked the front yard, and Greg sat down at a nice round oak table. He was just finishing his second cup when a local taxi pulled up and Parker Horton stepped out.

Greg thought he was going to be sick on the spot. That little girl, he thought. Oh my God, not the little girl. His skin felt like it was going to have to snap off him. He ran to the front desk.

"Horton? The guy who took Petra? Was he driving a silver Acura?"

"You know, I think he was."

Greg slammed his fist into the wall once, then again. The receptionist looked up, very alarmed. "Fuck! It was him," he said and the receptionist's mouth formed a shocked circle before her body caved in like a blow-up doll that'd been stuck with a big pin. Greg met Parker in the foyer.

"He got her," he said. "He got away from me. I'm sorry." Then he about-faced and returned to the desk. "Get me the police, hurry." The receptionist handed him the phone. As Greg spoke, he felt Parker come up behind him. If he could've faced him, he would've turned around but he couldn't look him in the eye. Not yet. Depending on what happened from here on in, maybe not ever.

"This is Greg Litner at the Warren School," Greg said. "We have had a kidnapping. The perp is driving a silver Acura Legend, license plate number Massachusetts 361 F02, and is probably heading off the Cape. He has abducted an eight-year-old girl, Caucasian, named Petra Horton. You need to set up roadblocks on every exit road off Cape Cod." He paused for a second and then exploded. "No, asshole, this isn't a fucking joke. Put me through to somebody with some brains!" Of course, in his mind, those were the exact words he was slashing himself with. The receptionist's eyes were wide with horror. The cop finally got the picture. They were sending a car right over. They would radio for roadblocks at both of the bridges off the Cape.

Greg couldn't put it off any longer. "This is Mr. Horton," he said to the woman at the desk, and then he turned to face him, dreading it, not knowing what to expect. Anything this guy did to him, Greg figured, he had coming. In spades. But when he turned, Parker Horton was just sitting on a wooden bench, built like a church pew, along the wall: his head was bent forward and he was crying.

"It's my fault, Mr. Horton," the receptionist blubbered. "He asked for her by name. He asked to speak to the director, and I...I'm afraid I...just assumed..." Then she started bawling too.

Mistake #4: he had never thought of the airport. Until they located the Acura in the parking lot at four o'clock, no one else did either. The local cops had never had a kidnapping, and in Greg's experience, kidnappers didn't usually have the cash to charter a plane. Or the luck, or the gall, or the cool. To take a chance like that, risk it all on a gamble that there'd be a pilot and plane available, that took nerves of surgical steel. And the amazing thing was, it had worked. The guy was definitely graced. Greg could only hope Petra was.

Greg felt like his insides were being chewed up by rats. The things the human imagination could come up with to do to other people was sickening. Greg knew this well. Every time he thought of that poor little eight-year-old, grabbed out of a special school for God only knew what purpose, he felt those rat teeth in him chewing, chewing, chewing while his hands were tied. He knew one thing for sure: it was his fault. He would not lie to himself about it. He had been the only person who knew what was happening and he'd blown it. No. He knew two things: he'd find Steve Dant and make him pay for this, in or outside the law. That would depend on how Petra was when he found her.

It had taken Greg too long to find out where they'd headed from Logan. The shift had changed and the ticket agents who'd come on duty had not seen anyone fitting Steve's description. Of course, no Steve Dant or Parker Horton or Petra Horton appeared on any ticket list going anywhere. No credit card payment, though Greg learned that Steve had returned the keys to his car and paid up, all honest and responsible. Strange guy. Greg had finally gotten a lead when he'd examined all the one adult/one child pairs of tickets and phoned the sales agents at home. The police were cooperative at this point, though he knew they would've been less so if they'd got a look at him drinking his French roast coffee in the Warren School faculty lounge while Steve Dant was flying away from Chatham in a chartered plane. He had skimmed over that part, though he refused to deny it to himself. As a matter of fact, he tortured himself with it. Anyway, the cops greased the way for him at the airport, went over the lists, got the home phone numbers. And then the crew from the trip to Syracuse returned and a stewardess remembered a good-looking guy with a little girl. She had served her an orange juice and noticed when she collected the glasses before landing that she had-n't even touched it. No, she said, nothing appeared to be amiss. The girl was tired, she thought; she just sat quietly, hanging onto her daddy's finger for dear life. It was sweet.

Greg didn't bother to tell her the truth. He booked a ticket on the next flight and boiled in his own mental oil until the plane finally took off. The New York State police and the FBI, once it was estab-lished that Dant had crossed state lines, had been alerted. Investigators would be tripping all over each other. Greg was tired. He could feel his skin sagging down to fill the bags under his eyes. He needed sleep and a long, hot shower, but neither would come his way for quite a while.

As he snapped his seatbelt shut, he closed his eyes. A picture of Parker Horton, crying like a baby, appeared on the screen inside his eyelids. Greg studied it as the flight attendant's take-off lecture com-menced in the aisle next to him. It was the saddest thing he'd seen in a long time. A man could go three ways when he got bad news, Greg thought: he could get mad, go numb, or be crushed. Parker had fallen into category #3 whereas Greg was in #1, and those two states did not mix. Greg had found it hard to move toward Parker and soften his voice.

"Parker," he'd said, "I'm gonna get this guy. I promise you."

Parker said, "Please find her" in a voice that sounded like a wail. That pressed down hard on Greg's nerves because it added whining and begging to crying, and that was too much. He'd given Parker a resounding slap on the back and gone outside to wait for the cops. Now, though, from hours away and feeling so worn down, he felt kindly toward Parker Horton. Parker had entered hell, and nobody knew how he'd act when he got there. And it wasn't as if any one way was right. It was just a reflection of who you were, and that didn't have the first thing to do with choice. Who you were was something you got stuck with at birth, and you spent your whole life dealing with it.

He must've slept sitting straight up all the way to Syracuse because the next thing he knew they were on the ground again. He could pick out the FBI guy in the crowd without even trying, so he walked directly over to him. "Greg Litner," he said, extending his hand. "Frank Lamica," the guy answered. He was clean cut, of course; suit, maybe thirty years old. Lamica took off and Greg kept up.

"The flight arrived from Boston at 3:59," Lamica said. Great detecting, Greg thought; so tell me something I don't know. "No car rentals; no hotel reservations made from the airport. We think he took a taxi. The driver who picked him and the girl up is on his way in. He was off in Hell's Half Acre somewhere, but he'll be here shortly." They hurried over the polished floor, their shoes making simultaneous clicks with each step, and then entered an unmarked door in the baggage claim area. "You got a description of this guy?"

Greg felt a stab of guilt. He had him on film, of course, in the camera in his shoulder bag right now, but he wanted to hold that just a little longer till he could have a chat with Christine Timberlake. "Yeah, I've seen him. And I got him on film." He hesitated a fraction of a second. "It's back in my office in New York."

"I'll send somebody for it," Lamica said.

"I'm going down there myself later. I'll develop the film and get it to you."

"Can you fax it?"

"Sure."

"Good."

They crossed the small windowless room to a long table. A map of New York State was spread out. "By 6:15, we had roadblocks up in a thirty-mile radius on all the major roads. That would've given him ninety minutes, plus or minus." He looked up at Greg. "What d'you think? You think he got through?"

Greg shook his head. "I don't know. The guy keeps surprising me."

"How'd you get onto him?"

"The mother of the little girl refused to tell her ex where the kid was. The ex hired me to find her."

"And you found her at the same time as this guy?" Lamica's eyes were a greenish shade of hazel and they dug into Greg like a dentist's drill digs into a bad tooth.

"I picked up on the guy and followed him there."

"How?"

"I saw him hanging around the ex-wife's."

"Really? Where is she?"

"Last I saw, she was being put in an ambulance outside her apartment, unconscious."

Just then there was a knock on the door and a young girl with one of those silly hairdos that went out three years ago in New York, all teased up in front like a Frisbee stuck on her head, came in. "Mr. Lamica? The man you're expecting is here."

"Good. Bring him in," Lamica answered. Greg was glad for the interruption. He didn't want to answer any more of Lamica's questions. The kid was fast at a time when Greg wanted to slow down and go back over everything piece by piece.

A white guy, late fifties and going bald, came in. His scrawny arms hung down from a short-sleeve shirt and his pants looked too big on him.

"You Harold Corbin?" Lamica asked.

"Yeah. What'd I do?" Corbin asked. It was a stab at appearing less anxious than he felt, Greg knew.

"Nothing, Mr. Corbin. Or maybe I should say nothing I know of." This was an attempt at humor, Greg knew, but it thudded down hard. "Sit down. This is Greg Litner."

Harold Corbin sat.

"I understand you picked up a fare here at the airport about 4:00 o'clock. Guy about thirty, thirty-five and a little girl."

"Yeah. I took 'em out to Rent-A-Wreck on Industry Avenue. I already told the dispatcher."

"And you left them there? You didn't wait?"

"Nope. The guy got out with the kid; he paid me; I took off."

"The girl," Greg said, "how was she? Did she seem...afraid or shook up or anything?"

"She didn't say a word. I think she must've fell asleep."

"What time did you leave here?"

"Maybe about 4:15."

"Let's take a ride out there," Lamica said.

"You don't need me to drive you, do you? I gotta earn a living here."

"No. Just gimme your phone number and that'll be it. Thanks for coming in."

"Ain't got a phone. You can always leave me a message with the dispatcher. I work seven days a week."

"O.K. Thanks."

All three men stepped back into the baggage claim area. Harold Corbin disappeared quickly through the door, climbed back into his cab, a maroon station wagon, and took off. Lamica indicated a grey Ford parked in the loading zone and Greg climbed in. The clock on the dashboard said 8:49. About twenty-six hours since this whole thing started in New York.

"Will this place be open?"

"Can't hurt to check. The office should be getting back to me with the name of the owner anyway." Lamica pulled away from the curb.

"Mind if I close my eyes for the ride?" Greg asked. "I'm beat."

"No, go ahead. You got about twenty minutes."

Greg fell asleep as soon as he let himself and woke up when the car stopped. The gate was closed and padlocked and the car yard was silent under the spotlights.

"Nothing here," Lamica said. "Waste."

"You never know what's gonna turn out to be a waste," Greg said.

"Right." He opened a stick of sugarless bubble gum and offered one to Greg.

"So, what next?" Lamica asked. "We got nothing on the road-blocks yet."

Greg thought for a second. "I think I'll go back to New York. Pick up the pictures, get some fresh clothes. Come back up in the morning. Drop me at the airport?"

"Sure." Lamica started the car and they drove off, each periodically blowing a big pink bubble and then popping it in the air.

Greg arrived back in his apartment after midnight. In the bathroom, he developed the film of Steve, hung it to dry, and fell into bed where he slept like a dead man until the alarm went off at seven. He got up, made himself some scrambled eggs, packed a light bag, and headed into the city to see Christine Timberlake at St. Vincent's Hospital, where she was now listed in good condition and scheduled to be released within twenty-four hours.

Assuming, he guessed, that Greg was with NYPD, the nurse at the desk brought him up to date. It amazed him how much people took for granted. Christine, she reported, was logged in as an accidental overdose. Yes, she had been struck: the wounds were more bloody than serious. Her stomach had been pumped. A massive amount of alcohol and six to ten seconals. No, it didn't really look like a suicide attempt, at least not a serious one. Probably her boyfriend smacked her and she put on this dramatic display to get even with him. Of course, it didn't do her much good because no one had called or visited. She was resting comfortably and would be released by tomorrow morning at the very latest.

He didn't expect a policeman outside her door and there wasn't one. He knocked and hesitated a few beats before stepping in. She was in a semi-private room, and the other bed was empty. It hit Greg that, since no one had called, she knew nothing about Petra. He was surprised Parker Horton hadn't crashed down the door in the middle of the night to rage at her. After falling apart like he did, he'd probably need to take it out on someone later...a weaker someone, naturally. Or maybe Greg had Parker pegged wrong. At any rate, the FBI would be here soon enough and they would break the news. It sure wasn't his place to tell her.

She was sitting propped up in bed wearing a hospital nightgown. There were dark circles under her eyes and her skin was some color between pea green and ocher. She had a bandage across her jaw and chin, and another one that ran along her hairline near the eye.

"Ms. Timberlake, are you up to talking for a few minutes?"

"Who are you?"

"I'm an investigator."

"Well, I can't really remember anything. I don't know who did it or how he got in or...anything. I think I...blacked out."

"Thirteen ounces of vodka and a handful of seconals will do that to you," he said with a warm smile meant to put her at ease.

She looked down at the bed, ashamed. "I had some bad news...and I guess...I..."

"You went on a bender," Greg finished in an upbeat tone. "You aren't the first or the last person to do that, believe me." He pulled a chair up to the bed. "I have some pictures I wanna show you. A person that was seen there. Will you take a look?"

"Sure, but I don't think it'll help."

Greg slid the photos out of the 9x12 manila envelope and passed them to her. He watched her carefully. Her face would tell him a lot about how she felt about Steve Dant. She thumbed through all three pictures and her face said nothing. Then she looked at Greg with the most innocent brown eyes in the world.

"Who is he?" she asked, and her question was so guileless and so natural that Greg knew in a heartbeat that she was telling the truth.

"You don't recognize him?" he asked because his words had not caught up with what he instinctively knew, and that was her answer: no.

She studied the picture closely. "He doesn't look familiar," she said, returning the pictures to Greg.

He took them and replaced them in the envelope. He was speechless. More than that. Thoughtless, as if he'd been hit over the head with a two by four and just hadn't put it together yet to fall down.

She looked at him curiously. "Are you all right?" she finally said. It struck him so funny that he started to laugh. There she was, all bashed up, pea green in a hospital bed, and she was asking him if he was all right.

"No," he said, "I'm not." He felt the giddiness deflating but he was still laughing a little. "I'm confused."

"Why?"

"Because, Christine, I've personally seen this guy in your apartment several times."

Her face showed how shocked she was. Very.

"I don't know what's going on anymore," Greg said. He felt like lighting a cigarette, though he hadn't smoked one in over ten years. She was staring at him, and it made him sad. "I'll tell you what I know if you think you're strong enough to hear it."

Her shoulders shifted back and he swore he saw some color seep into her cheeks.

"Tell me the truth," she said.

"I'm the investigator your husband hired."

Her chin lifted about an inch. "Then you're the son of a bitch who hired that punk to grab the envelope out of my hand." Her voice was steady. It had lost the natural inflection and came out all one tone which made her seem menacing in spite of the shape she was in. He noticed that her hands had automatically formed fists and she looked like she'd love to throw a punch into his solar plexus.

"No," he said. His forehead knotted up. "I don't know what you're talking about."

"In the post office. The letter from my daughter's school."

"I really don't know what you're talking about." He saw the wind go out of her sails and her eyes glistened with tears which never gathered the mass to roll down her cheeks.

"Well then, who was he?"

"I don't know. Tell me what happened."

Christine recounted the story. None of it rang a bell with Greg. "Christine," he said, "I don't know what to tell you. I was checking you out...checking your apartment out, and I saw this guy in it. I thought he was your boyfriend. I even followed him home. Then the night before last, I happened to get there when you were being taken out in an ambulance. This guy was in the crowd. I got the pictures then." He hesitated. "Could this guy be the punk?"

"Let me see them again," she said. He admired her control and he dreaded what he had to tell her next. She stared at Steve Dant's face. "I've never seen this guy. How could he get in my apartment?"

"I don't know."

"It's...creepy."

Greg took a deep breath. "Christine, it gets a lot worse."

She moved to the edge of the bed.

"When I saw him outside your apartment that night, I followed him. He left New York and flew to Cape Cod. I tried to follow him but he got away from me...and he got your little girl." He said the words fast. "He kidnapped Petra."

The color he'd seen in her cheeks drained out and her fingers gripped the side of the bed for support but she didn't say a word. The pain on her face was so sharp that Greg felt it stab into his own heart. Not knowing what else to do, he continued on.

"I trailed them to Syracuse and I'm heading back up there right from here. I came back here because I thought he was your boyfriend and you might have some idea about where he'd go."

"And Parker knows all of this?" Her voice sounded dead and cold.

"I called him from Chatham. He flew in and got there...a little too late."

"Where is he now?"

Greg hesitated. "The police thought he should stay at the school for a day or two in case there was a ransom call or something. I'll be talking with him shortly."

"And you had nothing to do with the post office guy? That's the truth?"

"I swear to God."

Christine's feet didn't touch the floor as she sat there on the edge of the bed. She looked like a little girl, and Greg felt sorry for her. He stood up. "I'm sorry this happened. I feel responsible. And I'm sorry I had to be the one to tell you."

"I'm glad you told me."

He turned and started for the door, but her voice stopped him.

"Wait," she said, "I'm coming with you." He turned to face her just as her feet hit the floor. "You're gonna have to help me," she said, "but I'm definitely coming with you." Greg could've said no. He could've turned and left but he had too much respect for that kind of fire in a female, the kind of strength that stood on wobbly knees and said, "Not without me you don't."

"Where are your clothes?"

She indicated a closet in the corner and Greg walked to it and pulled her tee-shirt and skirt from the hanger. The skirt, folded in half and hung over the crosspiece on the hanger, looked about the size of a postage stamp and the tee-shirt was stained with blood all down the front.

"I'll run down to the street and get you a new shirt."

"No. This one's fine. I'll get another one at the airport."

"O.K." He turned away from her to pull the drawer open on the metal dresser. Her black tights and her white sports bra were folded there. When he turned back to hand them to her, she was stepping into the skirt and pulling it up over the longest set of legs he'd ever seen close up on a woman.

"See if you can find my boots," she said.

They were in the closet, standing side by side. Jesus, Greg thought as he hefted them out, they weighed a ton. They looked like boots the Hell's Angels, the men in the Hell's Angels, wore for the annual get-together in South Dakota. Greg did not understand the fashions of today. Every item he'd seen of Christine Timberlake's was all wrong: the bra was too plain; the skirt, too slutty looking; the boots, forget the boots. And yet, put them all together and she looked like some futuristic goddess, a visitor from the time up ahead when everyone would have to scrape for food and water.

Or her child.

"Are you gonna tell them you're leaving?"

"They'll figure it out."

A scofflaw. Greg liked that. "O.K. Let's go."

The nurse did a double take when she saw Christine. "Miss Timberlake? Miss Timberlake! You can't leave." She scurried out from behind the partitions of the work station and chased them to the elevator. "The doctor hasn't released you."

Christine ignored her. The elevator doors opened and she stepped inside with Greg right behind her.

"Can I lean on you?" she asked. He put his arm around her waist and felt her pass some of the job of standing up off to him. On the street he hailed a cab and they got in. She sat against the other door and it flashed on Greg that the feel of her body running full length against his had been nice. When she slid over so far, she felt torn away, like Velcro. Of course, it was just a flash and it added up to exactly nothing.

"LaGuardia," Greg said to the driver.

"What's your name again?" Christine asked.

"Greg Litner."

She looked straight into his eyes. "I don't have any money on me, Greg. You're gonna have to pay for everything."

"Yeah, sure."

"I'll pay you back later." She closed her eyes for the whole ride. Greg watched her. He knew people were prone to all sorts of strange reactions because he'd seen the whole spectrum in his years of being the one to break the bad news. When you expected rage from the person, you got pity; if you expected tears, you got that terrifying laughter that was perched on the ridge of madness. Today, from Christine, he'd expected hysterical accusations, screaming and fist shaking, and he'd gotten silence. Stone cold, iced over, and completely polite silence. Very few people retreated to that particular fort from the front lines and they always put him on guard because he believed if you stuffed all that reaction inside it would bubble and ferment and sooner or later the gases would heat to the point of spontaneous combustion and the explosion would blow somebody's head off. Was that happening inside the ex-Mrs. Horton?

For that matter, what the hell was he doing with her? What was going on inside of him that he'd allowed himself to pair up with his client's problematic ex-wife? Talk about a conflict of interest. But no, he thought, when Petra got grabbed, all the points of conflict suddenly became unqualified, seamless, mutual interest. All bets were off. Everybody wanted the same thing now, so all the borders faded. Sort of made you wonder what they were doing there in the first place.

He glanced over at Christine, resting with her head against the edge of the window. She sure didn't seem like the bitch on wheels Parker Horton had described. Greg thought she looked like an angel, stunned to discover she'd fallen from grace and been booted out of heaven. And here she was, his partner in an investigation that could very likely uncover her own dead child, or something, in Greg's opinion, even worse.

Lamica met them at the gate. "You got the pictures?" he asked. "I wanna plaster them all over the news." Greg handed him the manila envelope. Lamica hadn't put it together that Christine was more than just the woman coming off the plane behind Greg.

"This is Christine Timberlake," Greg said. "The victim's mother."

Lamica looked up at Greg with noticeable irritation. "What'd you bring her here for?"

"Because I insisted," Christine said. Her voice had a rumble to it. Lamica turned to face her. He wasn't any taller than she was.

"It's not good for the family to be around during an investigation. No offense, but the emotions are distracting. It makes it hard on the team."

"Tough shit, Lamica," she said. "I guess you'll just have to ignore my emotions." It shocked the hell out of Greg. "...And you know what?" she added. "I don't think you'll have too hard a time, considering how careful you've been so far."

"Look, I'm sorry," Lamica said.

"Don't spend too much time on it, O.K.? Get to work."

Lamica shot Greg a look.

"She's right," Greg said. Lamica took off down the hallway and

Greg and Christine trotted along a half step behind.

"I got the data on Rent-A-Wreck. Let's go over there."

His car was in front, in the loading zone, and they climbed in. The last trip down these streets had been less than twelve hours before but it seemed much longer than that. The gate was unlocked and open when they got there, and a man with a long red beard was flopped in an old bucket seat outside the trailer drinking coffee out of a thermos. Lamica got out of the car, all business.

"You Richard Favre?"

"Who wants to know?"

"FBI," Lamica said, flipping open his I.D.

"Well, in that case, yes." Favre did not get up. Sitting in the car seat, his head didn't even reach the top of Lamica's thighs. Lamica thrust the manila envelope right under Favre's nose. Too aggressive, Greg thought. But it appeared that he was just along for the ride, so he kept his mouth shut.

"You ever see this guy?"

Favre opened the envelope and glanced at all three photos.

"Don't think so." He handed the photos back.

"Well, that's strange because I got a cab driver who'll swear he dropped him off here yesterday afternoon about 4:30. He had a little girl with him. A girl he kidnapped."

"Lemme see the pictures again." This time he looked at them carefully. Greg knew he was buying time. He could almost hear the computer inside Favre's head hammering him a readout for his next move.

"Yeah, now that I really look, I do remember him. He came in to rent a car."

Lamica gave him a disgusted look. "Why don't you trot inside and get the paperwork?"

Greg heard the computer inside Favre's head boot up again.

"I can't. There ain't no paperwork. He didn't see anything he liked."

"So how did he leave here?"

A slight hesitation. "He walked, I guess. I wasn't paying attention."

"Did he have bags?"

"I think he did."

"How many?"

"A couple."

"So he walked away with a couple bags and a kid...down Industry Boulevard and you don't think a thing of it."

"I rent wrecks, man. I get all kinds in here."

"How was the little girl?" This was Christine. "I'm her mother."

That jolted Favre and Greg saw it. He finally got so shook he stood up. "She seemed O.K. Sat right here, quiet as a mouse." He indicated the car seat. "Didn't seem scared or nothing. Is the guy your ex?"

"No, he's not," Lamica interjected. Greg knew that he didn't want to lose control of the interview, which was stupid, but kids acted like that when they were new on the job. They wanted to shake the tree, not sit on the ground and look at the apples all around them. The only cure for that was time, but meanwhile, Lamica was blowing this in a big way. As soon as they could reasonably get away from him, Greg would return here with Christine.

"I can subpoena your records," Lamica said.

"Hell, go on in and take 'em. I'm not stopping you. I didn't do no business yesterday. None."

Lamica took a few seconds to assess the situation. "Someone will be over shortly with a warrant for the records."

"Take 'em now for all I care," Favre answered.

Lamica headed for the car and Greg and Christine followed.

"Shit," Lamica said as he slid behind the wheel. "Well...I'll take the pictures to WSTM on James Street. Wanna come along?"

"Could you drop us at a hotel? We can touch base later."

"Sure. The Hilton's right on my way." He passed Greg a business card. "Keep me posted."

"Right."

At the hotel, Greg booked two rooms and then he hailed a taxi and they returned to Rent-A-Wreck. "Look, Mr. Favre, I'm not a fed. I'm a private investigator hired by the family. If something wasn't legally kosher with this guy yesterday, I don't give a shit. I wanna find the kid. Now is there anything you forget to tell Lamica?"

"Shit," Favre said. He sucked in his cheeks and looked at the cloud passing by in the blue sky overhead.

"Please tell us. It's my little girl," Christine said.

Favre's eyes darted from one to the other. "Look, the guy gave me five hundred bucks for an old Escort and we sort of skipped the paperwork."

"Good," Greg said. "Get us the license number and a description and we'll get outta here." He asked Christine to wait in the cab and stepped into the trailer after Favre.

"I got a record," Favre said. "This is my livelihood. I can't have the feds breathing down my neck. If they find out, that's it for me."

"Who's gonna tell 'em?" Greg said. "Not me." He hesitated. "But you want some good advice? Call the cops and report the car stolen now. When the feds get back, tell 'em you got motivated and took a stroll through the yard and saw the Ford was missing. Matter of fact, call Lamica back and tell him personally."

Favre's eyes were hungry. He wanted guidance.

"You sure?"

"That's what I'd do."

"O.K., man, thanks."

"Can you think of anything else?"

Favre thought for a few seconds. "Just that the Escort was on empty when he left here, so he had to stop for gas right away."

"Which way did he go?"

Favre pointed. "There's a gas station a couple blocks down. He might've stopped there."

"Thanks."

"Tell the lady I hope she gets lucky."

"I will."

Greg asked the cabby to make a U-ey and look for the gas station.

"What'd he say?" Christine asked, but Greg motioned vaguely toward the driver and said, "We'll talk in a while." The guy who ran the station remembered Steve and Petra. Steve had bought a map and asked for directions onto Route 80 North toward Watertown. Greg bought the same map, climbed back into the cab, and asked the driver to return them to the hotel.

Christine spread the map out on Greg's extra bed while he opened the "Horton" file and collected everything he had on Dant into a pile. There was quite a bit: his TRW, bank records, drivers license number, former addresses, pictures. He went through it slowly, line by line.

"What're you looking for?" she asked.

"I don't know."

"Can I help?"

"You're welcome to take a look at this stuff...see if something hits you."

"What is it?"

"Information on Steve Dant."

She stood up. "I don't think I can face that right now." She seemed moody. She looked out the window over the streets of downtown Syracuse. "I think I'll go down and pick up some clothes and things I need." She came toward him. "Got any money?"

He reached into his pocket, pulled out a wad of cash, and gave her two hundred bucks. "Will that do?"

"Yes. Thanks. I'll be back in a little while."

It was a nice feeling, peeling off a couple hundreds and handing them over to a woman who was going shopping. It had been a long time since he'd done that, but it still felt familiar. Norma used to stand in front of him with one palm up and the other on his dick. The more cash he gave her, the faster she rubbed. It was a little game they played, one of the little song and dance routines of their marriage. Of course, it wasn't really about sex. It just felt good to give things to her. When he realized he was staring at the door Christine had just left through and thinking about how nice she'd look in a pair of pearl stud earrings, he forced himself to snap out of it.

He reached for the phone and called Parker Horton at the Warren School. They had not spoken since yesterday afternoon and that wasn't right. The receptionist said Parker was with the police and asked Greg to hold. In a minute, she came back on and took Greg's number. Parker would return his call in five minutes. Greg checked his answering machine and called Favre at Rent-A-Wreck to see if he'd reported the car stolen. He had; that was good. The cops would get it in the computer in a New York minute. He had just hung up when Christine threw the door open and rushed in without knocking.

"Greg! I put the money you gave me in my pocket and when I took it out to pay for some stuff, I found this!" She was breathless and her hand shook as she passed Greg a small piece of note paper. "It's from him. It has to be." Greg took it by the edge and laid it on the bed. He read: "Christine, Gone to check on Petra. Don't worry."

"What does this mean?" Christine asked, and, of course, he couldn't answer. "He must've been in my apartment, but how did he know about Petra? I don't get it." She sank onto the bed and for the first time the tears started to run down her cheeks. "We have to find her. We have to do something," she said in a beaten and discouraged tone. Greg moved to her, awkwardly patted her head. His hand moved on its own and he stroked her shiny dark hair. He was all choked up too. He wanted to have the answer and he didn't.

"We'll find her," he whispered and his voice cracked like a teenager's. It sounded lame and stupid in his ears. And then the phone rang.

Parker Horton.

22

*P*arker hung up the phone after hearing Greg's report more confused than he'd been since he arrived at the Warren School and learned he was too late, and Petra was gone. Now Greg and Christine were in adjoining rooms in some hotel in Syracuse. Greg's discovery that Steve Dant was not Christine's boyfriend nor even her acquaintance created an eerie glow in the awful darkness surrounding Petra's kidnapping.

Steve Dant had not called the Warren School with a ransom demand, and Parker felt edgy and ineffectual sitting there waiting for the phone to ring. It was a world of women and children. Only the school's director was male—and, of course, the cops—but even so, Parker felt suffocated in a haze of the very worst aspect of the female sex which was, to him, the constant drive to communicate. The little girls in the school could not and would not communicate according to the rules of conversation and social interaction, but Parker thought they did very well in other ways. Some were so angry or so agitated that their mere presence in the room made what they had to say painfully clear. On the other hand, the nurses and psychologists, all women who were determined to elicit the normal kid out of the cloud of mental illness, seemed like well-intentioned blood suckers to Parker. Being there made his head ache.

But then, his head had been aching for a long time. He had put it in an imaginary brace after Christine left and gone on as if everything was normal. Things had even started to feel normal. He had a new girlfriend; he had confronted Christine and hired Greg Litner. But the whole tapestry unraveled when Petra was kidnapped. There he sat among the loose threads, unable to recreate the picture and totally overwhelmed at the prospect of starting a new one.

He stared at his reflection in the tinted mirror of a lamp base and saw a man he didn't know. He realized with a jolt that his Parker Horton mask had been unceremoniously pried off. The man in the dark, smoky mirror was beaten, defeated, down for the count. Studying him, Parker experienced a strange ribbon of intense heat in his chest. He had worn masks his whole life: one had the sharp angles necessary for a tough kid who would not back down no matter what; one was etched with the acid of pride; one was infused with a warm glow and a boyish smile that women would take a chance on. One was Parker Horton, workaholic. One was Joe Ostrobsky, born to lose. None of them had been genuine, not really. They were all exaggerated to make him better or worse than he really was. But here, helpless at the bottom, there was no need to maintain a front anymore. Not even a possibility of it.

There was a knock on the door. "Come in," he called. It was Susan, the receptionist.

"I brought you some coffee and a Danish," she said as she entered and placed them on the table in the school's guest suite.

"Thanks, Susan."

"You keep forgetting to eat."

"I know," he said with a small smile, "but I'm making up for it by smoking."

"Oh well, then I guess it's O.K.," she laughed. She hesitated a second. "Any news?"

"Not really. I just talked to Greg Litner, but..." His voice trailed off.

It was too much to tell her, and he didn't feel the need to discuss it anyway. He almost forgot she was there, but when he glanced up and saw her, expectantly waiting for something, he brightened his voice a bit and continued. "Anyway, I think I'll go to Syracuse. I can't stand waiting around here."

"Want me to find out about the flights?"

"No, I need something to do."

"O.K." She moved toward the door, but she stopped and the words flew out. "Parker, I just feel...I know I'm to blame for this and I'll never forgive myself. I..."

"You're not to blame, Susan," he said, "...and besides..." Suddenly he felt splayed by emotion and he heard himself say, "...besides, it doesn't help anything to fix the blame." It felt good to say that. True.

"Thank you," Susan said as she left. He wasn't sure why.

He took a small bite of the Danish. Strawberry. Way too sweet for him.

He hadn't told Greg he was coming to Syracuse; the idea hadn't entered his mind until he heard himself tell Susan. It felt right, though he doubted if he'd be welcome. He repacked his overnight bag and called the Chatham police to tell them where he was going.

The shuttle ride back to Logan was tense. Parker had imagined he'd be returning with Petra, snatched from Christine while she was in the hospital proving herself, beyond a shadow of a doubt, an unfit mother. For the first time he admitted to himself that his motivation for that was actually a complicated mixture of concern for Petra and a desire for revenge against Christine. He had refused to admit it before because he didn't want to acknowledge the viciousness beneath the surface of their armed truce. Admitting it felt like putting a match to a five-gallon can of gasoline. But now, he'd been blown away anyway, and it didn't matter anymore. Besides, who cared about what he was going through. The only one who mattered was Petra and nobody knew what was happening to her. And Parker didn't much want to let his imagination present the possibilities either.

This was the third time he'd lost his little girl. The first time was when she inched her way backwards into herself as he and Christine stood by helplessly. It was like watching her drown. The water got deeper and deeper and then closed over her head. A father could never forgive himself for not knowing how to swim out into the dark water and save her. The worst part was, Parker couldn't save Petra and he couldn't drown with her either. That was very cruel, he thought.

The second time he'd lost her was when Christine took her away from California. It was horrible enough to sit in his office and think, Now they're getting on the plane; now they're on the plane; now they're getting off the plane; now they live alone, without me, and I am nothing in their lives anymore. That was bad, but then discovering that all the pictures were gone and Christine had put Petra in an institution and would not even tell him where, that was worse. He would spin the old globe in his office and stop it at random with his finger. Was she there? He'd spin again. There? It was too much blankness for a man like Parker. He liked order: the chairs at the table pushed in, the magazines in a neat stack, the broom tucked behind the door. He needed to know where everything was before he could rest. Christine had taken Petra and hidden her, and Parker couldn't give up until he found her.

And when he did, then the third loss. Why does a stranger kidnap a child? How did Steve Dant pick Petra out of all the little girls in the world? Petra, who would not speak or cry out. Petra, already so damaged she was like a rag doll, placed in a chair and forgotten.

Parker tasted tears that had seeped into the corner of his mouth and felt them splashing onto the front of his shirt. He wiped them away but more came. It was extremely odd for Parker. He had cried, in private, exactly twice in his adult life: once when he'd closed on his condo in San Francisco, because he finally had a home, and again when a fire erupted in the fry oil at Paco's after he'd only been open two months. He had not cried when Christine left or at any time during the humiliating divorce proceedings. But since he'd arrived at the Warren School, he had not stopped crying and he didn't really care who saw him. He was way past that now.

He paid for a seat on the next plane to Syracuse. It hit him that he hadn't called the restaurant, or Lily for that matter, since the whole ordeal had started. He dropped his bag in front of the row of pay phones and dialed the restaurant. The head waitress, a conscientious type named Bernice, answered.

"Hi Bernice."

"Parker! Where are you?"

"I'm in Boston now," he started and suddenly he felt his throat start to close and he knew the tears were beginning to burn their way out again. "...on some personal business. I don't know when I'm gonna be able to get back. Can you run the show there for me for a while?"

"Well sure, but...is there something wrong?"

"Yes," Parker said. "Everything is wrong."

She was silent for a second or two. "Do you want to tell me?"

"No, because...I'm in a public place here and..."

"I understand. So you want me to just...kind of take over?"

"Would you? I'll square it up with you later."

"Don't worry about that."

"O.K. Thanks, Bernice. I'll be in touch."

"O.K. Bye."

He hung up and called Lily. The answering machine picked up and he left an abbreviated version of the events of the past few days. As he walked away from the phone, he realized that he was relieved not to have had to speak with her. Lily had never seen him weak. It would scare her, and he didn't have the energy to calm her and assure her that everything would be all right. He also didn't want to suffer through the petulant verbal attack she would no doubt make as soon as she heard his voice, and then listen to it transform into pity and apology when he finally explained himself. It seemed like such an unnecessary waste of energy, so predictable and so useless.

Parker arrived in Syracuse and took a taxi to the hotel. He barely noticed the city passing by outside the smudged window of the cab. It was faded, grey, and whipped, just like all the cities in the northeast. He felt agitated, an old feeling, about barging in on two people who didn't want him there. They would have already constructed a wall and he would be on the outside looking in. It was awful being the unwanted one, but he knew he could deal with it. He felt he had lived with it most of his life.

He skipped the front desk and went directly to Greg Litner's door and knocked. A few seconds later, Greg opened the door. He was in his sock feet, Parker noticed, and wearing black-rimmed half-glasses. Christine sat across the room in a Danish modern chair by the window, poring over a stack of papers in her lap. Though it took a few seconds, maximum, it seemed to happen in slow motion for Parker. Christine looked up as if the knock on the door was a major irritant.

"Parker," she said in a loud, shrill voice, "what're you doing here?"

Parker felt tired. He averted his eyes from Christine's and looked at Greg. "Can I come in?" he asked.

Greg shook himself out of his trance. "Sure, come in. Sorry. You surprised me." He reached up, slid Parker's bag off his shoulder, and leaned it against the wall. "Sit down. You want a drink?"

"I could use a beer." Parker stood self-consciously inside the door. His gaze traveled to Christine. Her face was still bandaged and the circles under her eyes were a deep maroon. He could see and feel her anger. It added more bulk to his incredible weariness. He could not even propel himself farther into the room.

Meanwhile, Greg bent down into the small hotel fridge. The wave of cool air against his face and the cold can of beer in his fingers felt good, a momentary distraction from the tension which had escalated to a whole new level. Greg didn't need to turn around to know what was happening behind his back. Mr. and the ex-Mrs. Horton were both stone silent, two fighters waiting for the bell to ring so they could come out slugging. Greg could not allow that to happen. He knew he had to intervene, and more important, he knew why. Her name was Petra. He straightened up, pulled the tab on the beer can, and handed it to Parker.

"Christine," Parker said, "I had to come. I'm sorry. I'm sorry about everything."

"That's great, Parker. That's great," Christine snapped as she jumped up out of the chair and started across the room.

"Cut!" Greg yelled in a harsh voice. He made a T with his hands. "Time. None of that shit, you two." He turned to Christine. "We got work here, so put it aside." He saw her eyes flare up and deaden as she made an about face and headed back to her chair. "O.K.," she said in a tight voice. She resumed her work without another look at Parker. Parker glanced at Greg and shrugged.

"Did you book a room?" Greg asked.

"No."

"May as well share this one then." Parker slumped onto the edge of the bed. "Christine is checking over the records I have on Steve Dant. I'm making some calls. Why don't you relax for a minute and then we'll fill you in."

"I'd like to clean up."

"Sure," Greg said, and he moved toward the phone and started flipping through the pages of his notebook. "We all have to cooperate," he said again, in an authoritative tone, to no one. "We have to function as a team. For Petra's sake." But how could they, Greg secretly wondered. How could they?

Parker stared down into an old kidney-shaped stain on the beige carpet. Christine studied him from under her eyelashes. Now that Greg had short circuited her initial anger at seeing him, she was somewhat stunned by his appearance. It was as if the room had mysteriously melted down and left her with only one incongruous image: Parker, his hair hanging loose; his beard, patchy; his face, pale and worn; his shirt, stained and wrinkled. It was extremely rare to see Parker disheveled, to see even a small crack in his cologned and well-pressed veneer.

Petra's father, she thought with a rising feeling of panic. Her father. Suddenly she didn't know where she was. She didn't know who she was or how she felt. Her jaw throbbed and a slate grey sadness pressed against her like fog.

Parker looked up and saw her staring at him. He rose quickly off the bed and went to her. "Christine," he said, his voice cracking like a teenager's. That confused her even more. Her heart burned with an odd and painful tenderness. Greg was right, she knew. Everything had to be put aside now. They could fire up their hatred again later, after the crisis had passed, when things returned to normal. But for the moment, staring at Parker's tortured face, she couldn't even remember what had gone wrong between them in the first place.

She knew Parker was waiting for her to say something, but her words were choked in sorrow. Impulsively, she reached toward him. He took her hand and pressed it between his. To Parker, it was like catching hold of a warm ray of optimism, and for that moment he was certain there would be some way for him to help. The three of them, together, would find Petra. They would find her in time. She would be all right. She had to be because none of them could face it any other way.

23

Steve felt comfortable with the strange, silent child. He studied her little hands, folded with thumbs tucked in at all times. Was she trying to fend off some invisible attack? He knew that feeling well and tucked his own thumbs inside his fists to see if it was comforting. He blocked out all the other sensations in his body and focused on his hands. Closed and clenched so tight, they seemed to form a barrier to the natural flow of energy out his fingertips. He glanced again at her fists. Did she want to keep life out or keep it in? Or was that the same thing?

As they had driven north toward St. Regis Falls in the Ford Escort, Petra had stared straight ahead and remained motionless. She was barely tall enough to see over the dashboard. Steve couldn't decide if she was even looking, but he suspected she was oblivious to the woods and fields and towns they passed through. Her stillness had not upset him. It was, after all, the desired state for most junkies, who wanted to remain forever suspended in a euphoric state that felt totally alive and totally dead at the same time. Petra interested him but he would not intrude into her private world. In fact, he thought, he had more or less proven that he would plant himself between her and anyone who was trying to storm her gates. He just didn't know why.

Steve had stopped in Potsdam, a half hour from his childhood home, to collect some groceries and other essential items. He needed matches and candles, bug repellent, a water jug, so many things. He bought a pair of lightweight pajamas for Petra and another little outfit that looked like it would fit her. He had nervously left her in the car in the parking lot while he buzzed through the K-Mart. He didn't like her being out of his sight, but he'd felt daunted by the prospect of dragging her around the store, about the attention she would draw, so he left her there in the car in the front row of the parking lot. Every time he emerged from the end on an aisle, he checked. Her little brown-haired head never moved.

At the cash register he'd noticed a display of animal crackers and had impulsively grabbed three boxes. He'd carried the purchases to the car and flung the bags into the back seat. Then he'd opened Petra's door and placed a box of crackers in her lap. She didn't respond, so he opened the box, shaped like a cage with bright pictures on the side, and placed a cracker in each hand.

"A lion for this hand," he'd said as her fingers closed, "and an elephant for this one. You keep 'em quiet till I get back." The Pick-N-Save grocery was right next door. He bought two bags of groceries. On his way out, he noticed a phone booth off to the left of the automatic doors. The cashier cheerfully gave him a roll of quarters and he placed a call to the *Expression* office. It was Saturday. The answering machine would pick up. As Steve fed the coins into the phone, he felt a collar of guilt close around his throat. Janet would be fit to be tied with both Steve and Mary Anne gone. But then, it was her ship. It was her responsibility to keep it afloat.

The machine clicked on. "Janet," he said, "it's Steve. I'm sorry but something unavoidable came up and I had to leave town for a few days. It's Saturday now. I won't be back in New York by Monday morning. So...I just wanted to let you know. Sorry for the inconvenience. Bye." He started to hang up and then returned the receiver to his mouth. "Janet? Is the machine still on? Listen, if it is, you should give that punk kid—y'know Alex who sits on the stoop?—you should give him a few days work. He's a smart guy and he needs cash. Then you wouldn't have to look for anybody. O.K.? Bye." He hung up the phone, feeling better. All Janet would have to do to solve her problem, if she had the nerve, would be to stand on the top step and yell, "Yo!" He climbed back into the car and they took off. It was 6:45; he'd be home in half an hour.

It was strange for Steve to turn onto Route 11B, as he had done so many times in his young life, and head east toward St. Regis Falls. He had not thought of his parents' home in a long time. It was as if it had withered up and blown away, out of his memory and most certainly out of his daily life. He found the trees along the highway to be claustrophobic and the early summer vegetation to be overwhelming.

That was what he remembered most about living there: the sensory deprivation of the long winter, with its white sky and snow in drifts that covered the windows of the house, and then the springtime, with its suffocating greenness, lush as a jungle and full of mosquitoes and black flies. Nature did not seem sedate and beautiful to Steve; it seemed uncontrollable and sadistic. And small town life, with its nosiness and gossip, put him on edge. From years away, he viewed St. Regis Falls as a haven for people with beer bellies and green teeth. Judging from the look of the trailers and shacks lining the edge of the road, satellite dishes and Little Bo Peep lawn figures had been added.

Steve cut off 11B up the mountain into the village. He passed the school where he'd graduated in 1977 in a class of nineteen students. The teenagers were still hanging out in front of the sub shop, balancing on the metal railing as they always had. Several stores were boarded up and a few buildings near the bridge over the St. Regis River had burned. His parents' house—now his own—was on the other side of town, up a dirt road on the edge of a desolate stretch of bad road called the Seventeen Mile Woods. It was state land. No one lived there.

The old Escort rattled and clanked its way up the side of the mountain. Steve was tense. With each curve in the road, he remembered more distinctly the utter nothingness he'd always felt about the place. He took a sharp left onto Wolf Pond Road. The house was almost two miles in. The road continued past it another half mile and then ended in a dead end at a hunting camp that had been abandoned for years.

There were no new houses on Wolf Pond Road, and the names on the mail boxes were the same ones that had always been there: Bashaw, Tatro, Duquette, Grytebust. He passed the last neighbor's house, about three quarters of a mile from his own, and continued on. Brush on each side of the road had grown thick. Steve expected that his house would be hidden in the tangle of pricker bushes and burdocks. He might even have to park in the road and hack down a few bushes before he could get in the driveway.

But no.

The yard around the house was not overgrown at all; it was mowed and the flower garden was a riot of daffodils, tulips, and irises. A wooden Adirondack chair, double size for two people, was placed under the huge old maple tree at the corner of the yard. The house needed a paint job and a new roof, but it looked both occupied and cared for.

He pulled into the driveway, wary that some squatter had taken over and would refuse to leave. Steve didn't want to fight for a house he never wanted. He was tired and the porch swing looked inviting.

It had been a ridiculously long day. He needed to rest, and then he would call Christine and find a way to tell her that he, a stranger, had managed to get to Petra in time. To save her.

"We're here," he said to Petra. "Let's go in." He undid his seat belt and got out, placing the bags on the hood of the car. When he opened Petra's door, he noticed that the box of animal crackers was almost gone. He'd been so preoccupied he hadn't seen her eat them. A rush of words of praise almost erupted from his mouth, but he stopped himself. He could give her the room she needed to eat. "Come on, Petra," he said, guiding her out. Her fingers were clamped around the white string handle on the box of crackers. It dangled beside her thigh like a small purse.

Together, they climbed the front steps to the porch. Steve called out a precautionary hello and cupped his hands around his eyes to peer in the windows. There was no sign of life. He slid a shingle to one side—the third one down from the porch ceiling, nearest the door, the old hiding place—and sure enough, a single key still hung there on a carpet tack. Steve used it to open the door and stepped inside.

Nothing had changed. The old upright piano stood in the exact same spot and his father's foot stool still waited in front of his armchair. Even the smell, a house closed up against the cold for long periods and not allowed to breathe, was familiar. He opened a window and stretched the expandable screen that was propped against the wall in front of it into the grooves in the casing and slammed the window down tight against it. Petra climbed into a worn armchair and ate the rest of her animal crackers while Steve walked through, opening windows, looking for some sign of who had been there. There was none. Without thinking, he pulled a string hanging down from the kitchen light and, to his astonishment, it turned on. He had never paid an electric bill, not once in the years since he inherited the house. Then he moved to the sink and turned on the faucet. Cold, pure spring water splashed into the sink, which meant the temperamental shallow-well pump was primed and working. Hesitantly, he lifted the receiver off the wall phone. No dial tone. At least that was dead. In the refrigerator, there were three cold Genessee beers. He cracked one open and went upstairs.

The same, everything the same. His mother's room, his father's room, his. The praying hands, the Jesus faces, the Virgin Mary. All the beds were made with summer spreads and a wool blanket folded across the bottom. And while there was a layer of dust, it was the amount that collected in a week or two, certainly not in five years. Steve opened the windows for cross ventilation and went back downstairs.

He took a pillow off the couch and threw it onto the swing on the porch and then went inside and brought Petra out. "You should get a little fresh air," he said, lifting her onto the swing. Her little body was tiny and her rib cage felt fragile beneath her Ninja Turtles tee-shirt. Petra would be long and lean, he thought, like her mother, and if her hair ever grew out, it would probably be just like Christine's. Petra had the same smallish mouth. Steve stared into her eyes from perhaps a foot away, with Petra on the swing and Steve squatting down in front of it. He felt mesmerized, hypnotized by this beautiful, damaged child. Suddenly he remembered the attendant back at the Warren School. It had been so chaotic and confusing at the time, and it had made no sense, but he remembered her words. She'd said that Petra listened to the fog horn, that she noticed it and listened to it. Steve had heard many fog horns in his years in the navy. The two tones, one low and the next one lower still, were totally familiar. And before he knew why, he found himself looking straight into her eyes and chanting, "Mmmmmmmmm.... ummmmmm mmmm, Mmmmmmmm....ummmmmmmm, Mmmmmmmmmm.... ummmmmmmmmmmmmm. His voice came from deep in his belly, vibrating through his rib cage and throat. He chanted in the same sad and lonely cadence of the fog horns in the water. And then he changed it to, "Pet....tra, Pet...tra, Pet...tra." It became a meditation to him. He thought he saw her eyes flicker over him for a brief second. Then they lost their focus. Steve sat down next to her on the swing. That was when he tried her thumb-tucking routine.

The sun was dipping down toward the tops of the trees in the distance, but long straight-edged shafts of light cut across the lawn. The grass was the color of early summer: bright and full of life. It had not yet reached the peak of color, the saturated, drunken hues of August. Who had cut this grass? Steve wondered. Who had planted the flowers and made the beds? Where was that person now? And if a stranger had moved in and taken over, why was the house the same?

It was silent except for the sound of the birds and the chatter of the chipmunks running in and out of the spaces in the ancient stone wall that had once marked the edge of a cornfield. Steve shifted his weight and the chains on the swing creaked. His shoulders dropped down an inch as he relaxed after the intensity of the last twenty-four hours. Just yesterday Alex had handed him the envelope from the Warren School. Today, Petra sat beside him on a porch swing. In many ways it was a miracle, Steve thought. His irrational intervention had saved Christine's daughter. It made Steve feel good. His chance to be a hero had come up and he'd found himself able and willing to do the necessary job. He got up and walked to the car to gather the groceries and put them away. He was hungry. Time to rattle the pots and pans.

He wasn't sure what kids liked to eat and Petra obviously wasn't going to tell him, so after surveying the contents of the bags, he settled on a batch of brownies from a Betty Crocker mix and a macaroni and cheese casserole with sliced tomatoes on the side. He decided to bring Petra into the kitchen and sit her on the counter. Maybe she'd watch him cook. As he led her into the room, it suddenly hit him that she hadn't been to the bathroom all day. That was probably way too long for a kid.

"Do you need to use the john, Petra?" he asked, leading her to the small bathroom in back of the kitchen. At the door, he hesitated. What did you do with a kid like this? Pull her pants down, stick her on the toilet, and run the water in the sink? Christ, he thought, maybe she wears diapers. It wasn't out of the question. But as it turned out, he didn't have to make the decision because Petra walked to the toilet, unsnapping her pants on the way. Thoughtful, Steve stepped out of the doorway and returned to the kitchen. She could take care of pissing and probably eating, if the animal crackers were any indication. That made her conscious in there. That made her half normal at least.

He set the table for two and scooped the warm macaroni and cheese onto her plate. He said nothing, just stretched a paper towel across her lap and put the fork in her hand. She ate, her eyes downcast. After dinner, he piled her back into the car and drove half way down the mountain to the Trading Post, a Mom & Pop store that sold beer, junk food, and fishing tackle. From the phone booth in the parking lot, he called Christine's room in St. Vincent's Hospital. He was panic stricken and rehearsed the lie he'd made up to tell her. He would say that he'd been visiting the next door neighbor's and had seen the door ajar; he'd opened it wide and seen her there; she'd very rationally asked him to go get her daughter and then passed out; he'd called the ambulance and done as she asked. Maybe she would buy it; maybe not. But she'd been so far gone, maybe she would trust him a little. His hands left wet marks on the receiver as he deposited his quarters. The phone rang and then an official voice answered.

"I thought I dialed direct to the patient's room," Steve sputtered.

"The switchboard picks up all patient calls after nine p.m.," the voice answered.

"What time is it now?"

"It's 9:05, sir." The voice had a trace of irritation in it now.

"Could you ring me through? This is very important."

"I'm sorry, sir. I can give you patient information."

Steve hesitated. "O.K."

Christine, they told him, was resting comfortably. He could speak to her directly after nine the next morning. He hung up. He considered leaving a message on her home phone machine, but if the hospital phones were off for the night she couldn't check it anyway. He would call her exactly at nine the next morning. It irritated him that he couldn't get through, that he'd missed the deadline by five minutes. He was amazed that hospitals even stuck to that rule at the end of the millennium when things were collapsing and falling to ruin in every corner of Planet Earth. It was straight out of the Victorian era, when rest was considered a first step in the cure rather than a last resort. Rest used to be a full-time, open-ended prescription, Steve thought. Now it was slotted in according to the convenience of a person's schedule.

He avoided the store and returned home. Petra fell sound asleep on the fifteen-minute ride, and he carried her upstairs and tucked her into his old bed. Then he kissed her pale, pink cheek. It felt cool, almost cold, so he unfolded the wool blanket and covered her shoulders. He left her there, with the plaster faces of Mary and Jesus for company.

The mosquitoes had taken over the outdoors, so Steve settled in the living room. He sipped another beer as he put his feet up on his father's footstool and gazed around. His inheritance. A hundred-year-old farmhouse full of nothing but bad memories. His house.

He studied the wallpaper. Scenes of a colonial-style plantation house in shades of green on a white background in a repeated pattern. He remembered when his mother had chosen it. She hung it herself, efficient as always. He would have been around ten at the time and his job was to pass her the brush she used to smooth it out on the wall. It was a tedious, awful day. The silence as his mother worked was broken by one word and one word only: "Brush!" Then she'd extend her hand and he'd place the brush in it. By the end of the day, he slapped it hard into her callused palm, but she didn't notice.

He had never planned to return here, not even if his parents had lived—especially if they had lived, he realized, for he would not have come now if they'd been here. He hadn't spoken to his parents even once in the years before their accident in December of 1989, and he hadn't put a foot in this house since he returned from the navy in the fall of 1982. He was twenty-two then, and despite all the years he'd spent with them and four years in the seamiest ports of Southeast Asia, he had mistakenly harbored the childish hope that his return would be a warm and happy occasion. He thought that in the years away, as he'd solidified from a boy to a man, his mother and father would've come to see some worth in him, even if it was just an extension of themselves, and would want to embrace it. But he hadn't called them from the bus station in Potsdam because he'd suddenly been afraid they wouldn't want to drive the thirty minutes to pick him up. He had hitchhiked home and hoofed it down the

Wolf Pond Road with his duffel bag on his shoulder, navy style. He wanted them to throw their arms around him and tell him how strong and good he looked. But when he'd come in the front door, they were parked at the dining room table having their usual ten-minute, silent supper.

"It's me!" he called as he appeared in the doorway. And there they both sat, mid-bite, like figures in a wax museum. He knew they were surprised; that was natural. What troubled Steve was he felt the thoughts behind their pasty faces and he heard the unspoken words: "What? You again?" It was like a swift kick in the stomach.

Of course, Lyle had stood and given him a firm handshake and a hard tap on the back, and Sarah had pecked his cheek and set another place at the table, but the conversation only sputtered a few times before it went out. They asked him about the navy, but he felt vocally paralyzed and answered in monosyllables. Then they'd recited the names of all the kids who'd been killed in drunk driving accidents since he left, and after that, there wasn't much else to say. He'd volunteered to do the dishes and by the time he'd finished, both of them were fused to their chairs in front of the TV. Lyle was drinking a Bud from the can, and Sarah was finishing the dregs of her coffee.

"Did you ever see this show, Steve?" she asked indicating the TV screen. "It's real good." She turned her attention back to it. Tears stung Steve's eyes and an overwhelming sorrow hit him in the chest. He had had to go out to the porch to compose himself. An hour later, his mother stood in the doorway and announced she was off to bed. Soon after, Lyle shut off the TV, called a good night, and went to his room. Steve lay full length on the swing and sobbed with his head buried in a pillow. His parents didn't care about him. Nobody loved him. And he felt certain no one ever would either. He would live in a love-vacuum his whole life and die in a rented room by some bus station. Alone.

He stayed for three days. Repaired the roof, fixed his father's car, put up the storm windows, patched the footings under the kitchen, and bought a big load of groceries. He'd worked feverishly to keep from breaking down again. And then he'd used a big chunk of his navy money to fly himself back out to California, where he'd disembarked from his tour of duty on the U.S. Constellation a week before. He rented an apartment in Long Beach, not far from the docks, and removed a half kilo bag of heroin from a safety deposit box he'd kept at the Security Pacific Bank since his ship had put up in Long Beach for repairs two years before. He'd sold some of the dope to another guy with a jones from his ship, and stayed high himself for a long, long time. Somewhere along the way he'd written Lyle and Sarah off. As far as Steve was concerned, it was just a formality when they died. They'd never really been there anyway, so what was the difference?

Steve got up and paced the house, restless. He stopped to peer out each window, but the night was pitch black and he couldn't see a thing. He opened the last beer, ate three brownies, thumbed impatiently through a six-year-old Sears catalog, and then went upstairs. Petra was sleeping quietly. He looked in each of his parent's rooms and decided to sleep in his mother's. It faced east and the morning sun would wake him early. He stripped to his underpants and stretched out. The bed sagged in the middle. He fell asleep quickly, giving in to what felt like a whole lifetime of exhaustion.

Hours later, in the darkest part of the night, the dream began.

First, the sound of the children playing in the distance. And the friendly feel of the water. But then the black shadow and the cold fingers, pushing, pushing the child under, and the water closing over

the face so it blurred under the surface with the mouth wide, screaming, and filling with filth that went into the nose and down the throat.
And the last breath, the sweet, sweet air that held the water back for
one sputtering, coughing second, and the laughter, louder, louder,
louder, louder, till the face, blurred and mottled, opened and the
greasy water rushed in again. It seemed to take forever to let go and
die.

Dread permeated Steve's body. He was helpless and could not
reroute the images away from him, away from his sleep. Each frame
of the dream had a double edge to it: the moment itself multiplied
a thousand times by what he knew was coming. Even in the sunny
part of the dream, a knot of panic formed at the very bottom of his
spine. Even in his sleep, he could feel his screams begin to form. As
the panic shot along the wires of his spine, it became unbearable.
And then he heard the screams in his own ears, wild and terrifying.
They went on forever, longer than usual because this time the dream
would not unlock and let him wake up. He saw the child's face under
the water, the blurry pink mouth where the water rushed in, and he
felt death in his hands.

Steve sat up, his arms fighting against the air and his eyes wide,
before he even knew he was awake. His fingers clutched onto the
wrinkles in the sheet, and he felt breathless. He looked around.
Where was he? The room was dark but still familiar. Then he remembered: his mother's room. He turned his head toward the door and
saw a shadow there, backlit in the misty beam cast by a tiny night
light in the hallway. A little girl, barefoot on the wood floor, her tiny
shoulders bony even through her tee-shirt.

Petra.

She stood as if in a trance, her arms at her sides. Steve thought
she must be sleepwalking and shifted to swing his legs out of bed.

But she moved toward him, purposefully. She took five big steps to the bed and climbed up. Steve lay back down and opened his arm. She fit herself in beside him with her head resting in the curve of his shoulder. She seemed to fall asleep in an instant. It comforted him, her presence there. Who was protecting whom? he wondered. Her child's smell, a little sweaty and a little sweet, calmed him. He turned his head to watch the black clouds move across the dark grey sky.

For breakfast, Steve made French toast. Then he undressed Petra and gave her a bath. The tenderness he felt for her amazed him. Seeing her skinny white legs stretched out in front of her under the water filled him with the desire to take care of her, and his self-consciousness about undressing and washing a young girl evaporated. She wouldn't do it on her own; that was clear. He dressed her in the outfit he'd bought her at K-Mart, a blue and white boat-neck shirt with a red anchor embroidered on the chest and a matching pair of navy blue shorts. Then he washed her dirty clothes by hand in the bathroom sink and hung them out to dry on the old clothesline in back of the house. The bag of clothes pins was in the same spot in the pantry, still full of the wooden clips he used to pretend were alligators when he was a boy. Petra sat on the porch, silent and unreachable, and he combed her wet hair into a side part and let her be. Later, they drove back to the Trading Post and Steve called the hospital, It was 9:15 when the switchboard finally rang him through to Christine.

He counted eleven rings and no one picked up. Finally, an operator came on and transferred him to the nurse's station.

"I've been calling Christine Timberlake's room and there's no answer," Steve said.

He sensed the slightest hesitation. "Miss Timberlake checked herself out of the hospital at 7:15 this morning."

"Was she...do the doctors feel she was ready to leave?"

"The doctor in charge did not release her."

"You mean she just walked out?"

"That's correct."

Strange, Steve thought. "O.K. Thanks." He hung up, baffled, and dialed Christine's home number. As usual, the machine picked up. He hadn't formulated a speech to leave her, so he disconnected, prepared himself, and dialed again, nervously waiting for the beep.

"Christine, are you there?" A pause. No answer. He blundered on. "My name is Steve Dant and you don't know me, but I helped you the day before yesterday when you were...hurt in your apartment. You asked me to go to Cape Cod to check on your daughter because you thought someone was after her. I put a note in your pocket, but you were so out of it...I don't know if you..." Click. The machine cut him off. Damn, he thought, reaching into his pocket for more change. Not enough. He would have to go inside, though he dreaded seeing Leonard LePage, the proprietor. Fortunately, a teenaged girl he didn't recognize was behind the counter. Steve bought some candy and a six pack and then hit her up for five dollars in quarters. He returned to the phone and tried again.

"It's Steve again. I got cut off," he continued. "Anyway, I'll try to talk fast. I went to the school and I saw a guy I'd seen near your apartment in the city when they put you in the ambulance. When I got to the school, they thought I was your husband and handed Petra over to me. I figured if they were that out of it, I should take her till the smoke cleared. She's safe with me." He hesitated for a beat. "I don't have a phone, but I'll call you later. Thank you. Goodbye." The machine clicked just as he finished. He felt better having made contact, but he wondered where she was. And why did she check herself out of St. Vincent's without her doctor's permission?

24

Christine stepped through the door between her room and Greg's and slid the bolt to a locked position. She needed some time alone, flat on her back. So much was happening and there had been no time to process any of it. Petra was gone and Christine was terrified, yet she felt hope so thick and solid it seemed impermeable. The note she'd found in her pocket confused her. It was like a sturdy sapling growing through the face of a cliff that she'd somehow grabbed a hold of as she fell: it made no promises, but she would hang on to it as long as she had an ounce of strength. It was not a vindictive note, she told herself. The writer of it, presumably Steve Dant, said he was going to check on Petra, not kill her or rape her or torture her. Or kidnap her either, but she couldn't dwell on that too long.

Christine closed the foam-backed drapes and lay down on the bed in the dark. She was tired. Bone tired. But she didn't want to sleep because it seemed like a betrayal of the vigil she was holding in her heart for Petra's safe return. Next door, Greg was following up on several possible leads: phone records from Dant's apartment and his job at the magazine on 14th Street; any property listed in his name in the County Clerk's office; any reason to come here. Christine liked Greg Litner. She liked his methodical, calm way of working. Watching him operate, she automatically believed that he never failed to solve the puzzle, no matter how convoluted. She also liked the feel of his big paw patting her head when she'd finally broken down in tears and the way his voice cracked with emotion when he tried, in his awkward, clumsy way, to comfort her with words. He was a man you could lean on, she thought. Not a bag of wind or a help-less executive type who could only snap, "Do something about it!" at other people. Greg could and would do what it took.

And now Parker was with him and that didn't matter one way or the other to Christine, which marked a major shift in her attitude. It was as if she'd fallen asleep in one relationship to him and woke up in another. In the first one, she'd come to hate him; she'd viewed him as her sworn enemy and felt so much contempt it turned her stom-ach. In the second, none of that mattered or even existed. He was not a threat, not worth her rage and perhaps not deserving of it. Christine wanted to lie on the bed and think about Parker because in her heart, in the small section of the human heart where the truth is always told, she knew Parker was the same and it was only her per-ception of him that had changed. And that was something definitely worth thinking about. Christine needed to be perfectly still in a dark room to consider such a big issue in her life. In the stillness and dark, she felt able to understand the world in a more fearless way than she could when she was standing up, participating in it.

If Parker wasn't what she thought, what was he?

More important, who was she?

Her breathing was deep and quiet, and her slim body seemed to sink deep into the mattress.

In the next room, Parker sat with his back to the wall that sepa-rated Greg's room from Christine's. A long shower and a change of clothes had restored him somewhat. He read and re-read Greg's notes on Steve Dant. It shocked him how much information could be collected behind someone's back. In fact, it sickened him. Greg said that clues were found in the most mundane places and had asked Parker to study each entry on every form in the file. Parker suspected it was busy work, but he faced it with meticulous attention to detail and obsessive care. In the old days, when the glue in their marriage had dried up and flaked away, Christine had viewed this precision as more proof of his fear of being out of control. Maybe it was. She'd said he was terrified by spontaneity, afraid to let things happen as they would. Maybe it was true. She'd said he immersed himself in details so he wouldn't have to look up and see how huge life is, how brimming with unexpected opportunities and trials. She'd accused him of burying his head in the details of his business to keep from facing the facts about his own shortcomings as a human being. In fact, he thought as a smile cracked over his lips, he distinctly recalled her standing in the doorway with her hands on her hips, telling him—and he could remember it verbatim—that he was only one step away in evolution from a robot. Funny how it made him smile now when it had festered in his memory for three long years.

He returned his attention to Steve Dant's bank records from California. Using a piece of folded typing paper to keep his place, he continued to move down the printout, line by line. He was midway through Steve's years in Long Beach when something made him stop. Another wire transfer, bank to bank, in the odd amount of $632.48. Parker checked back. This was the third one, one a year in 1990, 1991, and 1992. Quickly, he scanned the records for 1993. Nothing. It was probably unimportant, but he would mention it to Greg.

Greg was across the room on the phone, his chair tipped back against the wall. He'd been on the phone ninety percent of the time since Parker had arrived, making notes in his leather notebook and flipping through the pages to enter one fact here and another one there.

"Look, Lorraine," Greg was saying, "have I ever let you down? I know it'll come out of your own pocket but I'm telling you I'll reimburse you; trust me." He smiled as he listened. "O.K. I'll take you out for a drink too, but don't try to take advantage of me when I'm drunk like you did the last time." Another pause. "You did too, Lorraine, and you know it. You wanted the Big Boy and it was only my good manners that saved your marriage." Whatever she said sent Greg into a peal of laughter. "O.K. O.K. I promise. Now will you fax me the records? I need outgoing and incoming for the forty-eight hours starting Friday at seven a.m. Lemme give you the fax number of the hotel where I am." He recited a number. "I'll call you when I get back in the city and we'll continue to negotiate. Bye." He hung up with a chuckle, catching Parker's eye as he made a note in his book.

"She works for the phone company," Greg explained. "She's helped me out for years but she busts my balls every time."

"Sounds like you can handle her," Parker said.

"Oh, I can handle Lorraine," Greg answered.

Parker hesitated before he spoke. "Greg, could you take a look at something?"

Greg jumped to his feet and crossed the room as Parker laid out the September records, year by year, on the table. "There's a systematic wire transfer every September and I..."

Greg bent down close. "Good, good," he said. "Lemme look at this." He followed the complex line of numbers across the page. "The transfer is from Security Pacific Bank in California to...let's see here. The territorial code is 29 which puts us..." He stood up. "...not far from where we are, I'll bet. Good work, Horton."

"What? What is it?" Parker asked.

"The banks are coded by location, sort of like a zip code, y'know? This guy wires money every year at the same time to a bank in upstate New York. I'm gonna make some calls, see if I can find out which one." He crossed the room again. "This could be it."

Parker was pleased. It was nice to get praise from a pro like Greg Litner, even if he had no idea why. He watched him dial the phone again.

"Yeah...uh...I just deposited a check into my account in New York. The bank code of the check is 29. Can you tell me when it'll clear?" He adjusted his glasses and waited. "Why so long? Oh, three days is normal for an instate check? Well, O.K. Listen, which bank is it anyway?" He listened for a few seconds. "Key Bank in Potsdam, New York? O.K. Thanks." He hung up and moved to the map, still spread out on the second bed. "Potsdam...Potsdam," he said under his breath. "Fucking A! North on 80," he said.

"Do we have something?" Parker asked, looking at the circle Greg had just drawn around Potsdam.

"You never know," Greg said, "but it's a lead. I'm gonna go down and see if my fax came in from Lorraine." He disappeared through the door. Parker lit a cigarette, slid the window open, and stood near it blowing the smoke out over the grimy city below. He wondered if he should knock on Christine's door and tell her, but decided against it. Why push his luck with her? She was exhausted and needed her rest.

Seeing her face bandaged like that had given him a sick feeling in his stomach, though she'd looked a lot worse when he had snapped and beaten the shit out of her. She'd had black eyes and terrible bruises and her cheekbones were raw and skinned. Several teeth had loosened, though thank God they tightened back up over time. She'd had cracked ribs and a hairline fracture in her right wrist from when she went over the couch backwards and crashed through the coffee table. In court, she'd said he'd laughed while he did it. He hadn't challenged her because before the fight, when she accused him of all those things with Petra, he'd seen a streak of white, then red, that widened and obliterated the rest of his view, and he remembered nothing till after the cops came and cuffed him. He may very well have laughed. Many things could be expressed through laughter: good will, madness, defeat, contempt, evil. Which one did Christine think he was expressing, assuming she hadn't lied about it? Which one did the judge use to color the scene in his imagination?

Suddenly he remembered the sounds of Petra's baby laughter. The giggles tumbled out when he pushed her on a swing or tickled her round little belly. He remembered her breathless shouts of happiness when the ocean spray shot up over the side of their sailboat to soak her on a hot day. But then her laughter dried up and until that very moment Parker had not realized how incredibly much he missed it. Gone, it was even more powerful than it was when it was present. The sound of Petra chuckling had filled Parker with grace, but its mirror image was hopeless despair that had lodged in the marrow of his bones and rotted. The tears began again and he brushed his cheek with the back of his hand. His cheeks were already wet.

Greg came back in. If he noticed Parker's distress he gave no sign.

"Good old Lorraine," he said waving a short stack of papers, "she comes through every time." He divided the pile and handed several pages to Parker. "O.K. We got incoming and outgoing calls from his home and his job. Let's just check 'em over, see if we see anything." Sorting through the New York Telephone Company codes was perplexing at first, but once the individual service listings for calls began, it was ridiculously easy. From Steve's home, during the forty-eight hours Greg had records for, there was only one call and it was a number that both Parker and Greg instantly recognized: the Warren School in Chatham, Mass. The records from the office phone were more complicated—business had been conducted there all day Friday, after all. But after quitting time, only two more calls came in. One was a fax from the Warren School and the other one, at 6:52 p.m. Saturday, came from a number in the 315 area code—the Syracuse area. One more quick call and Greg learned that the call had been placed from a pay phone in Potsdam, New York. Same place Steve Dant wired his money every year.

Greg looked up.

"He's there," he said. "Somewhere near Potsdam. Let's get Christine and go." Greg would be at the door of the Key Bank at 8:59 the next morning. Dant's trail was getting hotter and so was the hope that Greg knew he should but couldn't bring himself to stamp out— the hope that Petra was alive and well, and Steve Dant was harmless. It was a long shot but he could hope.

Parker went next door to wake Christine while Greg argued with himself about the FBI guy, Lamica. Greg hated to bring the feds, with all their weight and muscle, into a delicate situation that would prob-ably require a real balancing act. On the other hand, he shouldn't withhold information with the girl's life at stake. He made a deal with himself. He'd phone Lamica with all the information from Potsdam the next morning. That would give Greg a few hours lead time. In the meanwhile, Lamica would see to it that Steve Dant's picture was flashed on every news spot in the Syracuse area. He studied the map again, wondering if the broadcast range for the TV stations out of Syracuse reached Potsdam. Probably. Greg hoped that anybody who'd seen Steve or knew where he was would have the sense not to try to take the situation into his own hands.

When Christine and Parker reappeared in Greg's room, Greg was assembling a 9mm handgun. It was a shock to both of them though they should have expected it, and if it became necessary to use it to get Petra back, they would not object. But the sight of a gun, casually being taken from its case and snapped together, will chill the average person, and both Christine and Parker were average people.

Greg glanced up and saw their faces. "Maybe you two should stay here and wait," he said, "because I'm gonna kill this guy if I have to." His voice and his eyes left no doubt that he meant what he said.

"We're going," Parker said. Christine glanced sharply at him. It had been so long since he'd made a decision on their behalf, yet it was still a familiar feeling. He turned to her. "Right?" he asked and she nodded.

"All right, but you know what you're getting into, so don't get in my way."

They collected their possessions, which didn't amount to very much, and abandoned the two rooms. Parker settled the bill while Greg rented another car. When it was brought to the front of the hotel, Greg slid behind the wheel and Christine got in beside him. It was getting dark now, and the humidity made the air smell dirty. It was good to get moving, out onto the open road with a clear destination in mind. Greg wore the gun in a shoulder holster, which was uncomfortable in the stagnant, muggy night, but he had hit the point in his investigation when there was no more time to waste. From here on in, assuming he wasn't off track about Steve Dant's whereabouts, every second counted. The gun was cumbersome but necessary; as far as Parker and Christine, it was absurd that they were along for this ride, but flexibility was Greg's strongest asset. Besides, he thought, this case had been cockeyed from the get-go. It was a strange thing to do surveillance on an ex-wife and stumble across that woman's daughter's kidnapper before he'd even perpetrated the crime. Very strange indeed. He glanced over at Christine.

She sensed his look, turned to him, and smiled. It gave him a slight feeling of vertigo and he turned his eyes back to the road in a hurry. Christ on a cross, he thought, I'm falling for this kid. She was twenty years younger and part of a different world, an East Village divorcee who wore spandex. It was amazing. How did things like that happen? He didn't have a snowball's chance in hell with her. Then he took another peek and the way she was looking at him told him he did. He felt like a kid, a sixteen-year-old. The thought that there was a chance of peeling off those tights and running his tongue down the inside of those thighs gave him a momentary hot spot at the back of his balls.

But that would have to wait, and depending on what was coming down the pike toward them, it might never happen at all. He hit the turnoff onto Route 11 toward Watertown and continued on. In Potsdam, they would find rooms and Greg would work out a plan for the morning.

They checked into a small motel called the College Motor Inn and had a late dinner of pizza and a salad composed of a bowl of iceberg lettuce with one tomato wedge, one black olive, and two green pepper rings. The restaurant had booths with Formica tables on one side for eating slices and a more elegant dining room with waitress service and a huge crystal chandelier over more booths with Formica tables on the other. They were all tired and conversation was minimal. Greg observed that the ice had melted between Parker and Christine, but the chill was still noticeable. He distracted them by outlining his ideas for the next day. Christine would go to the court house to see if there were any property deeds registered to the name Dant. Parker would check the library for old phone books and hit the mall where the phone booth Dant had used to call his job was located and try to get a positive I.D. Greg would be at the bank and he would find a way to weasel the manager into telling him why Steve Dant wired money into his bank every year. Greg would drop the others off and pick them up an hour later. He said he felt confident that they would know where to go next.

Back at the motel, he hoped he wasn't building them up for the fall.

25

$\mathcal{S}$teve left three messages on Christine's machine on Sunday before he finally gave up and decided to wait until Monday to try again. He didn't think it was good for Petra to be bundled into the car over and over. She needed to feel more rooted than that, Steve thought. He mixed a bottle of orange soda with a bottle of 7-Up, a drink he remembered loving as a kid, gave her a big glass, and together they sat on the porch swing and watched the humming birds raid the lilac bushes. Steve softly repeated his fog horn imitation for several minutes, holding her in his lap, and she fell asleep. He stretched her out on the swing and went inside to sweep the kitchen floor.

It was amazing to Steve how involved he already felt with Petra. To love a child, he thought, was probably the most natural thing in the world. If a normal person, with the normal juices flowing, suddenly found himself or herself in possession of a child, the bonding was probably always deep, fast, and seamless. Steve had felt like a faucet that had rusted shut, but Petra's nearness pried him open and now he felt his heart pouring out into her. A child was like an admittance card to an exclusive club operated for healthy people. If you had one, you wore it like a badge: I have a family, it said; I have a relationship; I have optimism; I am capable of caring; I have committed myself to loving this child. When Steve saw families on the street or in a restaurant, he felt excluded. Substandard. Unable. He had never wanted a child and no woman had ever offered to give him one. In fact, Wai Ping had had two abortions during the time they lived together in Alongapo, though Steve had no way of knowing if either of the babies was his. He had not cared. The fetuses she carried meant nothing. But years later, after he kicked his heroin habit, he felt little stabs of sorrow about it, as if he'd blown a once-in-a-lifetime opportunity. Now he wanted to nurture life, but the chance had passed him by while he nodded out on dope. It was too late, and he was sorry.

Of course, he knew that his present views were infused with fantasy. One look at Petra, asleep on the swing with a look of pure anxiety on her little face, her brows knit together in an expression of pain, told him that she was no badge of honor and success for Christine and her ex-husband. A dark cloud edged over the faces of strangers when they saw her and realized that no, she was not all right. No, she was not normal. There would be no adorable questions to repeat to friends, no smart-aleck responses to tsk-tsk about and secretly admire. Petra, deep in her cocoon, was a painful mockery of the very forces that sought to create children in the first place, and no adult, and probably no child, was immune to her sad poison.

Placing the truth of Petra back to back against the myth he'd built about having children depressed Steve. He finished his sweeping and wandered around the dining room and living room until he finally sat down at the old upright piano. It had always been there, and he had always played it. He ran his fingers up and down the key of C, then D, then G. The piano, oddly, was in perfect tune—or at least as perfect as it ever got. That was very strange, just as strange as the daffodils thriving in the yard and the beds all made up with fresh sheets and pillowcases. He did not know who had done those things, and he had found no clue as to why. But years on a junkie nod had given him a huge capacity to exist in the unknown and not try to define it. So, instead of wondering why, he played the piano.

He had not touched one since he'd been at the clinic, and even there he'd only sat down and let himself go one time. Making music, to Steve, was like working out a kink in an engine: his hands simply knew what to do. They directed him, not the other way around. And when the engine got fixed and started to purr, or a beautiful intense melody appeared by magic in the room, Steve leaned against the sounds, the harmony, and rested. He had never studied music and didn't feel there was a permanent place in it for him, but when the combination of circumstances allowed, then he played.

The music was blue and moody. Steve's fingers gently pushed the keys and he felt as if each one cried out in relief and pain, as if it'd finally been allowed to stretch after years of being confined, cooped up. He set the piano free as he played, and felt himself moving into a trance, hypnotized by the wails in the room. He had played a lot in this house, but never when Lyle or Sarah was home. They resented the racket. "Knock it off for a while, will ya?" Lyle had snapped over and over until Steve just stopped playing. They were relieved, he knew, and they never mentioned it again. The house became a cruel, silent crypt. Years later Sarah had glanced through Steve's high school yearbook. "Why do the kids call you Mr. Blues?" she'd asked as she turned the pages.

Because I play them on the piano if you wanna know, you fucking bitch, he'd wanted to yell, but, of course, he didn't. There was no use. "It's just a nickname," he said and she nodded and continued to look at the pictures of the graduating class. Just a few kids, and none of them, not one, had ever shown up at her door. Not even one. Ever.

When he realized his back ached and his fingers were sore, he stopped. A glance at his watch told him that over two hours had passed. He stood up and bent backwards to stretch. Then he let his head drop forward and did a slow neck roll. That was when he noticed Petra standing outside the screen door like a little ghost. Her body created a dark outline in the sun behind her.

"Hello, Petra," he said in her direction. "You're up from your nap, huh?" On impulse, he crossed the room, opened the door, and pulled her inside. He lifted her to his lap and sat down again on the piano bench. He rested his left hand on the keys and then opened her hand and placed it on top of his. Her hand looked tiny and pink on his as his fingers flew up and down the keyboard. He hummed the notes as he played and then the music took over. He scooped Petra's right hand onto his and played for another half hour, his knees bouncing Petra to the music and her little arms stretched forward toward the keyboard. The chords arranged themselves into a quasi-ragtime rhythm which ultimately propelled Steve to his feet. He danced around the living room with Petra on his hip, twirling and spinning until the energy passed. Then he stood her on the floor and flopped into his father's easy chair. As she stood there, in the two seconds before his frenzy ended, he saw her bend and stiffen her knees, not once but twice, two little dips. My God, he thought, she's dancing and he rushed back to the piano and pounded out the raggiest rag he knew, but she didn't move again. He stopped after a few minutes, hugging her tight and ruffling his fingers through her brown-black hair. "You wonderful girl," he said, his lips pressed close against her ear.

That second night Petra stayed in her bed the whole night and Steve had no nightmares.

26

$\mathcal{B}$y 9:35 on Monday morning, Greg knew exactly where Steve Dant was. A few curt questions at the bank, a look at the county property records, a glance through the last ten years' worth of phone books, and a ninety percent positive I.D. of Steve by a cashier at the K-Mart put Greg, Parker, and Christine back in the car, heading east on 11B toward a one-horse town in the mountains called St. Regis Falls. From there, they would find Wolf Pond Road and then Greg would park the clients somewhere and go in alone to get Petra. If she was there. If she was alive.

It had not even been forty-eight hours since Steve Dant had kidnapped Petra right out from under Greg's nose. During all that time, Greg had felt his heart race when he fantasized about the scene that was, as of now, set approximately thirty-five minutes in his future. You couldn't predict what you'd find or what would happen when you put yourself between a criminal and his freedom. You could triumph and be the hero or you could end up deader than a bag of hammers. Of course, you bet on yourself to come out on top, but each time, just before going in, you suddenly began to notice the things around you that the good Lord had provided, like the color of the sky and the beauty of the orange flowers, and it hit you hard that life was something worth having after all. When the confrontation got closer, he would definitely not indulge himself like this, but driving the car along the winding highway he allowed himself a little slack.

They were all dead silent. Christine had torn a loose piece of adhesive off the edge of the bandage on her face and she was shredding it, thread by thread, and staring out the passenger window at the brown and white cows in the fields. Parker sat in the back, smoking up a storm, staring down between drags at the cigarette in his hand in that strange, nervous way he had. The strain of not knowing what had happened to Petra had eaten away at all their nerves, and now, at what would probably turn out to be the end, they were each, Greg thought, praying for her in their individual ways. And part of those prayers was for the strength and courage it took to save the life of a child you had failed in every way. Or the courage to bury her and find a reason to go on living.

St. Regis Falls, Greg thought, looked decayed and shabby. The people standing on the sidewalk in front of the few operating businesses stared into the car in a nosy way that gave Greg the creeps; women were dumpy and dressed in oversized tee-shirts and stirrup stretch pants. The map they'd Xeroxed in the office of property deeds indicated that Dant's property was a few miles out of town, farther up the mountain. Just before they edged out of St. Regis Falls, Greg pulled into the parking lot of a Mom & Pop grocery store.

"I'm gonna call Lamica," he said as he exited. Christine and Parker nodded, shifting nervously in their seats. Greg climbed the three cement steps to the porch of the store and made the call with his back to the car. Big houseflies buzzed against the windshield. Christine swatted them away and wiped a bead of sweat from her hairline. She focused on Greg's pale yellow summer-weight jacket. She could just discern the bulge of his shoulder holster.

She had something that needed to be put into words in that moment. It was urgent. But breaking the thick, tense silence was difficult. When she finally said "Parker," it seared the edges off the quiet and startled them both.

"What?" he asked from the back seat.

"Parker," she said softly, "you didn't...molest Petra, did you?"

"No," he answered in a tired voice. "I just...loved her like a father."

Christine turned to face him. "I think I must have known that," she said. "I'm sorry, Parker." Tears streamed out from under the bottom rim of her dark glasses. "But it seemed like the only explanation for Petra, so I made myself believe it." Her voice was desperate. "I needed an explanation. It had to be you 'cause otherwise it would've been me."

Parker scooted forward to the edge of the back seat and put his arm around her.

"Was it me?" she asked.

"No," he said into her hair. He wanted to tell her what he'd figured out over the past few years, the result of obsessively replaying the scenes in his head. When the words came, they sounded hollow but they were all he had. "Petra is sick, Christine. And one of the awful things about...mental illness is what it does to everybody else. We all suffered from her illness. We all did things we can't explain." He wanted to say more but he didn't know how, so he closed his mouth. He felt dead inside, not victorious like he always thought he would when Christine finally broke down and admitted the truth. It was important but it alleviated nothing. "Why don't you come back here and sit with me?" he said, and she opened her door and climbed out of the front seat.

Greg stepped into the store and bought a six pack of cold sodas and three hard rolls with butter. When he got back to the car, Christine was in the back seat and both of them were crying. Parker had his arm around her in a grip that gave Greg a jolt of jealousy.

"Did you get him?" Parker asked.

"I left a message." Actually he had left Lamica the code for his own answering machine in New York and then called the machine and left all the details. He didn't trust the secretary to get them straight, though she wouldn't last long if she couldn't take an accurate message for the FBI. Lamica would be back in a few minutes, she'd informed him, but Greg didn't want to wait. He didn't want to hear Lamica's voice forbidding him to continue, ordering him to sit tight, butt out, until the big boys arrived. No. Greg was gonna get the kid. In the car, he checked his gun one more time. It was ready. He left the safety strap on the holster undone.

He handed Christine and Parker the sodas and pulled out of the lot. "It's about four miles from here. When we get close to the house, I'm parking you somewhere and going in alone."

Parker started to protest but dropped off mid-word. He knew Greg was right. In a way, he was amazed Greg let them tag along at all.

Greg slowed for each left hand turn until he came to Wolf Pond Road. "It should be two miles down on the left," he said. "Slide down in case he passes us coming out. It might look funny with you two in the back." Greg put on a baseball cap and a pair of sunglasses he'd picked up in the grocery store. He could feel the sweat trickling down across his belly and soaking into the waistband of his pants. He drove at a respectable dirt-road speed, checking the sheet with the names of the deed holders on the road against the names on the mailboxes. On his map, he saw that the road made a sharp, long curve and Steve Dant's house, the one he'd probably inherited from his parents, sat on the left. The power lines crossed the road just at the beginning of the curve, and the power company had carved out a maintenance road through the woods. Greg backed the car into it, well out of sight, and stopped.

"This is it," he said turning slightly. "You two stay put. If you hear gunfire, head back to that first house and call the police. Call Lamica too." He passed Lamica's business card to Parker and all three got out of the car.

"I don't know what to say," Christine said.

"Let's just hope she's here," Greg answered. He crossed the road and disappeared into the dense, thick underbrush.

"I feel like an asshole, sitting here," Parker said.

"We'd just be in the way," Christine answered.

"I know, I know." He tapped another cigarette out of the pack. It fell into the tall weeds. He retrieved it and lit it while Christine settled on the hood of the car to wait, unconsciously tugging at the bandage on her jaw.

Greg stayed in the cover of the trees and followed the road until he saw the house. It sat down in a little dip. He reached into his jacket pocket and withdrew a pair of fold-up binoculars that had cost him a small fortune and scanned the front yard. The Ford Escort was parked in the driveway with its hood up. There was a greasy rag thrown over the front fender but no sign of Steve Dant. Greg moved slightly so he could see the front of the house.

His heart did a back flip when he saw Petra Horton sitting on the porch swing. She wore what appeared to be a little sailor suit. Greg moved a few feet closer and studied the yard again. Empty. He began to move through the trees, picking up speed but staying in the shadows. Petra was the most important thing, much more important than Steve Dant could or would ever be. Greg arrived at the edge of the yard and paused briefly. If there was no sign of Dant in fifteen seconds, Greg decided, he'd run for the girl. Let the cops deal with Dant. He scanned every inch of the yard, all around the house. No one. It was about forty yards to the kid. He started to run.

He didn't see Steve's legs sticking out from under the car until it was much too late. How could he? Dant was on the other side of the Escort. He had the wheel off and was flat on his back working up inside the back of the wheel well. But he must've heard Greg's pounding footsteps because by the time Greg rounded the car, Steve was out from under it. He had a heavy-duty wrench in his hand.

If the gun had been in his hand, Greg would've shot him, but he'd been afraid to scare Petra and left it in its holster. In the split second when he saw Steve spring up with that wrench, like a snake he was so fast, Greg regretted that little bit of compassionate carelessness. Greg caught a glimpse of Steve's face as he flew toward him. He had the killer instinct. Greg recognized it. Then Steve hit him and they rolled into the grass. The 9mm was rammed into Greg's ribs as they tumbled. He couldn't get it free. Dant was strong and not afraid to use his fists.

"You fucking son of a bitch," Dant roared, "what the fuck are you doing here, huh? You don't give up, huh? I'm gonna fucking kill you."

"It's over, Dant." Greg spat. "The whole FBI's right behind me." He managed to pound Steve good, twice, in the kidneys, but Steve's elbow came up and Greg felt his jaw go. Again. The pain would register later, if he made it to later. Greg shoved Steve off and got his arm around behind his back and pushed it up till he thought he heard it crack in half, but Steve twisted and somehow got away. He got to his feet and kicked Greg, full force, in the face. Greg crashed over backward. Steve jumped on him, pounded his fist into Greg's kidneys. Greg felt the will go out of him and his face dropped to the ground. Blades of grass stuck up his nose and he could taste blood. Then Steve kicked him again and Greg closed his eyes.

Through the small slit of his eyelid, he saw Steve Dant take off for the porch. He's gonna take her away, Greg thought. He didn't know where he found the strength to do it but he reached inside his jacket and pulled the gun free. He rolled off it and eased it out. He tried to yell a warning but his loose jaw wouldn't form the words.

Steve took a flying leap to the front porch where Petra sat, fifteen feet away. Greg aimed and pulled the trigger. Even through the blur closing in around his eyes, Greg saw Steve Dant start to drop mid-leap into the garden full of daffodils. He pulled the trigger again. And then he heard the screaming, the terrible, blood curdling sound of an eight-year-old screaming bloody murder. Then it seemed like the light went out and Greg's arm dropped. His fingers loosened on the gun and it fell into the grass.

When Christine heard the first shot, she was already running. Parker yanked the car door open to go to the first house, like Greg said, but then he heard the second shot and the sound of Petra's voice, a sound no one had heard in four long years, and he tore after Christine. She was far ahead of him. He stopped and went back for the car. They might need it. Christine, at a dead run, rounded the curve.

Without being aware of it, she noticed Greg Litner face down in the grass and the other man, Steve Dant, bleeding a deep, deep scarlet through his white tee-shirt in two places. He had twisted onto his back in the little patch of garden in front of the porch. Christine saw those things as she ran, but none of it mattered. What mattered was Petra. Petra's voice. Shrill, hysterical. And, Christine realized, saying something. She was saying, "No." She saw Petra get up off that swing and run to Steve Dant. She saw her kneel down next to him and cover the red stains with her fingers. And the whole time, she was screaming, "No! No!" at the top of her lungs. It was a miracle. An ugly miracle, full of blood. But a miracle.

By the time Christine got to Petra, Parker screeched into the driveway in the rented car. Petra's hands and arms were covered with blood and she had Steve Dant's tee-shirt wound up in her fingers. Christine looked, for the first time, into the eyes of the man who had kidnapped her daughter. They were cloudy and full of fear, but his voice was clear.

"Christine," he said, "I got her in time. For you." Then he passed out. Christine reached for Petra but Petra screamed louder and Christine let her go. Parker moved toward Greg and checked his pulse. "I've gotta call an ambulance," he said, and he tore down the road toward the next house. When he reappeared five minutes later Petra was still screaming, and Christine was still on her knees, helpless, near their daughter. The screaming was shocking in its rawness and intensity. It cracked Parker's heart wide to hear it and to see his ex-wife, whom he still loved despite everything, helpless before her child's absolute and utter despair.

Steve Dant's tee-shirt turned a deep maroon. It spread to the patch of yellow flowers, trimming their edges with crimson. Greg Litner moaned, his eyes fluttered open, and he found himself alone in the green grass. When the rescue truck arrived, staffed by well-meaning locals with nothing but a sixteen-hour first aid course under their belts, they could do nothing more than wrap them all in blankets and cram them into the town's one ambulance for the long ride to the nearest hospital.

27

For Christine, it became a blur: police, doctors, oozing blood and shouted questions, and always, always Petra's voice, screaming until the syringe full of barbiturates did its work. Then Parker was there, his hand steady in hers, Petra slumped over his shoulder, her tiny face pressed into his neck. Over the half-hearted protests of the doctors, they carried her out. The sheriff, a country boy with a beer belly, cleared a path for them, away from the emergency room to the car they'd rented in Syracuse. They promised to find a local motel, to keep him informed of their whereabouts, to answer more questions, more questions, more questions.

But Christine could only think of getting away. Away with Petra, asleep on her lap now. Away with the sweet smell of her sweaty little head and the vision of her translucent eyelids and the tiny, sad mouth, so pink against her pale white skin. Christine's arms locked around her daughter, and she held her tight. You are safe, she thought. This minute. Now.

Parker made a left turn out of the parking lot, down a tree-lined street with huge Victorian houses on each side. He made another turn, down another street, just the same, followed the speed limit and noticed nothing. They came to an intersection: Main Street, Malone, New York. There was a hotel on the right, an old brick place with a porch. A sign in front advertised a $2.99 lunch special.

"What should we do?" he asked. "Check in there?"

Christine tore her eyes from Petra. It was a warm, lazy day, and Main Street was deserted. There were cars passing through, waiting at red lights, but only a few pedestrians paused in front of shop windows.

"Let's go back to New York," she said.

"Christine," Parker said, with more words to come, but then he looked at her and the protests faded.

"What?"

"It's about seven or eight hours," he finished with a sigh. "Are you up to it?"

"I want to get away from here," she answered.

The light changed and Parker stepped on the gas.

It was a long, long drive and Christine and Parker barely spoke. They were exhausted and needed the silence. Christine fell asleep with her head against the door. Parker noticed that she never loosened the grip she maintained on her own wrist, circled around Petra. Petra slept on. And finally the lights of the George Washington Bridge appeared and the city of New York spread out along the opposite river bank. Parker felt giddy as he bumped over the potholes and merged into lanes of high speed traffic. Down the West Side Highway, past the aircraft carrier and the cruise ships, the heliports. By luck, they got a parking spot directly in front of her building. They climbed the stairs, Petra stirring but not waking when Christine passed her out of the car to Parker and then again as Christine undid the locks and pushed her apartment door open.

She was not prepared for the mess inside. It was so long ago that she had left here, been taken out by ambulance. All of that had shriveled and disappeared for her, but here it was again, the proof. Parker, winded from the climb, laid Petra down on the white leather couch. Absentmindedly, he picked Christine's bag up off the floor and began to replace her things in it, the things the man from the park had scattered across the bleached wood when he robbed her and beat her three days before.

Christine saw that her bedroom was disheveled, her closet torn apart, like a stage set from some unfamiliar melodrama. In the bathroom, she quickly collected the red sleeping pills off the floor and flushed them down the toilet. She closed the medicine cabinet, pausing for a brief moment to study her face in the mirror. The adhesive bandage looked filthy and she peeled it off. Beneath it, the coarse black thread, knotted into each stitch, looked ugly too, but it didn't matter. She returned to the living room, where Parker was staring out a window, smoking.

"You want a drink, Parker? I think I have some gin."

He turned from the window. "Sounds good."

Christine went into the kitchen and placed two tall glasses on the counter. She filled them, remembering exactly the proportions of gin to tonic that Parker liked. It seemed so incredibly familiar. Behind her, she heard him enter the kitchen.

"You got a message," he said, indicating the answering machine on a shelf just inside the door. "Actually, three messages."

Christine handed him his drink. "Probably Sheriff What's-His-Name calling to give us hell," she smiled, hitting the button.

"Christine," the voice said, "Are you there?" A pause. "My name is Steve Dant and you don't know me..."

Christine dropped her glass and it shattered. Ice skidded across the worn parquet floor and the smell of gin and lime rose around her.

"...but I helped you the day before yesterday when..."

Steve Dant. His voice, all around her. What was he saying? Why was he calling her? What was happening? Christine could make no sense of it and Parker stood staring at the machine, his jaw loose.

Nervously, Christine stooped to collect the shards of glass off the floor. And that was when she saw Petra, moving off the couch straight for the kitchen. She opened her arms to collect her little girl, but in the doorway, Petra stopped, confused. Steve Dant's voice continued on. Petra turned her back to Christine and Parker and placed her hands on the answering machine. She pulled it off the shelf and cradled it against her chest.

28

At the end of June, on the northernmost peaks of the Adirondack mountain chain, it is hellish. The air is thick with three different kinds of fierce, biting insects. Black flies relentlessly swarm, mosquitoes multiply by the millions in mud puddles, and the no-see-ums bite for fun.

Steve Dant remembered this.

Yet he pictured himself on the porch swing during the two months it would take for stage one of his recovery. He had taken one bullet through the left shoulder. The second bullet, which had hit him after his body twisted in the air on impact from the first, entered his abdomen in the upper left quadrant, anteriorally, and lodged in the spleen. It required an emergency laperectomy, and two units of blood were used during the surgery. He was to be confined to the hospital in Malone, New York, twenty-four miles from the site of the shooting, for a period of not less than ten days. In any major U.S. city, he would've been on the streets in four, barring serious complications.

After sixteen hours, he was moved from the Intensive Care Unit to a semi-private room. The night nurse on that floor had a kid brother just starting out in the carpentry business, and Steve hired him from his hospital bed to screen in the porch of his parents' house. He specifically requested the finest mesh screening with no obstructions to the view in front of the old porch swing. Steve had a lot to think about and he wanted to stare at something timeless, like the mountains and the sky, as he did it.

No one had been allowed to question him in Intensive Care, but as soon as he was moved, a line of cops, FBI agents, and newspaper people fell in outside his door. Words like kidnapping, assault and battery, crossing state lines, possession of a stolen vehicle, assault with a deadly weapon, and the right to remain silent flew back and forth over his head until he finally called Tom Bource, Jr., the family attorney. Tom surprised him, stepping into the situation with all the authority and presence of a true professional. The papers soon referred to him as "a smart country lawyer" and he took to wearing a fresh carnation on his lapel.

Tom had shooed everyone away from Steve and taken his deposition at a leisurely pace that lasted the better part of a whole afternoon. Steve told him the truth, though now it sounded half-cracked, even to him. Tom listened without judgment. When he stepped back into the hallway, he had a prepared statement which he had memorized. A hospital security guard led him to the staff lounge where the reporters, cops, and gossip-mongers waited.

"My client does not understand the allegations against him. He traveled to the Warren School in Chatham, Massachusetts, to check on Miss Petra Horton at the specific request of her mother, Christine Timberlake. He left a note to that effect with Miss Timberlake, who was under extreme duress at the time of her request. In Chatham, Mr. Dant recognized a man whom he perceived to be a threat to Petra Horton. In his judgment, the school's security was lax, so he took Miss Horton for her own protection. He left three messages on Miss Timberlake's answering machine in New York City. He did not, at any time, in any way, seek to disturb, hurt, or threaten either Miss Timberlake or Miss Horton. My client deeply regrets the misunderstanding and the mental anguish that were caused to Miss Timberlake and the other concerned parties. Ladies and gentlemen, that is all."

Greg, in his hospital pajamas, stood in the back of the room, leaning against the wall. His mind was foggy from the drugs they'd given him when they wired his jaw shut. But even through the haze, he could put two and two together: it didn't take a genius, after all, to figure out that he himself was the guy Steve Dant saw in New York and on the Cape. So it was all a mistake, he thought with a shrug. It made him feel like laughing and crying at the same time. Still, there were several pieces that he couldn't fit in the puzzle. Somebody had to be lying. Was it Christine? Dant?

He shuffled back down the corridor in his paper slippers to his room. He felt dull, confused. Had he really shot an innocent man? If he had, he could kiss his license goodbye for good. On the other hand, he thought to himself, if he'd made as many mistakes as he assumed he had, he probably should hang it up anyway. It'd be hard to believe in himself again. He climbed into his bed and laid himself out, flat on his back. He was tired. So tired. When he rested up a little, he thought, he'd blow out of this town and try to figure it out.

But for now, he would just sleep.

29

Christine rose slowly to her feet. She stared down at Petra, holding on so tightly to the voice of Steve Dant. One part of her hated Petra, her own little girl who had turned her back on her and chosen another, a stranger. Yet she was simultaneously filled with gratitude to see her daughter engaged in life at all. There she stood, just to the side of the broken glass, her head dropping forward, her navy blue sailor suit wrinkled from the long ride and her deep and troubled sleep.

Christine turned to Parker. He made an unconscious gesture motioning her back, as if he wanted to keep a space clear for Petra, just in case she wanted to emerge.

Steve Dant's deep voice continued. "When I got to the school," he was saying, "they thought I was your husband and handed Petra over to me. I figured..."

"Who is he?" Christine frantically interjected. "Why is he saying this?"

"I don't know," Parker answered. "Shhh."

The answering machine clicked off. For a few seconds there was silence, and then that same voice returned. "It's me again. I...I don't know. I'll try you later. But don't worry. Petra is fine, when you get this message." Another click. Several short beeps indicated the end of the tape.

Petra did not move. Parker reached over her shoulder and hit the replay button. She tightened her grip on the machine as the voice began again.

"Petra!" Christine cried. She had an impulse to yank the machine away from her. "Petra!" But there was no response, just the unapologetic blankness that Christine could not penetrate. She slumped down onto the wide windowsill to listen to the stranger's voice. When Parker looked at her, his whole face a question, she shrugged. "I have no idea what he's talking about," she said.

"Maybe I should call that sheriff," Parker mumbled. Christine nodded, but neither moved toward the phone. Instead, they played the message again for Petra. But she could not fight the tranquilizers in her bloodstream for long, and her eyes soon started to close. Christine placed her in the middle of her big bed, the little white Radio Shack answering machine tucked in beside her. She stood at the foot of the bed, her hands clamped into fists, until Parker's shadow, blocking the light from the foyer, fell over her. She stepped out the bedroom door.

"I want to kill Steve Dant," she said. Then she seemed to fold forward from the waist. Her eyes were swollen and shining with tears. "But I'm taking her back up there to see him, Parker. I have to. He reached her."

Parker held her as a great giddiness descended on him. Nothing made sense, and yet, there they were, Parker and Christine in each other's arms like long ago, with Petra asleep in the next room. Maybe Christine was right. Maybe she should ride this crazy wave all the way into shore, back to Steve Dant, he thought.

For Petra.

When the traffic on Avenue A thinned and the neon lights of the bars had gone out, one by one, Christine and Parker fell into bed, a parent on each side of the child, and slept. The morning came quietly to the city. Parker held Christine's hands in his when he told her he wasn't returning north with her. "I trust your mother's intuition," he said. "I don't want to interfere."

"You could come," she said.

"I'm not ready to forgive this guy," he answered. But he promised to wait and hope, and when Christine leaned forward against him, she could hear the wild pounding of his heart where her head rested against his chest. "Thank you, Parker," she said.

Later, Christine turned onto the West Side Highway, heading north in the rented car. Three-hundred fifty miles, she repeated. Three-hundred fifty. The mileage markers along the side of the Thruway clicked by one a minute. So fast, she thought, as she focused on each one for the tiny second before it disappeared behind her. She tried to formulate a speech, the right words to say to Steve Dant, but there was no place to start and no way to order it, and she gave up. Her vision was focused on the mountains in the distance.

Petra sat beside her without moving, staring down into her lap, never making a sound. Occasionally a blister of resentment would form in Christine. She felt so deeply betrayed by her daughter, so terrified. Still, she drove on, fussing with the radio but finding only static.

A strong sense of dread overcame Christine when she turned down Main Street in Malone. Had the nightmare of Petra's kidnapping just ended yesterday? Had they been here then? Was it possible that she'd made this trip twice in two days, once to flee Steve Dant and once to rush back to him? And would he be able to explain it all to her? Would he be willing?

She made the turn at the old brick hotel, back down the same tree-lined street toward the hospital. She had spoken to the sheriff that morning, telling him about the messages on her answering machine, but she did not mention she was about to return. She wanted to give Steve Dant no chance to prepare for her.

In the parking lot, she undid Petra's seatbelt and gently pulled her out of the car. The afternoon sun was not bright, but Petra squinted as it hit her.

"Come on, honey," Christine said. "Mommy wants to take you to see somebody." The sound of her own voice startled her. It had been a long time since she'd spoken. It made her sad. A long ride with her little girl, but no conversation, no commentary on the shapes of the clouds, and no sharing of childish secrets.

She stopped at the information desk for Steve Dant's room number and felt the receptionist's eyes burn into her back as she led Petra toward the elevator. Did she have a right to be here? She felt out of place and on display. A policeman was seated in a plastic chair outside Dant's door, reading the local newspaper.

"Excuse me," Christine said.

The cop stood up.

"I'd like to speak to Steve Dant."

The cop's eyes darted left and right as if he suspected he was being watched. "He's with his lawyer," he mumbled, "but I'll tell him he has a visitor. Your name is...?"

"Christine Timberlake," she said, "and Petra."

The cop's eyebrows rose as he disappeared through the door.

"Sit here, Petra," Christine said, depositing her daughter in the plastic chair. "Mommy will be right back." She didn't wait for the policeman to re-emerge. When she stepped into Steve Dant's room, all three men stopped talking and turned to stare at her.

"I'd like to speak to you alone," Christine said. Tom Bource, receiving some coded signal from his client, said, "I see no harm in that," and headed for the door. Enroute, he collected the young police officer.

And so Steve Dant told Christine Timberlake his story. It was difficult for him. Humiliating. He rarely raised his eyes to meet Christine's.

"You were the one who hired that punk kid to get my letter," she demanded.

"Yes."

"Why?"

"At the time," Steve began, but he wasn't sure how to finish, so he said, "...it made sense. I don't know why."

"And when you went into my apartment, you thought that was O.K.?"

Steve's voice was barely audible. "I just did it. I didn't think."

"Have you ever done anything like this before?"

"No."

Christine stood up and crossed to the windows. She stared out for a long time before she spoke. "I want to hate you, you know that? But...because of Petra, I don't."

"And I want to like you," Steve responded, "but because you dumped her in that school instead of taking care of her, I don't."

Christine caught her breath. She turned to look into Steve Dant's eyes. "I didn't have the key to open her up," she said helplessly. "I hoped they would." But truthfully, she knew that no one had the right key to anything. No solutions were that simple. The work of the human, she thought in that second, is to find a way to tolerate that basic fact. Steve Dant's sad brown eyes told her he knew this. And to her absolute amazement, she blurted out, "Steve, will you help me take care of Petra?"

Steve let out a sad, low-pitched moan, one that had started long ago in his childhood. It hurt. God, it hurt to stand in the presence of a person who knew the worst about him and hear her say, You are somebody. You have value. Tears formed and fell down his cheeks, into the creases of his neck, onto the pillow case, soaking it till the ticking on the pillow showed through. Christine drew the straight-backed chair up next to the bed and they sat, fused together in the heat of their tension, until his tears had stopped and left him drained and pale.

"I'm gonna bring Petra in for a minute," she finally said, "and then I'm taking her to your house in St. Regis Falls. That's where we're staying." Her voice was defiant. "I think we have the right." She rose and walked to the door.

"Petra?" she said, taking her daughter's hand and guiding her through the doorway.

"Petra!" Steve repeated as she came quickly toward him.

30

By the Fourth of July weekend, the strange convulsion that had reorganized all their lives had passed and a new routine was forming. Steve had been released from the hospital. He had returned to his house with a shy but not unpleasant feeling. For the first time, he felt he belonged there, that he was part of it and it was part of him. He slowly walked from room to room, amazed at how the place had changed. It smelled of flowers and Christine's latest culinary attempt: focaccia bread. She had hidden the plastercrafts away in a drawer and rearranged the shabby furniture to make it more close and cozy. A collection of spicy-smelling soaps proliferated in the bathroom, and pairs of shoes in three sizes rested to the side of each stair; no one ever remembered to put them in their bedrooms.

Christine had been settled in Lyle's old bedroom when Steve returned. Petra was in Sarah's. Petra soon began to position herself right next to him on the porch swing, and occasionally she banged for a few seconds on the old piano though she still had not spoken. Christine and Steve, on the other hand, spoke non-stop as a way of covering their mutual embarrassment. Yet they had not become close. Rather, they circled each other in a sort of primitive ritual. Polite but suspicious. It did not feel bad to Steve.

It was Friday afternoon. Christine had taken Petra on a shopping expedition to Potsdam. Alone for the first time since he'd come home, Steve opened a cold beer and carried it to the porch. He got tired in the afternoon and had fallen into the habit of napping on the swing. Just as he was about to drift off, a car pulled into the yard. It was too early for Christine to be back, so he pulled himself upright, taking care, as always, not to strain his abdomen, chest, or shoulder stitches. By the time he reached a sitting position, the car, a Firebird about eight years old, was parked in the driveway and a woman in her mid-fifties was climbing out of the driver's side. Her hair was grey and cut short, and she wore a pair of baggy shorts that hit her just above the knees. Steve leaned forward. There was something familiar about her; perhaps the shape of her body or the no-nonsense way she moved. And then he realized.

"Aunt Nancy!" he hollered, using his hands to push himself slowly up off the swing.

She stopped. "Steve?" A smile broke out over her pale lips. "Is that you?"

"It's me," he called moving to open the new porch door for her. He felt warm joy wash over him, just as the waves of Jones Beach had tumbled this same pair through the ocean water more than twenty years before. She came through the door and moved to embrace him. He stepped back and instinctively raised his arms to fend her off. He saw the hurt drop like a curtain over Nancy's face.

"Aunt Nancy," he said quickly, "I'm all bandaged up. I was shot." She laughed and came back toward him, much slower.

"Well thank God that's all it is. I thought for a second there you turned out to be a cold fish like your mother."

Steve kissed her cheek, which was just beginning to wrinkle and sag.

"No," he said. "No."

"Where can I touch you?" she asked.

"Around the waist is O.K." She slid her arm around him and they walked together into the house.

"I saw you on the tube," she said. "First you were Jack the Ripper; then after they found out about the little girl, suddenly you were Mother Theresa. I had to come up here and see for myself."

"I'm glad you came."

And he was. Whenever he looked back on his childhood, the events and emotions of it jumbled together into a lifeless black fog. On the other side of the scale was that one bright, shining week he'd spent with Aunt Nancy. She had genuinely liked him, he knew. It had crushed him when she said he couldn't come and live with her. And then, when she'd brought him home, there'd been angry words between Nancy and his mother. He had heard them from under the covers of his bed. Then the sound of the car door slamming and the car starting and Aunt Nancy just disappeared from his life like a beautiful soap bubble that burst into nothingness.

Nancy, Steve learned, had kept up the house. She had paid the taxes when they were publicly listed as delinquent after Steve stopped bothering with them two years ago, and she'd come up on long weekends and her summer vacation. She still lived in Queens, still rented, still worked as a bookkeeper for an auto parts ware-house. She had attended Lyle and Sarah's funeral, summoned by Tom Bource, Jr., though she hadn't seen her sister in fifteen years at the time of her death.

"My mother wouldn't talk about you," Steve said. "She wouldn't say why either. But I got the idea that it was because you were living with your boyfriend or something."

Nancy paused. "In a way, I guess that was it, but my boyfriend...wasn't a boy." She turned to Steve. "Her name was Terry."

Steve was silent. And then his little boy's question burst through all the years, and he blurted out, "Is that why you wouldn't let me come live with you?"

"Sarah would never have let me take you. Or Lyle either for that matter, though I never gave a damn about what he thought about anything. No offense." She laughed. "I used to call him 'Two Seconds of Sperm.' That was all he added up to if you ask me—one second for you and one for William."

And that was how Steve Dant learned, for the first time in his life, that he'd had a baby brother, fourteen months younger. And that brother had drowned in the St. Lawrence River at a beach in Massena near the seaway. Stunned, Steve demanded the details. Nancy told the story simply. Steve was two and a half. He and William were playing with buckets and shovels in the edge of the shallow water of the children's wading section. Sarah insisted she had only drifted off into sleep for a minute or two. She woke up when the yelling and shouting started. William was dead. The young mother who pulled him from the water too late tried artificial respiration, but William's body was so tiny and she was afraid. She reported that Steve, laughing and smiling in the bright yellow sun, had been the one who pushed him under. And held him there.

Steve felt sick. His mind fell backward. The dream, he thought. The dream.

"Sarah closed down after that. Wouldn't talk about it. She hid all William's pictures and heckled Lyle till they bought this place where nobody knew them. She could never forgive herself." Nancy hesitated. "Or you. She tried, Steve, but she couldn't."

Steve's eyes smarted with tears. "But I...I..."

"You were two years old." Nancy reached for his hand. "Sarah was crazy. Don't tell me you never figured that out." They were both silent, paralyzed by the ache.

By the time Christine and Petra returned, Nancy and Steve had carefully placed their painful past in one corner of the new relationship between them. They would examine it, together or in private, from time to time. Steve saw curiosity light up Christine's eyes as she was introduced to Nancy and it made him feel good. Another place was set at the table. The first corn of the summer had hit the farm stands, and they boiled up a huge pot for dinner. Nancy took Steve's room and Steve moved to the porch swing, which was his favorite place anyway, now that the bugs were kept at bay by the fine-mesh screens.

Late that night, long after the "Happy dreams, see you in the mornings" had been said and the lamps turned out, Steve sat up watching the random flashes of the lightning bugs in the yard. They made him angry because they were so tiny and powerless against the night. He was restless. Nancy's news, stirred into his psyche like soup with a big wooden spoon, changed the flavor of his early memories. He pictured Sarah's pinched face, and for the first time he felt her guilt and shame. He thought of Lyle, how he'd explained how the waves worked before Steve's trip to the beach with Aunt Nancy, and he understood his father's generosity. He could've so easily sent Steve off without a warning to sink or swim as fate would have it. But no. He also felt white hot bursts of rage. He, a child, held responsible for life and death and hated because he symbolized the wrong one. And Nancy, exiled for no reason. And William, drowned in the river, age one year. Agitated, Steve pushed through the door into the yard.

The night was dark though there were a million little stars. He looked up at them. They looked a mess in the sky. There is no order, Steve thought helplessly, no order. But then he looked back at his house, breathing with new life, new people, a new family, and in his heart he knew that, of course, there was.